HOOLIGAN

HOOLIGAN

A NOVEL

PHILIPP WINKLER

Translated from the German
by Bradley Schmidt

Arcade Publishing • New York

First English-language Edition

First published in Germany in 2016 under the title *Hool* by Aufbau Verlag GmbH& Co. KG

The translation of this work was supported by a grant from Goethe Institut.

This is a work of fiction. Names, places, characters, and incidents are either the product of the author's imagination or are used fictitiously.

Arcade Publishing books may be purchased in bulk at special discounts for sales promotion, corporate gifts, fund-raising, or educational purposes. Special editions can also be created to specifications. For details, contact the Special Sales Department, Arcade Publishing, 307 West 36th Street, 11th Floor, New York, NY 10018 or arcade@skyhorsepublishing.com.

Arcade Publishing® is a registered trademark of Skyhorse Publishing, Inc.®, a Delaware corporation.

Visit our website at www.arcadepub.com.

10 9 8 7 6 5 4 3 2 1

Library of Congress Cataloging-in-Publication Data

Names: Winkler, Philipp, 1986– author. | Schmidt, Bradley, translator.
Title: Hooligan : a novel / Philipp Winkler ; translated from the German by Bradley Schmidt.
Other titles: Hool. English
Description: First English-language edition. | New York : Arcade Publishing, [2018] | "Copyright ? 2016 by Aufbau Verlag GmbH & Co. KG". — ECIP galley
Identifiers: LCCN 2017060026 (print) | LCCN 2018001363 (ebook) | ISBN 9781628728682 (ebook) | ISBN 9781628728675 (hardcover : alk. paper)
Subjects: LCSH: German fiction—21st century. | Friendship—Fiction. | Families—Fiction.
Classification: LCC PT2725.I549 (ebook) | LCC PT2725.I549 H6613 2018 (print) | DDC 833/.92—dc23
LC record available at https://lccn.loc.gov/2017060026

Cover design by Erin Seaward-Hiatt
Cover photograph: iStockphoto

Printed in the United States of America

For my parents

TRANSLATOR'S NOTE

Heiko Kolbe, the narrator of this novel, is torn between feelings of obligation for his family and for the surrogate family he has found in the hooligan scene affiliated with his local professional *Fussball* club, Hannover 96. The "96" in the name refers to the year the club was established, 1896. *Football*, in its various translations, is how the rest of the world refers to what Americans call "soccer." In this book, to better reflect Heiko's *Fussball* universe, we've retained the term closest to the one he would use in German.

One difference between European professional football and the franchise model of North American soccer is the possibility of relegation. Depending on the size of the league, the two or three teams with the worst record are relegated, or sent down, to a lower league, and are replaced by teams ascending from that league. This system enhances the stakes for a team's performance. Several of the novel's most exciting scenes revolve around the possibility of Hannover 96 moving up or down.

Fans like Heiko and his friends, who avidly follow a team despite its bouncing between the highest league and lower tiers, are the opposite of fair-weather fans. The most faithful fans might even place a higher priority on attending a match between their club's "U23" reserve team, comprised of players only under the age of twenty-three, than on the commercialized games of the main team. It's also common to follow both the main pro club like Hannover and a local small-town team, such as TSV Luthe, based near Hannover, as Heiko and his friends do.

Heiko's world is peppered with references to past and current Hannover players, such as the former goalies Sievers and Robert Enke, the coach Michael Lorkowski, or other stars from the 2000s like Bernd Schneider, Ansgar Brinkmann, and Roberto Carlos.

Hannover 96 and Eintracht Braunschweig are archrivals in this book and in real life. Because of the vagaries of success and league structure, some archrivals seldom meet on the field except in a cup match.

Finally, the ultra fan movement has been relatively diverse and includes groups of both right-wing and left-wing ideologies. While most ultras are primarily focused on supporting their local team, hooligans are mostly interested in organizing and carrying out brawls with other hooligans. Heiko and his friends Kai, Ulf, and Jojo, gradually move up within the Hannover hooligan scene. Although there is some overlap between the gang and the right-leaning Wotan Gym run by Heiko's uncle, Axel, it would be a mistake to equate the hooligans with a right-wing gang. However, Axel rules the group with an iron fist. Although *Hooligan* might at first glance seem to be just a novel about a crazy sports fan, it is worth noting that identifying with a team with a history stretching back more than one hundred years—outlasting numerous forms of political organization and spanning two world wars—offers a stable kind of tradition. It is natural that the book's working-class protagonists gravitate toward teams like Hannover 96.

HOOLIGAN

I warm my new mouth guard between my palms. Use my fingers to rotate it and squeeze it a little. It's what I do before each fight. The plastic holds firm, with just a small amount of give. It's a fabulous piece. You almost can't get any better. Specially made by the dental technician. Not one of those mass-produced cheapo jobs you can toss after two weeks 'cause the edges cut into your gums. Or you constantly want to gag from the horrible fit and the chemical smell of the plastic. By now, almost all of us have one of these mouth guards, except Jojo with his paltry janitor's wages. Kai, who always has to have the finest shit. Ulf has no problem paying for it. Tomek, Töller. And some of our boys who have the right jobs. Uncle Axel, of course. He's the one who discovered the dental technician a couple years ago. Specializes in contact sports and takes care of martial artists all over Germany. I hear the people from Frankfurt go to him and some of the boys from the East. From Dresden and Halle, Zwickau. Probably have to lay out their whole month's check from the government, I think, and run the tips of my fingers over the ventilation holes.

"Hey, Heiko!" Kai pokes me in the side. "Your phone." The knock-off phone buzzes between us on the seat. I reach for it, my fingers shaking. My uncle watches me in the side mirror. I press the button with the green symbol.

"Where are you? We're waiting," the voice of the guy from Cologne I organized the match with comes through the phone. I roll down the window so I can see better, look for any points of reference.

"We're on highway B55 near Olpe. Should be right there."

"Hit Desert Road. Turn right off the second traffic circle. On Bratzkopf, straight till you've passed the city limits. Woods on the left. Can't miss it."

Before he hangs up, I remind him one more time about our deal. Fifteen men on each side. Then I hang up.

"Well?" Axel asks without turning around. He's still watching me in the side mirror. Despite the sun's reflection, I can recognize his piercing gaze. How he's scrutinizing me closely. I pass along the directions and stress that I reminded the guy about the agreement.

"I heard," he says and turns to Hinkel, who's at the wheel as usual. Axel repeats the directions. As if Hinkel didn't hear me, or Hinkel could only drive that way if the directions come from him. I notice how Kai is looking at me from the side. The corners of his mouth spread. In solidarity. If I look at him now, he's probably rolling his eyes. Telling me, fucking hell, what a control freak. Something like that. But I don't react, just see whether Hinkel takes the right turn. He grunts, which probably means he understood. Hinkel grips the wheel, his meatloaf hand at twelve o'clock. Beads of sweat are trapped in the long hairs on the back and glitter in the sun. It looks like a comb-over in the wrong place. He lets the other hand dangle out the window.

Tomek, sitting on Kai's left, scrolls through his phone with disinterest. It's an East Bloc thing. Always the same Slavic face. Good mood or bad. You can't tell the difference. He'd probably have the same expression if he won the lottery. It wouldn't be surprising if he's pissed off. After all, Kai called shotgun before him. Probably doesn't even know it. Now he has to sit exactly where Jojo bled all over with his destroyed nose. Jojo's snorter really suffered. And the seat padding too. And besides, that's clearly the spot you don't want to sit on hot days. Behind Hinkel. Even with the window open.

Kai lifts his ass an inch above the seat and slips his powder tin from the back pocket of his Hollister jeans. He unscrews the lid and shovels a pile of blow onto his thumb, holding it under one nostril then the other, snorting. The car is jostling quite a bit, but he manages not to lose any. He throws his head back. His gelled boxer haircut scratches over the greasy seat cover. He holds out the tin for me.

"Want some? Maybe then you won't fill your pants." He grins. I grin back and say, "Better to have your pants full than your nose, Ms. Winehouse." He laughs. It's been quite a while since I last took something. He extends his middle finger while screwing the lid back on. My uncle clears his throat loudly. Kai shrugs his shoulders and deposits the tin back in his jeans. He knows very well Axel can't stand it when we mess up our heads with something before a match. Even stuff like coke, which clears your brain. But that's one thing even Uncle Axel can't get from people. That's why he usually lets it slide, so long as no one gets carried away. Besides, Axel's been known to sample the goods. A lot of people need it for their nerves. Well, that or just 'cause they're junkies. But Axel doesn't bring along anyone who can't get a grip. At least not to the important matches. Like today. When it's really about representing Hannover with honor. Kai may be a heavy hitter when it comes to blow, but he's too good to leave home. Against him all those pumped-up boys seem as mobile as bulldozers. And thanks to me, he holds back a bit before the matches. Besides, my uncle knows very well he couldn't always count on me if he left Kai on the bench. The yellow city limit sign from Olpe flies by the passenger side window of the T5 VW van. I lean forward, my face between Hinkel and my uncle.

"Now go straight—"

"Straight to the first circle, second right," Axel interrupts me. I fall back on my seat and respond to Kai's rolling his eyes by rolling my own. He hands me a cigarette. I light it and take a long drag. The space between the metal supports of the headrest in front of me is completely filled by my uncle's meaty red neck. His shoulders, so angular, as if constructed with a carpenter's square, protrude to the left and right of the seat. I exhale a plume of smoke toward the red surface between the braces and say, "Exactly."

We turn off onto a dry forest path. The sand crunches under the tires. We're immediately enveloped by the shade of the rustling trees. It's good to be out of the direct sunlight, and I notice how the slight cooling makes me somewhat calmer. It started when we left Olpe. That feeling that always comes just before things go crazy. I don't know if it's comparable with stage fright, I never had stage fright, after all. At any rate, it feels like something in my stomach begins to float. As if my belly was filled with helium and pressing up against my lungs from below.

"There," Hinkel says and points ahead with his fat, hairy finger. The three of us on the backseat crane our necks just to see something. A fair ways down the path we see the motorcade from Cologne. The guys stand around in front of their cars. Axel turns around and stares through the back window. I instinctively move my head to the side so he can see better but then immediately think to myself that I should cool it. I look back too. Everything's okay. The others are behind us, like before. No one got cold feet and turned around. I would have been very surprised.

"Park here," my uncle orders. Hinkel maneuvers the van as best he can on the grass strip between the forest path and the bushes. The others park behind us. We get out. The guys from Cologne park the same way. Just on the other side of the path. When the gig here is over, everyone will get back in their cars and disappear in opposite directions.

Axel walks around the hood of the car, positioning himself in the middle of the path, legs spread wide. I take my mouth guard out of the case and don't let my uncle escape my gaze. Tomek takes up position beside him. They put their heads together. I lean toward Kai and ask him for a cig. He tries to fumble the pack out of his tight jeans. I hold out my hand, keep on looking over to Axel, who is inspecting the guys from Cologne, hands on hips.

"Come on," I say, "any day now."

"Take it easy," Kai mumbles. I sway, rocking from one leg to the other. I go over to Axel and Tomek when I finally have a cigarette between my fingers.

"What?" Axel bellows when he notices someone approaching. Then he sees it's me. His jaw relaxes somewhat and he briefly rests his paw on my shoulder and pulls me closer.

"I just counted them," Tomek says with his Polack accent. It sounds like "cow-ted." "Fifteen men plus camera."

"Everyone got their red T-shirt on?" Axel asks. Could turn around and look himself, I think, but bite my tongue, of course. I passed out the T-shirts before we left. Precisely so we wouldn't have to be waiting around now.

"Everyone does," I say.

I want to add what I've worked out regarding formation. That we should try to put the massive guys in front. Like a breakwater, more or less. That way, we could catch a little of the first impact, even if it's at the cost of speed. But Axel raises his hand to signal I should be quiet. I haven't even said half a sentence. One of the guys from Cologne walks toward us. I'm guessing he's the guy I was in touch with.

"Okay," Axel says.

I don't know who to, exactly.

"Heiko. You make sure the others are ready."

He holds his hand out in front of me as if wanting to block my path, which isn't necessary, and goes toward the other guy, who has stopped in the middle distance and was waiting for one of us. I feel completely taken for a ride. After all, the agreement between Axel and me was that I would handle all the logistics this time. I try to swallow it. Tomek pats me on the arm. There is a faded tattoo of some woman on his hand. I look at him briefly, then at the ground, saying, "Fuck it," and grind out my cigarette.

Kai stands in front of the van with a cig in his mouth and examines himself in the tinted windows. He plucks at his short spiky hair. Everyone else is wearing the red T-shirts I passed out. He has a red Fred Perry polo on. At least he left the collar down for once. I step next to him, look at him first, then myself.

"You actually know how insane you are?"

Kai doesn't react, keeps on rocking from side to side and rolls his cigarette between his lips, humming. My face next to his in the dark brown-tinted windows. Expressionless. Corners of my mouth pointed toward the ground. Brow furrowed. Dead serious. At least my hair is shaved back down to a millimeter. A huge shadow pushes across the reflection in the car window.

"Hey, ya losers. It's been a while," says Ulf. "Ready?"

"I was fuckin' born ready," Kai says and slams his right elbow into his left palm, making a slapping sound.

I blow air through my lips. "You're a retard," I say. I turn around and look at Ulf, who's at least a head taller than me: "Way too long."

"Tell that to Jojo's crooked nose."

We laugh. Ulf gazes down the path. He asks why my uncle's down there shooting the shit again. If it wasn't my turn this time. I nod, but simultaneously lift my shoulders, what do I know?

"Come on, you know Axel," Kai weighs in. "Little uncle doesn't like to hand over the reins."

"Fuck it. He should do what he wants," I say. Ulf shrugs his shoulders too. The XXL shirt stretches tight around his chest and biceps. His collar looks like it might burst any second.

"You set this up here, after all."

I nod again, say I actually don't give a fuck so long as there's finally another rumble. We haven't had a single match since the new season started. Hinkel and a couple of the other old warhorses come back from taking a piss, breaking through the bushes. All of them form a semicircle around Axel. Skulls roll from shoulder to shoulder. Arms are stretched. Hands are shaken loose.

"Straighten up now! Let's go!" Axel calls.

I swallow my mouth guard. Bite down. The nervousness is only just an aftertaste. We form three rows across the width of the path. The adrenaline courses through my body. I get light-headed.

The squad lurches forward. Axel and Tomek are a step ahead of us. Ulf and Kai next to me. Fucking hell, he's grinning, and it gets me started. Then I look straight ahead. At the wall of shaved heads and white shirts pushing toward us. They become faster, bellowing, "Hanoi whores!" Several raise their fists.

Now we accelerate. Watch our footing. You need firm ground to step on. Otherwise you've already lost. They're running. We are too. Don't stumble now! Don't step on Axel's heel! Soon. I feel hands on my back pushing me forward. As if that was needed. Any second now!

One last howl. The forest falls silent. Then bodies slam into each other. Fists and legs are swung. I still see Axel basically sucked into the Cologne throng. A guy in front of me. A fist comes toward me. I take the swing. Duck under the blow. Throw myself against him. He doesn't fall. Fucker's too stable. He's huffing and puffing. They fly past all around me. Entangled. Tilted. In a headlock. The bald guy in front of me is ripped. Who cares? Raise your block. Fake a move to the left. He had the same idea. Is surprised. His punch is hasty. Slides past. Land a jab against his jaw. He groans. Stumbles. Not a clean hit. He comes hunched over, hands raised. I want to juke him again, then someone slams into me from behind. No chance. His fist slams directly onto my collarbone. Probably aimed for my face. Lucked out again. But my collarbone yowls. Seems to vibrate. Fuck it, I tell myself. I jump forward. Fake right. Juked him out. Fucker wasn't expecting that. He whips his hands up. Kidney shot. He bends over but is able to stay up. His hands instinctively go toward his kidneys. Tough luck! I slam a haymaker straight into his ugly kisser. Folds like a pocket knife, bends over and groans. Spits his mouth guard in the sand. Teeth covered in blood. Stay down, damn it! Stay down! I look around. Not too long! He stays down. Begs off, eyes clenched in pain. My vision is narrow as a bottleneck. I peer through and see Kai. In a clinch. Fucker from Cologne is tugging at his polo shirt. Kai tries to pull free. He pivots, his opponent comes along and raises dust. Another white shirt behind him. No fucking way, you bastard! The guy lifts his leg as I charge. Catches my groin. I'm a fucking idiot! Lose my footing, but catch myself with my hands. He's already on top of me. Gets a knee to my side. Breath knocked out of me. Try to catch myself. My hand slips and bends in an unnatural direction. Pain shoots from my wrist up into my shoulder. A taste like Styrofoam in the back of my mouth. No time. He comes. I push off him. Create some space. The goon falls for it. Gives me time to get up. My hand is numb. Not my elbow. My left straight-arm connects with his blocking arm and pulls it to the side. Then I slam my elbow into his trap. He goes down. Coughs. Gags and holds his face. I wait. Keep moving. He removes his hand, looks at it. A wide, shining cut over his left eye gushes. He stays down. I'm winded myself. There's just isolated, exhausted skirmishes that slowly disentangle. I put my hands on my hips. The air jags through my lungs like shards of glass. Fucking cigs! Now light one up. Some commotion behind me. Töller stands in the bushes, a good two meters away. Tatters of his T-shirt hang from his upper body. I go over to him, see he's standing over a guy bleeding with a split lip. The guy holds his hand feebly in front of his face, but Töller gets in two more shots and is screaming at him. I grab Töller's arm. My other hand around his waist and pull him away.

"Are you crazy, Töller? He's had enough!"

He pushed against me halfheartedly. "The piece of shit hit me in the balls!"

I pull him back out of the bushes. Several people come over, want to see what's going on here, but I raise my hands. Everything's fine. Everything sorted out. I use both hands to shove Töller, who wants to get past me.

"Take it easy, man! It had to be an accident. Even if it wasn't, just fuck it." Then I raise my finger. Hold it up close to my face, point at him.

"If I catch you punching someone on the ground one more time . . ."

"What then, Mr. Kolbe?"

He turns away before I can answer, waving me off.

"Hey!" Axel's voice booms through the trees. His shirt looks almost freshly washed. He spreads his arms in a question, his hands open. I show him that everything's okay. Ulf comes over. His collar is torn. The skin underneath is scratched and red. He congratulates me. I ask him why, but then I notice. Most of the people on the ground are wearing white T-shirts. The reds are standing. They're chanting: "Hann-o-ver! Hann-o-ver!" My shoulders feel lighter than they have for a long time. My stomach is as though filled with lead and crashes to the bottom of my torso. I crouch down next to Ulf's massive legs, rest my forearms on my knees, and try to breathe. My ribcage feels constricted. The collarbone flickers with numbness. My left arm is heavy. I spit my mouth guard into my hand. It covers my palm with blood. My face pulses with hot pain. I look up at Ulf. "Hope there's a second round."

When I slunk off at the rest stop just after putting the Ruhr Valley behind us, spreading the individual parts of the burner phone on the adjacent field, Kai and Töller got into it with a group of Polish truck drivers over some ridiculous shit. But Tomek was able to defuse the situation and shortly after that, when I came back, they were standing there together and passing around an unlabeled bottle of booze. Axel was just about to rip into Kai and Töller, them nodding in unison, asking what that shit was about, starting something after a match, and who the fuck had put that shit in their heads. But Axel didn't really sound all that into it—after all, we still had the fresh taste of victory on our lips.

So we arrived back in Hannover just before midnight. Everyone climbed back into his car. Even Ulf had to go, otherwise Saskia would bitch him out at home.

Kai and me drive back to the main train station together. I just want to go to bed. He still wants to head to Raschplatz and party; in other words, go out and find someone to bone.

We guzzle a quick pilsner at our local. Then I take the last regional train out to Wunstorf. Kai kept trying to convince me to come along, but I had no interest in shitty tunes and Beck's for the price of a used car. Even though he doesn't like being dissed downtown either, when you're looking for someone easy to screw, your best chances are there. But you should demand to see the ID of the person you go off with, to be on the safe side.

It actually happened to Kai once. He went home with a sweet little piece. 'Cause the parents were on vacation. And then there was a class schedule hanging in the kitchen, tenth grade, on the fridge. He claims he's never gotten his pants back on quicker. I think he went to a brothel that same night, got himself a professional significantly older than the girl. As an ethical correction, more or less.

As far as I'm concerned, there's only two ways you can drag me into the dives on Raschplatz: either it's Kai's birthday, or I'm so sloshed I don't understand a thing.

———

Arnim's farm is just over a half mile away from the train station in Wunstorf, where I'd parked my VW Polo hatchback from the eighties. When you're heading on the county road toward the autobahn on-ramp in Luthe, there's a field lane you have to follow till you hit the small patch of woods that surrounds the house. At night, I need almost half an hour, 'cause Armin hammered into me immediately after I moved in with him, you have to switch off the lights as soon as you leave the county road. If there's something he can't stand, it's unwelcome guests. Especially law enforcement.

I turn off the long, tree-lined lane into the driveway. In the pale, indirect light I can make out Jojo's Volvo next to Arnim's old pickup.

I climb up the peeling porch steps mumbling to myself, "Please don't let him be blown away. Please don't let him be blown away." All the while, I imagine Arnim standing over Jojo's corpse with his gun in his hand, one foot resting on the perforated belly like Captain Morgan, and looking at me and asking, "What? Unlawful entry, my boy."

Standing outside the front door, which is actually made up of two doors, the normal one and a screen door, I listen to the darkness for a moment. When I hear Jojo's voice, my prayer, which I didn't believe in anyway, evaporates.

I open the screen door. It hits the doorbell mounted above: Arnim's "alarm system." The familiar yapping starts up behind the house. A rectangular beam of light falls in my direction through the kitchen door. Then Arnim's heavyset silhouette pushes through.

"Who's there?" he calls. I see he already has the gun in his hand.

"It's just me, you mad dog," I answer and toss my duffel bag into the darkness of the living room. It hits the cushions of the old sofa with a thump. I hear Jojo call my name. The dogs are still yapping away excitedly. You can hear the clatter of the pen when they jump up against it.

"Shut up!" Arnim's bellowing turns into a phlegm-coated cough. He grabs the rifle by the barrel, sits back down at the table, and bangs several times on the windowpane with the gunstock. I expect the glass to break any second. But nothing happens except for the thundering frame.

Jojo jumps up. His short, tight curls bounce. We give each other a five and pat each other on the shoulder. I immediately feel my collarbone, which seems to stretch across the whole shoulder. Jojo's nose is still completely swollen and glows like a grow light. I grab a can of Elephant beer from the cooler and sit down at the kitchen table with the two of them.

"Well? What?" Jojo wants to know. I tell him about the successful trip to Cologne, and how Axel once again didn't want to hand over the reins, despite our agreement. Jojo greedily took in every little bit. Every now and then he groans and says how he fucking wished he could have been there, etc. Arnim gazes emptily into the darkness lurking outside the yellow-shaded windows. His lungs wheeze strenuously, doing everything they can so he doesn't suffocate right here and now. I look at him, amused. He doesn't usually get it anyway. I don't even want to know what kind of crazy things are shooting through his head again. Jojo squeezes his beer can, producing a rhythmic clacking sound.

"Have some good news."

"Spit it out," I say, and have difficulty detaching from the hypnotic up and down of Arnim's paunch.

"I got the position!" Jojo's voice did loops from the happiness.

I ask what position he's talking about: "What?"

"Well, not a position. I mean, because it's not a paid job. It's a volunteer position."

I stare at him, not understanding.

"He's now a coach with the football here," Arnim says, takes a sip, and looks away again. Maybe the old dude understands more than I gave him credit for.

"How? What?"

"Yeah. No. So. The coach of the B team had to quit. Stroke. And Gerti's filling in. Yes, and I have his position now. Coach of the C youth team."

"Fuck yeah, man," I say and hold my can out for Jojo to clink. "Cheers." We knock cans and drain the elephant piss.

Jojo had started a couple years ago. It was back when he was going through a really rough time. After the thing with Joel, which was hell for all of us. But that Jojo's father would really fuck things up a couple months later, truly no one could have seen that coming. We were already afraid we wouldn't ever be able to get Jojo out of his deep hole. No one wanted to leave him alone, and we divided up shifts. Then, on some random day, Jojo got up, finally took a shower, and went to the practice field in Luthe. Not a word to anyone. And would you look at that, co-trainer of the under-fifteen U15 development team. That had gotten him on track again. Even to the extent he went back to his old boss at the retirement home and apologized for drinking on the job. And once again, look at that, Jojo had his janitor's job back.

"I thought to myself, I'll change a couple things. Regarding the practice program. Do things different than Gerti did," circling the top of his beer can with his fingertip, "maybe integrate a couple of things we practiced with Joel, back when. I was meaning to ask you. Maybe you have the sketches we made back then. You remember? With the drills on them and all that."

I nod to myself and sigh. My gaze repeatedly drifts down to the surface of the table.

"It's been an eternity. Not sure I have them with my stuff anymore."

"Yeah, not here, but maybe back at your dad's place."

"Jojo, hey, seriously . . ." My mouth tastes like Styrofoam again.

"Yeah, just check the next time you're there."

He thanks me and drinks. A stream of beer misses his mouth and flows through his stubble and over his chin. He wipes at it with the sleeve of Joel's old Hannover 96 warm-up jacket. Only then does he realize what he'd just done.

"Well, shit," he mumbles and tries to rub the tiny beer spot dry with his bare hand. I kill my can and slam it on the table.

"Well, I'm so fucking tired. Think I'm gonna hit the hay now."

Jojo downed what was left and ground out his burned-down cigarette, which he'd forgotten in the ashtray.

"I'll head off then," he said.

We hugged, patting each other on the back. We don't actually do hugs, but for some odd reason we're in sync in the exact same moment, making it an honest hug and no embarrassed spreading of arms and leaning back and forth and end up just shaking hands.

We go to the door. I wanted to turn the porch light on, but nothing happened. I yell over to the kitchen that the damn outside light is already broken again and hold the door open for Jojo. The bell rings and riles up the dogs again. In the kitchen Arnim yells I should shut my trap.

"And congrats again," I say and hold open the porch door, 'cause it'd bang shut otherwise.

"Come over to practice sometime or something. I haven't told Ulf and Kai yet. And," he balls up his fist, "awesome how you guys smashed Cologne."

Jojo climbed into the Volvo, turned around, and putted down the drive. I raise my hand in parting. Then the car disappears behind the birches and willows arching over the driveway.

I get another beer from the kitchen. Arnim's chin is resting a couple inches above his paunch and trembling from the snoring. I take the rifle with me, placing it on the sofa on my way upstairs, and grab my duffel bag. The stairs creak like the bones of an old man.

As I walk through the dark hallway, I hear wings beating behind the first door on the left. It sounds dry. Like sandpaper rubbed together. The pungent smell of bird crap is pervasive. I unlock my room. The piece of hard rubber stapled at the bottom of my door scrapes over the old wooden flooring. I have to use my knee just under the lock to push the door shut. Then I turn on the light. Duffel bag to the corner. Open the beer. There's still a pack of cigs on the table. I stay standing in the middle of the room for a moment. Alternate between drinking and taking a drag. Feel my body. Feels like it's been wrung out. Has been, actually. I smile to myself, contented, then the pain shoots through my jaw again, and I dim it with more beer. Already half-empty again. Only now do I notice I haven't eaten anything since this morning. Was too nervous. While standing, I take off my shoes with some effort. Then I undress completely. My clothes make a small pile among many in the room. Need to go to the laundromat again. Fuck it, turning it inside-out works, too. My real phone is still on the power cord attached to the outlet next to the door. I pull it out. It sparks, but it doesn't catch me. Three messages, five missed calls. All five over the course of the day. All of them from Manuela. Then a MMS from Kai, which makes me laugh. He took a selfie, shirtless and thumbs up. Behind him there's some bimbo, legs together and bent over on the bedspread, pointing her naked ass toward him. Her head can't be seen. Behind it I recognize Kai's bedroom.

"That was fast," I write, "new record?"

A text from Uncle Axel: "Good job. See you at work." I don't write back. The third message is from Manuela. Sent a couple hours ago: "Heiko, where are you at?? Please call me back, but not so late. We go to bed around 10. It's about dad. Finally were able to get a spot in rehab. Hugs and kisses, your big sister. PS. Greetings from Andreas."

Of course, her retard fucktard husband sends his regards. I read the text again and press my thumb to the power button until the screen goes black.

I stand in the bathroom and study myself in the mirror. My face is distorted by the cracks in the glass, and I have to concentrate to fit the pieces in my head like in a puzzle. Otherwise I look like a mutant or something. But I'm not too far from that either. The left side of my face is a little swollen on the cheek and glimmers red to purple. On my mouth, there are two globs of congealed blood, which I leave where they are. Got off okay this time.

Even the collarbone appears to be okay. Though it may hurt like hell now, that'll be gone in two or three days, max. I rest the beer on the lip of the sink. Next to it, some damp dust rolls into something that looks like a delicate gray maggot. I hold my hands up in front of me, turning and examining them directly and in the reflection. Blood has collected under the skin on all the joints and who knows where else. There's a remnant of blood I must have missed at the sink in the rest stop toilet. Not my blood. Here and there scratches, with dirt in the furrows. I look at myself again. Not the mutant reflection, but rather the composite, true puzzle-me. As I'm standing here in the flickering light, surrounded by tiles that don't even look white by day anymore.

"Good job," I repeat, and try to look myself in the eye, as if there was a real person standing behind the mirror, someone who should be praised.

I climb into the shower. A family of silverfish scurries into the cracks between the tiles.

Damp footprints follow me into my room. I lock the door, slip into some boxers, which immediately absorb the shower water I hadn't dried off, and lie down on the mattress. The water covers my stubbly hair like a blanket of mist and cools my scalp. I cross my arms behind my head. Close my eyes. I think about Yvonne. About her pretty face and her eyebrows, which are as free as a cloudless sky.

———

It was after the match between the under-23 reserve teams of Hannover and Braunschweig. I think people still called them amateurs or second-string back then, though it wasn't very long ago at all. Today the team is officially called the U23. That was in Eilenriede Stadium's good old curves. Normally, I can't take the ultras seriously. They get so excited they piss in their pants, but you have to give it to them, they really fired up the old cauldron that day.

We were supposed to meet afterward in Hannover's city forest. In the central fir section, I think. At any rate, it had to be as far
as possible from the street and, of course, the cops. Eight against
ten, because we couldn't raise more people. Young crew against
young crew. Young Dogs against the Cool Hogs. It sounds stupid
if you say one after the other. The bit about the Young Dogs was
my idea. Supposed to be a kind of play on words. There are the
Red Wolves, and so we were the Young Dogs. When Kai found out
what I wanted to call us, first he burst out laughing and then he
threw a fit.

"You can't call yourselves that! Sounds like a group of fag Boy
Scouts," he tossed at me.

I just shrugged my shoulders and said it doesn't make a rat's
ass bit of difference what we call ourselves.

"Y'could at least have made it Young Dogz! With a *z* at the
end."

"Are you a damn gangsta rapper now?!"

"Nah, dude, but . . . I mean . . ." he said and took another pick-
me-up. "Or look, how about Bloodhoundz? Get it? Because blood
is red, like us. Just not such a faggy name."

"Come on, drop it. It is what it is."

"Look at it from the other side," Jojo said. "Better than an old
fucking rap group from Cologne."

"Which is also true."

Everything went so damn fast. Had to go damn fast because even
if we were in the woods, we were still in the middle of the city. The
cops could bust through the undergrowth any moment, lights
flashing. Alerted by a concerned walker taking an evening stroll.
Luckily enough, it was raining, which meant not many people

were walking around. But you could slip on the wet ground, which was already covered with moisture, so you watch like mad so you don't fall on your ass. At any rate, the Cool Hogs weren't so cool when we beat the living shit out of them with just eight of us. They bounced off Ulf like the raindrops that kept pounding our faces. And the rest of us did a respectable job.

I was going at it with one of them when I grabbed his lid and threw it at him. He was so distracted I had plenty of time to aim and knock him out. I hope I'll never forget the sound of him splashing in the mud. They had more or less already lost when I saw one of them reaching for something hanging from his belt. He was going at it with Kai. I'm still of the opinion I saw something flash. So I went over. Just thought to myself, no fucking way, you butt-fucker, and kicked him in the back of his knee, and then wound up. All the way. There was plenty of time. And thumped a really brutal haymaker against the side of the guy's head. Kai looked at me in surprise and at first I didn't know why he was so wide-eyed. Must have been quite a punch. The guy from Braunschweig lay there. Lay there with his face in the rain-soaked glop, like a fish out of water. And twitched like crazy, and there was blood running out of his ear. Didn't know what I should make of it. All the adrenaline and the rage over all that shit and the booze from before, at the game. All I can remember is how quickly Kai got Tomek. He'd seen the whole thing. Axel was busy with something and had sent Tomek as a minder, to report on how we did. Really gave them a beating. Tomek and Kai immediately carried him away. I just stood looking back and saw how two guys from Braunschweig took him, swung his arms over their shoulders, and dragged him off.

Axel didn't want to believe I'd seen a knife. But I'm still of the opinion there was one. Only no one thought to check the grass later. After all, everyone had to get the fuck out because you could already hear the sirens howling over the tips of the trees. But Axel was pretty impressed all the same. With two fewer. Against Braunschweig. He called it an important victory for Hannover and didn't mean the match between the two second-string football teams. I told Kai about the knife too, and he couldn't get over it, enthusiastically roaring my praises, and when I asked him if he'd seen the knife, he said something like, "Not directly, but I think something definitely fell into the grass. Definitely!"

———

I take the causeway to reach my father's house. It's on the other end of Wunstorf, in a street with other former farms. The street is basically a dead end, even if the town is too lazy or broke—or both—to put up a sign. At some point the asphalt just stops and gives way to a field that stretches out into the plain. On a day like this you have such a view over the flat land that you could almost fall into the sky. Even on cloudy days, you can usually see all the way to Mount Potash, which looks different depending on the weather. Sometimes white like the salt on fries, sometimes gray like concrete.

One time I broke in with Kai, Jojo, and Joel at the grounds of the potash and salt company there. Stomped up to the top where the salt is harvested. Jojo and Joel had brought a kite they wanted to fly, and it really soared. Kai and I didn't know exactly why we wanted to go there. Then we got the wild idea to jump off, but it was a major fail. On one side it went down steep for what must have been at least a hundred feet, which would have been instant death. And on the other side, where we were, it was flat enough that we'd have been back on our feet within a couple of meters. At some point, Kai got going so fast from the incline that he lost his balance, staggered, and rolled down the slope like a barrel. He came to rest at the base of the hill, motionless, and the three of us were flipping out, but when we got close to Kai's body, just lying there, he jumped up and laughed his ass off. His clothes were torn to shreds and he had bloody scrapes all over. A flap of skin was hanging off his shin. I can still remember how Joel immediately had to puke when he saw that.

I press the doorbell, and before I can waste a single thought on immediately turning on my heel and getting back in my car, my sister is already opening the door.

"Heiko. Nice. Finally. There you are."

She opens her arms, and I take a hesitant step toward her. Then she pulls me close. I feel stupid because I'm just standing in Manuela's hug, my arms hanging at my sides. She squeezes several times, so I give up and place a hand on her arm too. This appears to finally satisfy her, and she lets go and says I should come in. I follow her into the main hallway, which leads to all of the rooms in the house. She walks ahead of me and disappears behind the kitchen door to the right. My eyes have to get used to the hazy lighting. Due to the sheer size of the space and because there aren't any windows, with the exception of the glass front door, it's usually shrouded in darkness. At the height of summer this was always the best place to be when I wanted to cool down. Stripped to just my underwear, I would lie down on the black floorboards and doze until my mother or Hans would rouse me with a kick, saying I shouldn't be lying around where people walk. The old glassed-in cabinet is still against the right wall, next to the kitchen. It was already there when the house belonged to my grandparents. I pause right in front and look at the things behind the glass. If a stranger came in, they'd probably ask what kind of taste-impaired people lived here. Admittedly, I ask myself the same thing again and again, but at least I know the strange hodgepodge comes from the fact that three generations have lived here. My mother's spooky porcelain figurines—angels, cats, and dogs—perch on top of my grandma's placemats that she crocheted herself. The figurines were apparently not worth taking. Next to them stand little golden Buddha statues with fat bellies and wooden elephants decorated in purple and gold. Mie's contribution to the jumble. Only now does the idea occur to me that it might not have been Mie who put them in. No real Thai thinks stuff like that is good. It's more like the bullshit that's hocked to Western tourists, making them pay through the nose. Maybe my father brought it back and set it up because he thought that way Mie would feel more at home.

"Heiko, are you still there?"

Manuela's head peered sideways out the doorway. The glasses she didn't need and only had to look more like a teacher were dangling from her neck. I hear Hans's voice from the kitchen. He's saying something. But I can't understand him.

"All right, Papa," she said, and then again to me, "Come on. The coffee is getting cold."

How carefully she pronounced the words. So deliberately prim, just so she wouldn't say it wrong. Made the hair stand up on the back of my ass. I almost hit my head on the low ceiling, that's how long I hadn't been there. Manuela bustles around the small kitchen. Sparse light falls through the window and the patio door. Mie is standing at the sink and washing dishes. My father is sitting at the table, left and right arms resting next to his plate, which is already full of large crumbs. "Hey," I mumble. Mie briefly turns and whispers a hello. At least I assume so. It used to make me furious how quiet she always is. Today, because I don't have to live here anymore, I couldn't care less. Even though she's discrete, I still see Manuela give our father a poke, and he too produces a "Hey" before he loads another piece of cream-filled almond cake on his plate.

"Sit down, sit down," Manuela asks and immediately pours me a coffee. I pull out my cigarettes and place them next to my plate. Manuela instantly produces the ashtray and sets it noisily in front of me on the table.

The next minutes, in which no one at the table exchanges glances, are tortured. Mie places a dish with brown balls next to the plate with the cake. Then everyone is finally seated.

"What is that, Mie?"

"Kai nok . . ." and I don't understand the rest because it's Thai and fades into silence.

She appears to ponder how you could translate it but doesn't come up with a solution. Also because Manuela nods and says, "Aha," as if she knew exactly what was in those steaming bull balls.

I remove a cigarette from the pack, and while I light up, Manuela loads a piece of cake on my plate. Only then does she ask, "Cake?"

I wave my hand vaguely and tap the ash off my cigarette. My father looks over for the first time. He stares at my cig and runs his tongue over his upper lip. Even though it's been years since he shaved off his old porn stache, I still haven't gotten used to the view of his naked upper lip, which is covered in beads of sweat.

"Can I bum one?" he asks and didn't look at me for a single second, speaking only to the pack.

With relish, I take a long drag on my cigarette, knock off the ash, take another drag, and place it on my ashtray.

Then I flick the pack. It slides across the table, past Manuela, and slams against Hans's plate. He takes one out and pats down his pants pocket. Doesn't find anything, and now he looks at me, the butt already between his lips.

"Have a light?"

His eyes are simultaneously watery and glassy. Like an ashtray that someone had accidentally poured liquid into. I flick the lighter right after.

After the whole smoking thing is over and Manuela has quit her hacking, she finally gets to the point. Her disapproving gaze, which fits perfectly with the strict bun she's tugged her hair into, remains unchanged. She can't stand us puffing away but has to go along because she's in the minority and not inside her own four walls. At least she's learned to have an ashtray handy in situations like these, because neither Hans nor I give a rat's ass where we put our ashes.

"It's nice to finally be sitting together."

No one reacts. Only Mie is smiling somewhere between embarrassment and approval.

"But there's also an occasion," Manuela continued. "I was finally able—I have to say with the help of Andreas's good connections—to secure a spot in rehab for Papa."

Hans lets loose a scornful grunt that sounds so vulgar, as if his mouth was an asshole. But Manuela doesn't let herself be fazed. That's from her years of experience.

"And he has—," she cleared her throat, "will be going to Bad Zwischenahn until November."

"Hmmm," I murmur past the piece of dry cake in my mouth. I'm afraid she must have baked it herself.

I'm wise enough to refrain from asking what all this has to do with me, because I have absolutely no interest in a full-on bargaining session. In a second, she'll be getting around to saying why it'll all be my business.

"I'll probably take him there personally next week," because she wants to be truly sure that he'll go, but of course she doesn't say that.

"Of course, someone will have to tend to Papa's pigeons during that time"—aha, so that's the way things roll—"and because I really won't have any time to take care of that too, with my job—and the kids are so demanding at their age—and I have so much to prepare and get through before and after school, with corrections, I just can't manage it, and because Mie's terrified of the birds, we were thinking"—she looks at Hans, probably in the hope she'd catch his gaze, but he keeps staring at his cake—"I was thinking that you could do it, Heiko. You used to always help Gramps feed the birds, right? So you must still know how all that works."

It's at least twenty years ago.

"That would be a great relief for all of us, Heiko." She appears to have repressed the reason why I never again set a foot in the shed, never helped my father with the feeding after he'd taken over the pigeon breeding from grandpa. Suits her agenda.

While I'm busy scarfing down the last piece of cake, I mentally scroll through various excuses, none of which is substantial enough that Manuela wouldn't throw it right back at me.

The rock-hard corners of her mouth loosen, and her eyes, which seemed almost rectangular, relax a little. She probably noticed I couldn't think of a good objection. I really, really don't want to do it, but once again, some sort of important connection between my brain and my facial expressions is apparently MIA.

"So it's a deal," she decides and is the first to take one of Mie's meatballs. She bites down and is only barely able to twist her mouth into a smile. I can see her fake a smile for Mie. Mie smiles back, unsure. Then I look at my father, who's having a staring match with his cake and probably thinking only about the next can. I can't blame him. I don't feel any different. Sitting here, at this table, in this house. With my biological family. Damn it to hell, what I want more than anything is to get drunk with the next best can of beer. Nothing here makes any sense, I think to myself, and pat the table, saying, "Good."

This pulls everyone else out of the thoughts they were just lost in. I down my coffee, get up, and reach across the table for my smokes.

"Got to get movin'," I say, "lots of shit to do."

No one was expecting that exit, not even my sister, who's stuttering away, immediately searching for some random thing we could still discuss. No. Way. I turn on my heel, knock on the doorframe in parting, not looking back, and am through the hallway, out the door, maneuvering my VW hatchback down the driveway.

———

Wotan Boxing Gym is a former factory building in Hannover's Stöcken district. Uncle Axel once told me they used to produce fountain pens or ballpoint pens here. The company went belly-up. Axel, who owned part of a bar next to Steintor, had his share paid out and bought the joint for next to nothing and opened the gym. The clientele is mostly made up of less-than-success-ful martial artists, pals from the security scene, and bikers. And unfortunately, a good deal of right-wing riff-raff. You shouldn't be too surprised at that if you name your gym after a Germanic god. If I had my way, none of the skinheads would be allowed in. But as the gofer I have next to no say. Adjusting equipment, sort-ing weights, wiping up sweat and blood here and there. Besides, you can catch wind of plenty of things you shouldn't list on your résumé. I've already been doing the job for five years now. Since I flamed out of school after wasting my second chance. But despite the shit I've seen here and have to listen to, day in, day out, I can't imagine anything else. No suit busting my balls. Axel usually lets me do my own thing. I can work out whenever I want. And I earn more than enough to pay the bills.

Right now, I'm checking the protective covers in the corners of the boxing ring and tightening them as needed. We have a regulation-size ring and two smaller ones for sparring.

"Mornin', Heiko."

Gaul sticks his head, ponytail, and full beard through the ropes. His hands, holding tight to the ropes, are covered with skulls. Did it himself. With whichever hand was free. Gaul is a biker and part of the Hannover chapter of the Angels, the big-gest in all of Germany. He's the Angels' tattoo artist. But we still all go to him. Of course, he doesn't do our tattoos at their club-house, keeping to his kitchen table at home instead. But he's used the needle on me in the gym's locker-room, too. He doesn't have outside customers because he works at the gym, in a manner of speaking. As well as several other clubs and bars. His main job is hustling stuff for the motorcycle gang. Anabolic steroids aren't for me personally, but I'd be the last to dictate what others can or can't do.

I pull the knots tight, slip through the ropes, and sit down on the edge of the ring. We shake hands. I like Gaul because he's a straight shooter through and through. And he's not a big mouth. But I wouldn't want to owe him anything. Not after one or two involuntary tattoo sessions I've heard about him giving people who couldn't or didn't want to fork over something.

"How you doin'?" I ask.

"Draggin' along." I nod. "Hey, you already talk to your uncle today?"

"Nope, why?"

"We need the locker-room a little bit later for a couple minutes. Axel's busy but said you could open up for us."

"Sure."

"I'd need you to stand in front of it and make sure no one disturbs us when we're inside. Shouldn't take too long. Quarter hour. We'll come in through the back, you'll lock up after us and then go up front so no one tries to get into the locker-room from the hall."

"No problem."

"Good man. Then I'll just pop out and make some calls."

In the meantime, I'm scrolling through my Facebook news feed, even get so bored I sweep the entryway, and I chain-smoke at the back entrance. Axel's office door is closed the whole time, and he doesn't come out once.

At some point I'm out back again, puffing away, and Gaul and two other guys from the gang roll up on choppers. They're trailed by an unmarked delivery vehicle that expels four Turks or Arabs with faces that look like bulldogs. One of them is lugging two chunky black leather bags.

Gaul and his colleagues nod to me. One of the Rabs stops in front of me when I get up from the folding chair and grind out my cig with my foot.

"Who's he?"

I'd like to tell him it shouldn't interest him a flying fuck, but Gaul says, "Works here. A friend."

I walk ahead of them, into the hallway with four doors along the walls. Axel's office on the right, on the left the storage closet, service entrance to the locker-room, and straight ahead at the end of the corridor, the entrance to the gym. I unlock the door to the locker-room, hold it open for them, and lock it behind them. Then I go up front to the gym. I again check the door to the locker-room I'd just locked and remain standing in front of it.

I can't understand what's being discussed in there. Don't want to know either. Should have brought a chair in case this takes a while.

Tall-boy Töller came in, duffel bag slung over his shoulder. Came to the hooligans the same time as my uncle. He's even a little taller than Ulf but more of a beanpole. Not a wall of granite like Ulf. I can't completely get behind Töller. Everything he says sounds like a provocation. It can really get on your nerves long-term. But we actually do have similar points of view. Regarding keeping your political views to yourself on the field, for instance. He has just as little patience as I do for the brown diarrhea a lot of guys spew. And Töller knows his football. His general knowledge doesn't stop in the midnineties. He's still a true Hannover 96 supporter. Of course, all of us are, but with a lot of our boys—and this isn't just the case in Hannover—sometimes you hardly know it's about football and representing your hometown, so to speak. But what he pulled against the boys from Cologne recently, that's one of the reasons I can't really stand him.

I step to the side and block his way because he wants to slip past me. Hold up my hands.

"Sorry, can't go in there right now."

"Huh, what? Why not?"

"Just can't do it right now. Have to wait a couple minutes."

"Kolbe, I have to be back at work in an hour. So let me get changed now so I can pump a little."

"Can't. Just. Right. Now."

"Why not?"

"Töller, I said you just can't right now. Closed. You just have to wait a minute."

He runs his free hand through his dark blond hair and groans in annoyance. Then he pushes past me and turns the knob on the locker-room door. Nothing happens.

"Fuck this shit!" Then he tried the knob once more and spoke toward the door: "Who's in there? Open up."

Fucking idiot, I think, and push him aside. I can hear some kind of metallic click behind the door. Then Gaul's voice: "Heiko? Heiko, what's going on out there?"

Töller looks at me. His forehead is wrinkled and his nostrils, big as boreholes, flared.

"Nothing! Everything's okay!" I call back. Then to Töller: "Now get lost. Go smoke a cigarette. I'll let you know."

He finally seemed to have caught on that he'd better knock it off with the macho act. He shoves the front door open as hard as

31

he can and steps out for a smoke. But doesn't take his eyes off of me and the locker-room.

A couple minutes later someone knocks on the door. I say I got the message and go around to the back door. I open the door. The Mulachos leave without a word and walk past me without a single glance, climbing into their van and revving around the curve.

Gaul and the other two, whose names I might know but can't think of right now, come out with backpacks that hang low and heavy. Gaul keeps standing by me while the others are already in the back.

"What was that all about?!" Gaul hissed through tightly clenched teeth. I can actually feel how he's pulling himself together so he stays peaceful.

"I'm sorry. To—" I just barely manage to shift it. "Someone came in and wanted to go into the locker-room."

"That's exactly why you were supposed to be standing there, so something like that doesn't happen. The thing almost went to shit."

"I'm really sorry, Gaul. Didn't take my hands off the wheel."

He stares deep into my eyes. Probably is trying to find out if I'm serious or if it happened because I didn't give a fuck.

"All right, we're good. After all, nothing happened." He pats me on the shoulder. Then they drive out of the yard, machines producing a deep base gurgle. His hand left a faint sweaty palm print on my T-shirt.

I go into the locker-room and look around. Everything back to normal. I unlock the door to the gym and wave at Töller, who's still standing outside, that he should come in. Then I go back to the back door. Ask myself if Axel's even there or if he was sleeping the whole time in his big boss leather chair. I knock twice and push the door open. He is, in fact, sitting on his massive office chair made of black leather. The surface of the oak desk is cleared in the middle. Three lines of blow are lined up in a row.

"What's up, Heiko?" he asks in a sharp tone of voice. The two skinheads with hollow faces turn in their chairs in front of his desk and toward me. A third is leaned over the desk, straw in hand. At the sight of me, he straightens up and interrupts his sniffing session.

"I'm busy right now. So if it's nothing important . . ."

I forget to answer him and, one after the other, examine the bozos, whose faces I recognize from somewhere. I just can't place it.

"Nah . . . um . . . it's okay," I say and want to move my body back into the hallway.

"Hey, Heiko, wait a sec," Axel says and snorts the remaining coke that's still hanging on his nostril. "Let's chat about Cologne sometime soon. A little debriefing. Okay?"

He winks conspiratorially, which confuses me so much I only stupidly nod and leave an "um" hanging in the room. The drugged, wigged-out eyes of the three skinheads follow me out. I close the door.

———

It just wasn't working anymore. Much as I wanted it to work, for *us* to work. It was equally clear I couldn't change myself and she wouldn't change. No question. That's what we'd told ourselves from the beginning of our relationship. Sure, other people wouldn't see it as real, but that's what it was. Which was also fine by me. Me and my bros were just starting to learn to play the third half—as people rightly call it—and I wasn't about to let something mess it up. Least of all a woman. On the other hand, it's Yvonne and not just any girl.

At first I kept thinking how perfect it would be. She needed plenty of space too. I never thought it'd be possible to meet anyone so compatible with my lifestyle. And then it wasn't as it seemed, but for reasons I couldn't have imagined. Goddamn! It's almost funny, but after a while I guessed she had another poker in the fire besides me. Poker . . . how fucking fitting. Always talking through everything took forever. I was never good at things like that. At least with words. And saying what's going on inside yourself, and all that emotional crap. But the conversation always heads in that direction. Without me really being prepared for it. She said it wasn't as bad as all that. That she just needed it. She has everything under control. I just have to leave her alone. After all, she accepted me just the way I was too. With the brawls and the "football crap," as she called it. Such a goddamn fucking crock of shit!

She threw all my clothes she could gather into the hallway and locked the door. I didn't even do anything about it. Like stick my foot between the door and the frame or yell she should cut it out. She said I should go, and I accepted it. I collected my clothes, went into the kitchen, and ate the meal we hadn't finished that evening. Could have just left right when she said it, but I think I was trying to draw it out. Maybe she'd reconsider and come out of her room. But, of course, she didn't. She never did. Never once in my experience did she change her mind when she'd made a decision. Not even with the smallest, least important things. I went into the living room, turned on the tube, and sat on the couch for a bit. Pet the cat next to me, which was having a hard time finding a comfortable sleeping position and was punishing the slipcover. I tidied up a bit. Put dishes in the dishwasher, carefully stacked her stupid magazines on the glass coffee table, and washed the backup utensils and hypodermic needles and syringes in the bathroom sink, returning them to their leather case. Then placed the case in its spot in the drawer in the living room cabinet. I would have preferred to slam the case against the wall. Actually, why not? For some reason, I was cleaning up like a zombie, with my head empty and stuck on straightening up. I took my things, pausing in the open doorway to the apartment, listening to Yvonne's place one last time. Then I closed the door behind me. As I went down the stairs and ran my thumb over the jags of the key in my bag, our two-year relationship shrank with every step into a tiny, compressed ball.

———

Kai's done with his classes. Even though that means he has to take an ass-load of finals on balance sheets, human resource management, and some other business crap, he still prefers to hang out with me all day at the gym and starts drinking around noon. I always skip a round of beer so I'm halfway able to do something when necessary. But there's nothing to do. And Kai's presence distracts me from the dull bits of conversation I overhear all day long. We're just sitting next to the front door, smoking, drinking, and Kai shows me pictures from Aztec stadium in Mexico City. His big dream. Just once in that ginormous stadium which used to hold more than 110,000 people. These days it still has around 95,000 seats.

"Sure, but seats, dude," I say, "it's fucking lame."

"You don't really believe the hombres stay seated, resting on their asses. There's a real fiesta!" he bellows and accidently knocks ash on his new, snow-white Le Coq shoes.

"Oh, fuck."

He licks his thumb and tries to wipe away the ashes. Gaul comes around, greets us, and goes in. We watch him go. Inside, he's approached by Latze, the six-foot-six bouncer who's smiling like a fat kid in a candy shop, and they go into the locker-room together.

"If Latze swallows any more bull shark hormones his biceps will explode someday," Kai says and giggles.

I laugh. Wave him off.

"Nah, it's only hot air anyway."

"You think? I can go in there right now and tell Latze you want to challenge him to a round of arm wrestling. Won't take long at all. Wham bam, thank you, ma'am."

He acts like he would really get up any second and do it, but then he sits down again and continues sipping on his can of beer.

"But even if the stadium is awesome," I say, "and I do have my doubts, I have to believe some of the atmosphere gets lost in a huge arena like that. Even if, who would play there anyway?" I don't wait for an answer: "Nope. Celtic versus Rangers. That," I point my raised index finger at him, "would be something! The oldest, longest-standing fucking derby in the world. That's where religions collide."

"But then the Rangers would have to move up to the top league."

"You're right about that, too," I say.

The beer almost slips from my hand when my uncle rips open the door and bellows, "Can you step into my office, Heiko?"

"Where'd he come from all of a sudden?" Kai says in a whisper, though Axel's already back inside.

"I shrug my shoulders, drain my can, and toss it to Kai, who catches it and sets it down next to him.

On the way to Axel, I try to decide whether I should ask what those Nazis were doing in his office the other day. The question had been rolling around my brain the whole day, but I just couldn't think of an answer that would be any of my business. After all, I keep my nose out of everything else that concerns the gym.

I open the door to Axel's office.

"Hey, hey, hey. Don't people knock these days or what?"

I apologize and want to close the door.

"No way. You're going right back out and doing it the right way."

You gotta be kidding me, I think to myself, but do as ordered: go back out in the hall, close the door, wait a second, knock, he says, "Yes?," I open the door, my uncle says I should come in, and I close the door behind me and plant myself on a chair and just think what the point of the preschool show was?!

Axel sorts through some documents on his desk. Acts as if nothing had happened. He actually praises me for the good organization of the Cologne match. It could have run a little more smoothly here or there, without going into detail about what he means exactly, but it was really quite good for the first time. In the end, everything turned out all right. We took home a win. No cops. Bottom line, a success.

I'm about to interrupt him and ask about the right-wingers when he says he's proud of me. I think I wasn't hearing right, but he takes a deep breath and says, "As you probably already know, I can't do this forever. It's a pity, even so, but at some point things come to an end. I'm not so shortsighted to think that I can stay fit forever. There are enough idiots out on the field that tell themselves who gives a damn what happens afterward, but not me," and he rapped his knuckles on the table. Maybe it was supposed to be some kind of superstitious knock-on-wood thing. "Heiko"—he moved so close to the desk that the edge pushed into his stomach muscles—"we're starting to build something. For Hannover. Put the city on the map, once and for all. So that no one talks about Stuttgart, Frankfurt, Dresden, Magdeburg, hell if I know, without having to mention Hannover." He balls up his hands into fists that immediately go red because of how fast the blood shoots into them. It's like he's the leader of the bodybuilding political party or something with this little motivational speech. He pulls back from the table again, leaning backward and making the chair squeak under his weight. "I hope I can pass the whole thing on to you someday. That I can hand the reins over to you and not any old Johnny-come-lately. What they're missing. What we have. That's brains, Heiko"—he taps his finger against his temple, where veins ran like pipes—"brains."

I take it all in. I filter out how absurd it all seems because I've never heard Axel talk this way. So I take it all in and almost ovulate for joy or enthusiasm or the hell if I know. Finally, really start something. Show all of those goddamn son-of-a-bitch operations in Germany they'd better pay attention to Hannover. Must pay attention. Maybe he wouldn't be such a bad politician.

"Listen up. I want to introduce you to someone. We're gonna just drive over to Wunstorf and visit an old friend of mine. Who you can learn plenty from. I've learned plenty. From him. All right?"

Once again, I don't open my mouth, and I'm just smiling and nodding like a true brownnoser. Even if I know it's not really me, only the simple fact of sitting there and listening to it all, even if I'm truly happy about it, I'd like to slap myself upside the head and tell myself I shouldn't be acting like a hypocritical yes-man.

"Then you can call it a day. Your car is parked at the train station in Wunstorf, right?"

And again, I just nod.

"Just give me a call when you're finished with your royal audience or whatever kind of faggy stuff you're up to," Kai had joked, and I climbed into Axel's plush Audi.

We rolled down the autobahn at two hundred kph. Axel's way of driving doesn't leave room for questions, although there's probably a big, fat, red question mark on my forehead when we turn off into the parking lot at the branch of the regional hospital in Wunstorf. The local funny farm. I'm supposed to wait outside, and Axel says he'll bring out his friend.

"Then he can get a whiff of fresh air."

I take a seat in a wooden shelter set aside for breaks in the hospital's park.

I'm already smoking my third cigarette and there's a scent of freshly spread potting soil and summer thunderstorms. It hesitantly begins to rain. Here a drop. There one. Then more. All around me, the rain falls in thousands of spider legs. I flick the glowing cigarette butt into the already soggy bed of flowers. The automatic doors to the front entrance open. Axel comes out. He's pushing someone in a wheelchair.

Through the rain, which was already letting up, I hear him: "Oh, oh, oh, we're gonna get so wet." He's pushing the wheelchair and its jockey out in front at a trot. It rattles a lot over the cobblestone path. As if the sight of the guy in the wheelchair wasn't bizarre enough in itself. This guy is huge. I'm talking about Ulf and Latze proportions. A goddamn fridge of a guy. Or rather, he must have been at some point. Now he looks like his skeleton and inner organs shrank but his skin stayed the way it was. I don't mean he looked all wrinkly. I'd guess he's roughly my uncle's age. It simply looks . . . wrong. Off, somehow. As though it wasn't a natural process. At any rate, even in his state, he still seemed far too large for the wheelchair, which is probably a completely standard model. But he still gave me the impression of a sad clown on a kid's tricycle. This was heightened by the puffy orange bomber jacket he almost disappeared into.

Once they're nearly under the roof with me, I'm able to make out the guy's sunken face better. On the cheek more than anywhere else, it's like one of those beat-up plastic bottles you can massage as much as you want but you'll never get the dents out. I suddenly have a kind of déjà-vu feeling. I ask myself if I've ever seen this guy somewhere, but try as I may, I can't picture it. His head is pocked, strangely pointy, and looks like he would normally shave it, judging from how the hair's sprouting from his scalp. Only it doesn't grow evenly but in thin, isolated bundles.

Axel pushes him under the roof. I don't know if I'm supposed to stand up or not. I just stay seated.

"Dirk, this is my nephew. Heiko." Axel pronounces the words clearly and distinctly. Emphasizes every single syllable.

It feels like Dirk needs years to lift his face in my direction. Two shimmering pools of spittle have gathered in the corners of his mouth. For some reason, I feel nauseous. His eyes pan slowly and imprecisely in my direction. They're topped by bushy eyebrows that look like those fat, hairy caterpillars you can see in documentaries on the Amazon.

I say, "Hello," and wave without lifting my arm, as if he weren't sitting directly in front of me.

The sight of this ghost made my testicles contract. I'd already seen plenty in my day, but him . . . A taste of soggy cardboard spreads through my mouth.

Axel crouches down between us so anyone who walked by here would think we look like a conspiratorial group. He rests his hand on the puffy sleeve of Dirk's washed-out bomber jacket, from which a hand with scabby yellow fingernails protrudes. And the back of his hand. Only now do I notice it. On the back of his hand up into the sleeve, and as I assume, probably even farther up his arm, there's a blackish, tumor-like crust growing rampant that looks like a smoker's leg kneaded into a lump.

"My nephew here. Heiko," Axel emphasized loudly once again, "he's really talented. One of our best." I briefly squint over to Axel and then back into the milky eyes of Dirk, which don't seem to have any spark, from my perspective. "Has proven himself multiple times. He's capable of stuff, Dirk. He's a good one." Axel gets really close to Dirk's ear, but doesn't reduce his volume. Dirk begins to nod very slowly. His mouth opens and closes to a hardly visible degree, like a goldfish. I hope I don't look like that when I'm nodding in agreement because I can't think of anything better.

My uncle turns to me. Back at normal volume: "Me and Dirk. We used to be the best. Always at the front of the pack. What am

I talking about? Leading the way! Together we made that tired bunch into a hard-hitting squad. I couldn't have done it without Dirk." He briefly ponders, looking at the ground, then back at me: "A little like you and Kai. Dirk and me. We were always that tight."

"Understand."

"You, Dirk. We're no spring chickens anymore, hey?" Axel doesn't wait for an answer. We could be sitting here till the month after next. "And at some point, you really have to let go, right? That's when I thought of Heiko here. My nephew. The best of all." He swipes his hand in the air between the three of us in emphasis. I have to look away out of embarrassment. The rain has stopped. Individual drops slip heavily off the leaves of the flowers and onto the soil. A neon-yellow butterfly flies past the wooden hut. I watch it go, till my gaze snags on the two warhorses in front of me.

"But of course, none of that happens unless Dirk gives his blessing, right? You're okay, Dirk," he literally croaks in his ear. I notice how my uncle's voice flutters, but just slightly, so you hardly notice. Dirk's face pans toward the source of Axel's voice like in slow motion. The black bulges also protrude from the collar of his jacket, up his neck.

"All right?"

Axel appears to be out of patience. I repress the impulse to light one. Then finally a reaction. He nods. His goldfish mouth forms an: "Okay." Strings of drool connect his lips.

It's enough for Axel: "I'm glad. Well, we're all cooled down after that rain. I'd better bring you back inside. So you don't catch anything out here. Say good-bye, Heiko."

I say bye and watch the two of them go. I want to pull one out of my pack as Axel and Dirk have turned onto the path toward the main entrance, when Dirk yelps all of a sudden. At first I don't get that it's him, but it absolutely doesn't sound like Axel. It can only be Dirk's voice. I hear him caterwauling the metro song, but unbelievably off-key, till they disappear past the sliding doors of the building. That he wants to build a subway from Mannheim to Auschwitz. My forehead is buried in my palms and I spew as much vomit between my feet as I possibly can.

———

The meal was over. I'd just accompanied Yvonne back to her car. She had to go to her night shift. "Nice that it finally worked out for us to meet," was what Manuela had said in parting, and she gave me a sideways glance, "I was afraid that we'd never get to know you. Heiko is such a tough nut to crack. Never opens up."

Yvonne smiled, unsure whether or not to take it as a joke. She apologized again that she'd come in her work clothes: "We can't change at the hospital because the nurses' locker-room is being remodeled at the moment."

Manuela assumed a generous smile and shook her head. Her long, dangling earrings made her seem at least ten years older.

"Don't worry about it. I hope you have a quiet shift. I bet it's hard work at the hospital." She went back to the patio to help Andreas and his parents clean up the picnic table. Damian was kicking my birthday present through the garden, which was bathed in evening light. I had even gone to the trouble to get him the official ball from the '98 World Cup in France on eBay. Best ball ever.

I kissed Yvonne on her pale forehead and watched her climb into her Ford KA hatchback and drive away. Once again, she'd hardly eaten a thing all evening.

I wanted to light another cig on the patio.

"Heiko," Manuela said, "can you please not smoke around Damian?"

I flipped the pack shut.

"But he's playing on the grass way over there," I snapped at her and pointed at my nephew, who was at least five meters away.

"But it blows over to him."

Which wasn't true. From the trees beyond the property, I could see the wind was blowing in exactly the opposite direction. And even if it wasn't, we're outdoors, damn it, I told myself.

"Besides, I don't want you to set a bad example for him. If he sees that his uncle smokes, then he might want to, too."

"He's six!"

"Heiko, please," Andreas butted in.

So I went around the corner, where Damian couldn't see me, and crouched down, leaning against the wall, smoking in silence. At least the evening was almost over now. It was cooling down.

For me, it felt like the meal had lasted forever. The most exciting thing was Damian's torrent of words. They just bubbled out of him, about the first grade and who his best friends were, and so on and so forth. The business chitchat between Andreas and his father, who'd sat across from each other in their checkered shirts, looking more and more like clones and less like father and son, made the time go by all the more slowly. Manuela wasn't much help either, not missing a chance to praise Andreas's many varieties of salad. She couldn't produce something edible if you put a gun to her head, I'll admit that. The food was actually good. Electric grill. But you don't really need to eat outside if you're not going to use charcoal.

Hans's place at the table opposite Yvonne had remained empty the whole time, so Mie sat there alone and smiled silently at the circle. My father had made her load up a plate and carry it to him in the living room because he wanted to watch TV. I could see him from the patio, through the window, the bluish reflection of the tube flickering on his face and then disappearing again.

I heard voices from inside. Only then did I realize I was sitting right by the kitchen window. Andreas and Manuela were talking. It sounded like they were loading the dishwasher. Andreas's parents joined them.

"We'd better go. I have to leave early tomorrow morning," Andreas's father said.

Manuela and Andreas thanked them emphatically for coming and for the generous presents for Damian, and I just thought, Good lord, how long do people need to say good-bye? At some point Andreas walked his parents to the door. The kitchen fell silent moments later. Manuela had stopped loading the dishwasher. And then I heard her suddenly start to sob. She sucked up the snot. Then another moment of silence. Then it started again. She seemed to be holding her hand in front of her mouth. I tried not to move so she wouldn't know I was accidentally listening in.

Andreas returned.

"Dear, do you . . . ?" He stopped. Must have noticed she was crying. Then nothing. It took me a minute to get that he'd simply turned on his heel and left my sister alone in the kitchen. No clue where it came from, but I stood up next to the kitchen window, but without showing myself, and whispered, "What's going on?"

Manuela didn't seem at all surprised my voice was suddenly coming in from outside. If she was, I couldn't tell.

"It's just . . . Heiko. I just can't stand it sometimes."

I wanted to press about what she meant exactly, but she added: "Seeing Andreas's parents. And us in contrast. How Papa doesn't even come to the table. And Mama . . ." My molars ground together so hard my jaw hurt. "Heiko. I hate Mama for it. I hate her for just running away. I hate her for not caring about us at all." I wanted to tell her I felt the same way. That it wasn't a family. And it never had been. At least not as long as I could remember. I wanted to tell Manuela she was my sister. I mean: of course she is. But, saying it, I wanted to say something else actually. But instead of saying that and more, what I could have said, I said nothing at all. 'Cause once again I couldn't manage to find the words. Then it was too late, because Mie came into the kitchen with the rest of the dirty plates. We haven't spoken about it since.

I went back around the corner of the house. My knees were soft as sponges. Damian called from the patch of lawn, asking if I could play another round of football before he went to bed. I said I'd come right away.

Andreas sat at the picnic table. There were red splotches on his cheeks, which didn't fit with his otherwise tidy appearance. He just looked at me. Took a swig of his nonalcoholic beer and looked at me again from beneath his eyebrows. I walked by him without saying a word.

———

The week's almost done. I can't put off feeding the pigeons anymore. They're free-flying and might be less than stupid about finding something to eat and drink along the way, but, after nearly a week, I still have to make sure everything's in good shape. Otherwise, they'll shit the coop full to the brim. Besides, Hans is in withdrawal. Or as Manuela calls it: rehab. At least that way I don't have to cross paths with him.

I parked a little ways down the street. I don't want Mie seeing the light from my headlamps when I turn into the drive. I have no clue if she'd ask me in or anything, but she'd certainly come out to say hi, and then we'd be standing there and looking at each other, and no one knowing what to say, how to end it halfway okay.

From the front, no light is visible in the house. But what if she's in the kitchen right now and looks out? Well, then I can't do anything about it. But maybe I'll get lucky and she's in the living room or already asleep. So I slip through the narrow space between the shed and the fence. There used to be a well-worn path you could take to go from the driveway to the garden. Today it's overgrown with weeds a meter high, growing from the wall of the shed to the gutter on the roof—stinging nettles and thistles. I was smart enough to dress in long pants, though it's brutally hot. Even after sunset. The heat of the day is so heavy and oppressive the plants just sag to the ground at night and lie there till the next morning, only to start up again.

The garden is surrounded by the house on one side, the neighbor's property on the other, and the shed next to the street. It extends out back at least twenty meters in a rectangular shape. Judging by the high grass, which covers the entire garden like the thick fur of a huge animal, Hans hasn't mowed for months. Wouldn't be possible now either. All you could do would be to go in with a scythe. The one place trampled flat is the area between the patio, the coop, and the house, where a garden hose is attached to a faucet.

I wade through the hip-high grass, which keeps wrapping around my legs as I go. I'm lucky. There's no light coming out of the kitchen. And because there's a clear sky with a moon that's nearly full, I don't need a flashlight to see. In the twilight, the coop seems like a bulky, black torture chamber where people get locked away or suffocated or something. The monotonous cooing of the pigeons only reinforces this impression. Can't get over the fact I'm doing this. Just hope none of the neighbors looking over the fence sees me sneaking around the garden. They'd call the cops because they'd think I was breaking in.

All at once, the grass in front of me rustles and something scurries away. It causes a very slight furrow to form that closes soon after. Then, at the end of the garden, a cat jumps onto the fence and looks back. The pair of eyes glow at me. Then it hops down over on the other side and disappears. "Fleabag," I whisper, and though I don't believe in that kind of bullshit, I can't help but see it as a bad omen. I want to walk over to the patio because I assume the bucket with pigeon feed is there, when something squelches under my foot. I raise it. A black, formless blotch is visible.

"Oh, no way." I whisper a curse because I think I've stepped in a pile of shit. The stench creeps into my nose, but it's not the stench of feces. It smells of rot. I risk a glance into the kitchen. Everything's still dark. Then I whip out my phone and light up the pile.

"What the hell?" I bend lower so I can better make out what I've stepped in. Then my phone nearly flies out of my hand when I see it's a dead mole I've squeezed the innards out of irreversibly.

"Holy shit," I say and have to gag because I get a full dose when I inhale. I take two quick leaps out of the high grass and over to the flattened area in front of the coop. I spit a couple times and scrape the sole of my shoe on the patio flagstones. Bits of the mole still cling to it.

I quietly curse my sister and father, and most of all myself for agreeing to this, but there wasn't any point. I'm here now anyway. And I don't want the birds to have to crouch in their own filth and catch something from some bacteria or something. It's not the pigeons' fault, any of that.

And still, with the feed bucket I found on the patio in hand, I take a couple deep breaths and grab my crotch to reassure myself I still have the necessary balls before opening the door to the coop.

The pigeons look at me with their beady, seemingly dead eyes. All of them focused on me. As a kid, I never noticed how one of those tiny, black eyes can make you pretty nervous. Then all this calm cooing from every side. As if they were scheming something. I try not to think about it anymore and let my gaze sweep over the rows. All sitting in their roosts. None of them croaked yet. I shine the light from my phone on them, and then I notice my mistake: how the hell can I clean out the roosts when the pigeons are sitting in them? There aren't any newspapers on the ground I can just change in. I'm a fucking idiot!

"Fuck it. You can take a couple more days the way you are," I say and decide the coop isn't too full of feces. I bend over to reach the water and food trays, and that's when I make the next mistake. My gaze hits the opposite wall. At that spot. That very goddamn spot. For a moment, I can't move anymore. Like I'm frozen. I will myself on with some sort of inner strength, reaching for the tray. Spilling water and some of the feed. Whatever. Just get it done! I quickly fill the long tray with feed. Set the bucket back down.

Go over to the side of the house. Dump out the old water and put in new. Put it in the coop. Close the door. It sticks. The old rusty hinges catch somewhere. I push against it with all my might. The brittle wood creaks and finally gives way. I slam the door. Simply leave the bucket standing in the coop. Just get outta here. Get the images out of my head. I cross the grass and weeds with long strides. The tops of plants are hanging from my jeans, and I hear my beating heart in my throat. Only when I'm sitting in my car does my heartbeat slow.

———

That weekend, while we were at Timpen watching the Bundesliga live scores, like every year we had a discussion about whose turn it was to get the wreath or bouquet. And just like every year, we'd all forgotten who'd taken care of it the year before. I thought it was me, but I couldn't prove it. So this week I called up our regular florist to order a wreath in green, white, and black. Even though 96 was always called the Reds, because that's what they took the field in, those were the team's official colors. I picked Kai up at the station and together we drove to Luthe. To the cemetery on the edge of town, near the fields between Luthe and Wunstorf.

Jojo and Ulf are already waiting at the gate. We greet each other, and I get the wreath in 96 team colors from the trunk.

Why'd you dress so fancy?" Ulf asks Kai, who looks down at himself. He's wearing a tight-fitting black shirt. Sleeves rolled up. Black pants and black Lacoste shoes.

"You're not gonna get started on that. Heiko was saying the same thing in the car."

"He's not getting buried again, right?" Ulf joked.

"You should be able to dress up for once to honor a deceased friend, you fucktard. Am I right, Jojo?"

We turn to Jojo. He's standing at the edge of the field, one hand forming a canopy for his eyes, looking over the fields at the sky.

"Something's brewing over there," Kai says and peers in the same direction. We've been having heat thunderstorms nonstop since the beginning of the month, but unfortunately they only bring brief periods of cooling. It's still so unbearably hot you could change your sweaty clothes three times a day.

"The shoes are still hanging there," Jojo says, without shifting his gaze.

We follow his gaze. Only when you protect your eyes against the sun and look very closely can you see the shoes hanging from the power lines in the glaring light.

"That's unbelievable," Kai says. We're standing in a row at the edge of the field and shielding our eyes, "that they're still hanging there."

"Almost ten years," I say.

"And they haven't fallen down," Ulf says.

"Or no one took them down."

"Almost ten years," Jojo murmurs to himself. Maybe just to realize for himself what an eternity has gone by.

I kneel down and place the new wreath in front of Joel's grave. In the meantime, the sun has retreated somewhere behind the clouds. There's a creaking sound in the distance. I rejoin the semicircle made by my friends and clasp my hands over my crotch like the others, head bowed. No one says anything.

Even after nearly ten years, I feel strange standing here like this. I'm guessing the feeling won't ever go away. How bizarre is it to stand in front of a polished slab of stone representing a person six feet underground? I feel the sweat collect between my fingers, and I stare at the tombstone. Joel Seidel. Seventeen years lay between his birth and death. Seventeen pitiful years. Out here in the cemetery, I'm always aware of how long Joel's been dead. Precisely here. When we come together to memorialize him. Whenever I come here, he dies again. Because out there in my normal life I think he'll call any minute, come over with Jojo, or we can go see him at practice. Admire his dribbling skills again. Bernd Schneider. Ansgar Brinkmann. The white Brazilian . . . my ass! Joel Seidel, that was the white Brazilian! The dribbling machine from Luthe. Here in the cemetery, his face disappears before my eyes.

No one says anything. Maybe others mourn differently. Someone says something to the deceased. Gives a speech. Reels off an anecdote. We do that too. But not here. We can't think of anything as soon as we walk through that gate. No one dares say anything. And so we're standing here, hands clutched in front of our balls as if we were forming the wall on a free kick. He could do free kicks like no other. Direct free kicks. Bent into the corner. Roberto Carlos from Lower Saxony. I could say all of that. But I don't. I don't know why. I just stand there, stare at the ground, and feel strange.

Kai and Ulf are the first to turn away and go back to the road. That relieves me too. Relief sounds brutal in this context, but much as I'd like to express my respect and grief, the fact that I'm standing here is just so much fucking torture. I sneak a glance at Jojo, who's standing next to me. He's stock still. Doesn't make a sound. But his upper body is racked by soft shudders. As if he had hiccups. I look at his face. His eyes are pinched tight. His lips are rolled inside his mouth. I can't stand it, so I leave him with his little brother for a moment.

We're standing in the middle of the cemetery with our hands on our hips, looking at the ground or up in the sky. Huffing away in the hope it brings some relief. The worst thing is it was only the first half. We're still waiting patiently for Jojo. He should have all the time he needs. We're only a couple yards away. Then he finally comes over. As he takes an obligatory deep breath, I place my hand on his shoulder and press tight.

"Well, then," he says with a cough, picking up the bouquet he'd set down when we'd arrived, and goes ahead of us to the next row of graves.

No one could have guessed beforehand how all this would play out. Which is why, at the time, it wasn't possible to find two graves next to each other. Which is why Jojo and Joel's father are one row over.

It's a large tombstone. "Dieter Seidel" is engraved there. There's still space on it for his mother's name. That's fairly macabre. What must it be like for Ruth, Jojo's mother, to come here every day? To her son's and husband's graves, and see the extra space on the stone. Jojo positions the bouquet, briefly pausing in a crouched position, and asks us for a lighter. Kai hands him his, and Jojo lights the votive candles spread across the grave that have gone out. He very carefully removes the lids, tilts the candles, fills them with flame, and then sets them back down using both hands. Doing some things with both hands is much more respectful than with just one hand. Shaking hands, for example.

The clouds slowly start to dump on us. The thunder has already moved closer. I catch Ulf sneaking a quick glance at the sky. Then his eyes look straight at the ground.

This time I'm the first to leave the grave. It takes unbeliev-able strength to be the first. You don't want to seem as if you want to quickly put the whole thing behind you. But I can't leave this burden on Kai and Ulf. I take the first two steps backward. Then I turn around in a fluid movement, making the rocks squelch under my soles, and go to the main gate. I wait to smoke until Jojo is back with us.

We make plans for the evening, in the gambling hall. Blow some money, that'll help, Kai says as we climb in. The first thing the ones in the front seats do is rub their faces.

On the way home from picking up some cans and frozen pizza at the supermarket, we gradually shed the heavy cloaks of grief. Have to somehow. And Kai tells us, with growing excitement, he has something to show us later that'll drive us crazy, but he doesn't want to reveal any more now.

"Wait till later, dude. I want to present my discovery to all of you. It's fucking awesome."

We're sitting at the bar in the Midas gambling hall, which is located in a former supermarket behind a Mongolian buffet. For the hell of it, to try something new, we're drinking the traditional beer from Cologne in the typical miniature, kid-sized glasses. It's still early in the evening. The constantly ringing, blinking machines on the walls are just sparsely manned. The rows of lights divide the hall into islands of red and blue. Where no light falls, it's so dark you can hardly see anything. You can tell the newbies by the way the first thing they do is fall on their faces in the areas where there's no lighting.

Jojo walks in. We immediately turn and wave him over. He orders a cup of coffee. It's surprisingly good here, for a gambling den.

"Coffee? What's wrong with you?" Kai asks, but I quickly punch his bicep so he leaves Jojo alone. I lean back a little to be able to see Jojo, who sits down to the right of Kai and asks: "Where'd you leave fat Ulf?"

"Had to go home. Saskia had something planned. Who knows what?"

"Well, great." Kai slams his palms on the bar, which makes the barmaid glare at him, and he waves a kiss back at her. "I discovered something really awesome. I wanted to share it with all of you."

"Spit it out, whatever it is. Don't piss me off, Kai!"

"All right."

He raises his hands as if he were surrendering. Then he pulls out his iPhone and goes into the Facebook app. He has his head over the phone. Pulls back conspiratorially.

"Come a little closer. . . . *Closer*," he whispers to us.

So we moved closer to him.

"Not so close, Jojo. You have coffee breath."

"Go fuck yourself, asshole."

"Come on," I say, "either you show us the pussy you nailed or I'm going right back to the machines and make myself poor."

Kai giggles and grins with his shark-like grin.

"It really is a pussy, just not like the one you're thinking."

He enters a name in the Search function that doesn't ring a bell for me, and then shows the profile page of the person he was looking for.

"Yeah?" I say. "Some random asshole."

"Really, Heiko," he shakes his head back and forth, pretending to be insulted. "Then take a closer look, please."

"What am I supposed to . . . ," and now the scales fall from my eyes: "All right, okay. Then just some random asshole from Braunschweig."

Kai moans and says, "Dude, do I need to press the phone into your pupils so you finally get it? You can't tell me he doesn't look familiar."

I take another look at the profile picture. Blond, side part, short hair. Stupid druggy grin. Disgusting wart on his cheek. I recognize it as one of the hooligans from Braunschweig.

"Yeah, fuck me," escapes me.

"Let me see," Jojo says, and Kai passes the iPhone to him.

"But what does it mean? That you're going to the other side, you traitor? That the heart in your chest is changing colors?"

"You're kidding me," he says with laugh. "Nah. A classmate of mine was born in that filthy town. I've been stalking her for a while on Facebook. Of course, I've been checking out her friends too, if there are a few hot ones there, and then I notice his infamous face. And this is where things get interesting: typical Braunschweig. Of course, the dickhead is too stupid to keep his profile private. It's all Greek to him."

"Do you even know where Greece is?" I ask.

"Shut the fuck up! Anyway. He's one of the people who are constantly posting pictures and have to inform everyone where they go to drink and everything. With links to friends and place. The whole fucking program!"

Jojo returns his phone and says: "You don't mean—"

Kai interrupts: "Yes, indeed, my dear Watson. That's exactly what I mean."

He turns his head from me to Jojo and back. His mouth is gaping with euphoria.

"What do you think? Should we teach the stupid idiots a lesson in data management?"

I hook the wings of my nose between my finger, drawing a breath between clenched teeth, and say, "Let's get something straight: you want to go to Braunschweig. *To Braunschweig.* And mess this guy up bad?"

"The scales have finally fallen, you genius."

I reach for a beer from the tray and walk over to the wall of machines.

"What?" Kai asks, and I turn toward them again.

"You're probably wondering what Axel would think about a stunt like that. He'd be heating up hell for us! He'd kick our asses so hard we'd have to clean the shit off his boots afterward."

I sit down in front of a machine, shake my head, mumble to myself that Kai's nuts, and down the beer. He isn't giving up and comes over to me.

"Dude, wait a minute. Axel doesn't have to know a thing. It's just something between the four of us. Well, the three of us. We can't rely on Ulf anymore, that old fart."

I shake my head again and feed the money-eating machine some change. Kai grabs my hand, making me look at him. Now he's completely serious for once.

"You keep on saying what a snooze-fest those old guys are. That they don't have any new ideas. Finally daring something again. This is the chance, man. And if it goes well, and it will, from then on, all people will be talking about is Hannover. Then even your uncle can't be pissed at us."

I pull away, dodging the question: "I don't know, Kai. For me it sounds like too many chances for it to go south."

"*You*," he emphasizes the word aggressively, "were the one who told me Axel took you to that insufferable junky in the madhouse. Because he wants you to take over the leadership someday. Wouldn't this be a chance to show initiative? To prove you have everything under control? Can take the reins? In your way, Heiko, not Axel's?"

My head slumps momentarily under the flood of thoughts Kai is pumping into my head. Then I try to concentrate on the game.

"Come on, at least let me play a round," I say.

———

I can remember exactly how we were lounging around on the battleship-sized sectional and zapping through the channels. Then we found live coverage of the memorial service on one of the news channels. It was taking place in Hannover's completely overcrowded Market Church.

"Look at that, it's Sievers!" said Kai, who stood in the patio doorway, smoking. Jojo hadn't made a sound since the day before, when Robert Enke took his life. I thought it was pretty spooky.

"Come on, turn it off," Ulf said. "Who has the remote?"

We grope the cracks between the sofas before Jojo just stretches out his hand and turns off the television. Ulf and I exchanged glances after looking at Jojo, who was staring at the black screen, hands folded over his lap, remote in his right hand.

"Let's go there."

Ulf's face, furrowed with worry, expressed what was going on inside me too. He asked Jojo if he was certain. "I mean sure," he said, "Enke was the best and everything, and this whole thing is fucking tragic, honestly, I'm on the verge of tears myself, but do you really think it's such a good idea?"

"It's the right thing," Jojo answered and turned toward us.

Kai had disappeared onto the patio to put out his cigarette but had heard everything. He came inside, clapped his hands together, and said, "All right, let's go then."

Jojo whipped his head around. The fastest motion he'd been able to achieve in the past two days of robotic slow-mo. Kai returned Jojo's gaze but not with the same seriousness as on Ulf's and my face. He raised his eyebrows, smiled at Jojo; I looked at him sideways, making him smile. Like so many times before, I thought to myself, just how does he manage to get people to react that way? It's Kai's personal magic, and though the word "magic" sounds completely gay, somehow it just fits. The guy is completely charismatic. Through and through. An arrogant loud-mouth, for sure, but an asshole with a certain vibe.

Ulf and I had a tough time saying no, so we all climbed into Ulf's station wagon. He'd bought it even before his house. There were no brats in sight yet, but if you saw the way he acted or his hustle, all that was missing was the coffee cup with the label "World's Best Dad" or some other bullshit. So we drove the mommy taxi out of the suburban hell that's Garbsen and into the city, and left it at the parking garage behind the train station. Me and Kai wanted to grab some beer in the station. We were at the cash register when we saw Ulf and Jojo standing outside in front of the shop. Jojo was rocking from one leg to the other, and once we paid he led the way. The general mood changed after we got past the square in front of the station and the horse statue. It was mainly occupied by people passing through with shopping carts who didn't give a rat's ass about what was going on in the city. Kröpcke Square was full of people. Most wearing at minimum a red scarf. Many decked out in full 96 gear. Jersey, hat, banners, and flags. Many were carrying candles and flowers. It seemed so surreal. I'd never experienced anything like it. Like a flash mob of blind dates made up of 96 fans who were all still waiting for their date, all full of silent nervousness. Typical for people from Hannover. You meet up at the Kröpcke clock or in front of the train station, at the statue.

"I'll be right back," Jojo said and pulled out his wallet.

"What's he up to now?" I asked.

We watched him push through the crowd of despondent gazes, stopping in front of one of the street vendors.

"You can't be serious," said Ulf.

"Not really, right?" I said. And I didn't mean Jojo but the guy who'd blatantly set up shop with a selection of candles he was hawking to mourners.

"Dude," I started, and could already feel the rage shooting into my fists, "I'd really like to go over there and give that cock-sucker some business."

Ulf said something intended to keep me from giving him a beating right then and there. Even if he deserved it. So just to be on the safe side, I memorized his face in case I happened to run into him on the street someday.

Jojo returned with four red candles, for the price for which you could have gotten a small personalized funeral wreath. He handed one to each of us, and we waited for the procession to start. I can't remember anymore how we found out about it, that a procession to the stadium was supposed to happen in the first place, but it felt like everyone in Hannover and the whole area knew about it. It was probably in all the papers and talked about at every kiosk and supermarket till.

It started soon after, and this huge throng of 96 supporters drifted right through the city. We kept to the back of the crowd. At the margins. Even though Jojo imitated the other mourners and walked silently in front us, for some reason I couldn't give in to the mood. Which is why most of the time I was going on about meaningless shit with Ulf and Kai. I was still surprised Jojo would let himself get drawn into the whole mourning business. Of course, it's all good and stuff, but if I had everything pressing in on me like Jojo, I don't know how I'd hold up. I can't stop thinking about Joel anyway.

I felt different when we got to the north entrance to Lower Saxony Stadium, where the fan shop is at. You could barely raise your cigarette to take a drag without touching the back of the person in front of you with the cherry. That's why I mostly avoided spending time at the train station, the Passerelle mall, or the shopping streets in the city. Everywhere always so fucking packed with people. Cheek by jowl. Another reason the whole ultra thing wouldn't have been my cup of tea. Sure, it was cool in a way to be in the stands, on your feet, screaming your head off, and guzzling the watered-down stadium piss. If it wasn't for all the teens and wannabes among the few good men you can find in the fan sections. I guess the feeling I had from my childhood wore off at some point. Reverence for the stadium and the stands, ruled over by people like my uncle. Probably goes back to the damn commercialization. Everyone calls it the Lower Saxony Stadium still,

PHILIPP WINKLER

but every few years a new company buys the naming rights, and each time a piece of tradition fucking disappears. But what's even more important is when you're one of the oldest in the block at some point and surrounded by middle-class kids who only have the balls to make a scene when they're surrounded by fences and security.

People for as far as the eye can see. Many were crying, embracing one another. Joined by the press, which caused the bile to rise in my throat, leaving a sour taste in my mouth, and made me pull the hood of my windbreaker down over my face and draw the zipper up over my chin.

Kai put words to what I was thinking: "People, there's way too much press and piss here for my taste. It's giving me ulcers and making my sphincter pucker."

It sounded like a joke, but even Kai had lost his gift for levity. He pulled his hoodie tighter over his noggin so his eyebrows disappeared beneath the visor.

"Jojo," Ulf said, and tried to grab him by the shoulder.

Some kind of Jackie Chan sense let him guess that Ulf wanted him to turn around. At any rate, he pulled in his shoulders and said, "Just wait a second," and then wriggled his way into the sea of mourners. We could see him for quite a while because of his mop of curly hair, which was still quite long then, twisting through countless shoulders. A short time later, he was out of sight, even for Ulf, who stuck up over the mass of heads like a shiny bald lighthouse.

So we waited for Jojo to come back after whatever it was he wanted to do. But because even Ulf had grown restless in the meantime, we separated completely from the herd. We were waiting for him on Robert Enke Street which was still part of the

Arthur Menge Shore Drive, and from the other side of the street we watched the slideshows of Enke that were being projected on screens in front of the North Curve bar.

"Best keeper we ever had," Ulf declared, arms crossed.

"Together with Sievers, you mean," Kai answered and spit to the side without watching out for people passing by.

"Sure," I said, butt between my lips, "Sievers was a beast on the line. The best at the time, controlling his area"—I weighed the situation with my hands—"definitely Enke. And not only that. The best damn keeper Germany ever had. He was calm like no one else and had reflexes like fucking Superman."

Ulf clucked and said, "Besides, he wasn't a pampered sports car–driving idiot like most of the pros these days."

We nodded in unison, and at some point a "Best man" slipped out of me. Without my really consciously wanting to pronounce it.

"This is all so fucking sad," Ulf added.

Jojo joined us just as Kai was returning from North Curve bar with three cups of beer. Judging from Kai's gaze and the fact that his nostrils were flared like he'd been caught picking his nose, I guessed he hadn't just been taking a piss in the bar's toilets. Kai was passing out the cups when he saw Jojo and wanted to give him one of the three beers.

"I'll be right back. Getting another."

"Forget it. Here." Jojo returned the beer. "I want to go. Can we go?"

We asked what was wrong and tried to keep up with him as he led the way with slow strides and swinging hands. He eased off just enough so we could catch up, then pulled out his phone and showed us a photo he'd snapped of the thousands of candles and bouquets. They seemed to stretch for hundreds of meters on the stadium grounds, and in the picture they morphed into a single indefinable mass of dots of light.

I pressed Jojo on why he wanted to get out of there so soon, and in the effort to keep up with him, my beer sloshed out of the thin plastic cup, spilling over my fingers and dripping on my pant leg.

"Maybe," Jojo said, "I just kneeled to put my candle down. But maybe then I had to think about Joel as well. And maybe a little raindrop fell on my face. And maybe, just maybe, I smashed one of those press fuckers who thought it'd be a great shot."

Kai and I briefly stood in shock and then had to make up two strides to catch up with him.

"What's going on?" Kai asked. I couldn't miss the way his voice went higher with excitement.

"I just told you. I was back in the crowd quickly and vanished. Before anyone really caught on to what happened."

I think Kai wanted to pat him on the back, but I silently made him understand that he should control himself.

And so we padded back, zigzagging via the narrowest alleys all the way to the city center. We looked around and behind us, but no one was there, of course. There's legitimate caution that can become paranoia—which necessarily make it less legitimate—and there's just being wet behind the ears. Which we were, in a sense, I have to admit. As if anyone could have found us in that mass of people, if they would've even tried.

On the ride back from the city, I sat on the backseat with Jojo. He was looking out the window the whole time. The cold early-winter wind hissed through the slits of the cracked windows and made

Jojo's curls bounce excitedly. I could simply have looked away, but for some reason I didn't. And the constant twirling of his hair was driving me crazy.

I asked him if everything was okay, quietly enough so Ulf and Kai in the front wouldn't have to hear. Kai had put on a personally mixed dubstep CD, but we only had to tolerate it at half-volume because Ulf was able to control it, thanks to the knob on the steering wheel.

"Yeah," he said without looking over, "yeah. You know . . . ," then silence for a while.

I thought about what I could say. Fucking hell, I was never good at this kind of thing. Can't even do it today. Express my feelings, as Manuela would say. I just can't think of anything, my brain gets blocked, and instead of producing something sensible, I just get angry. But not in that moment, strangely enough. I wanted nothing more than to be beamed out of the car or something, but fuck it, I thought, Jojo's your friend, and that means more than just hanging out and getting drunk.

I was growing more and more impatient, and if Jojo hadn't said something, I bet it wouldn't have been long before I became typically enraged. All at once, Jojo bent forward so his head was floating over the middle console. He looked straight ahead through the windshield and spoke so loudly everyone could hear.

"I want to go to the spot."

"What kinda spot?" Kai asked.

The music was turned down. In the rearview mirror I saw Ulf glance back every couple seconds.

"To the train crossing. You don't have to come along if you don't want."

"Wait up, wait up. What the hell are you talking about?" Ulf stammered. I'd known as soon as Jojo had said the word "crossing," but I didn't make a sound. Couldn't.

"Where he killed himself."

"Who?" Kai asked, and turn around for a sec. Maybe to make sure Jojo hadn't gone crazy. Had a mad stare or something.

"Enke."

The station wagon bumped into the curb and briefly howled in pain when Ulf shifted into the wrong gear.

"Sorry, Jojo, I don't really mean what I'm about to say, but"— Kai raised his voice—"are you fucking nutso or what?!"

Jojo slumped against the door. His gaze wasn't obviously crazy. So not at all. But strangely calm and very focused. I can't really remember exactly. But it definitely seemed spooky to me.

We were out in the country. In Walachia. In the middle of the night. Dark as a bear's backside. The station wagon's headlights were the only source of light far and wide. The nearest lights were more than a mile away. Some random villages close to the sub-urbs. We followed the paved road that for its part roughly followed the train tracks. At any rate, we guessed we were still close to the tracks because every now and again we could make out the swaths that cut through the fields and meadows. We passed through some woods. No one said anything for a while, with the exception of Ulf's increasingly annoyed groans. Well, and of course the approximate directions from Jojo, who had Ulf turn here and there. From one nameless road to the next. When we came out of the woods and Jojo craned his neck to see if the tracks were still nearby, we saw it all at once. Various headlights that melded into a single, frayed cone. A couple hundred yards to the left of us.

In the middle of nowhere. Accompanied by some flashing police lights making silent circular patterns in the broad fields.

"There," Jojo said and needlessly pointed in the direction, almost puncturing Ulf's cheek with his index finger.

"Jojo, dude, what's the point?" Ulf asked.

"Try to get as close as you can," he just answered.

Of course we didn't get close. A little farther on, the road went to the left, but naturally it was blocked by the police. We stopped on the curve. Jojo insisted. A cop, who was pretty drained and understandably annoyed, walked right up our car, saying he'd had enough of the rubberneckers. What kind of sick puppies we were, and if we didn't all want to spend the night in a cell together, we'd better get moving. I think it was the first and last time I'd ever agreed with a piece of shit cop.

Luckily, Jojo restrained himself and Ulf did the talking. He nodded in agreement with everything the patrol cop had to say. Even apologized. Then we kept on driving.

I think we all thought it'd finally be okay, but less than five minutes later Jojo said that Ulf should let him out.

"Are you crazy, seriously?!" Kai bellowed and raised his hand in question.

Completely calm, Jojo answered, "Guys, I don't expect you to understand. Go home. I just want to sit here for a while, somewhere out here, and think."

"Can you tell me how you think you'll get back?" Ulf asked and pounded the balls of his fists against the top of the steering wheel.

"Taxi."

"Hey, fuck it, okay," Kai groaned, "just let him be. If he needs it." He planted his face in his hands and rubbed his eye sockets.

His elbows were resting against his knees and his feet against the dashboard.

Jojo was half out the door when I spontaneously unbuckled, grabbed my phone from the seat, and opened the door.

"Heiko." Kai's chin dropped.

"It's okay, I'll stay with him. We'll take a taxi home. We'll be able to explain where we are somehow"—I bent inside the car—"at least I hope."

It was cold. As cold as it can be when you're in the middle of the-hell-if-I-know-where. Ulf started the motor but rolled down the window once more.

"If the cops were watching us and saw how we stopped and everything, they'll probably send someone over. So I'd suggest you guys get the fuck away from here. That's exactly what we're doing, too."

I thanked them and they left us. The red from the taillights moved down our bodies like mercury in a thermometer.

We stopped the next field over and approached the illuminated site of the accident. Until Jojo said it was enough, and he was good there. I could see ant-sized figures scurrying through the lights on the tracks. We climbed on top of a shed with three walls that stood in the fenced-in field. It smelled of manure, and the wind whistled by our cheeks. There was an old bathtub sitting in front of the shed, which apparently served as a watering trough for the cows or horses that grazed there during the day.

Soon we didn't have anything left to smoke. But we sat there till dawn, and talked between the waves of silence. About Joel. About Tonga. About their father, Dieter. And my father, too. At some point I kept nodding off, and Jojo said we should leave. It wasn't far to the next town. We got breakfast at the village baker. We nodded off in the taxi till the driver let us out in Wunstorf.

————

My window was open last night. I must have been so fast asleep I didn't hear a thing. The windowsill is covered with a film of water, and a large dark spot has formed on the wall below it. I press an old towel against the sill. It's immediately soaked. Then I look outside. Raindrops fall from the leaves of the old oak that stands next to the house. I can see only an even, gray surface through the treetop.

I go down to the kitchen. There's a scrap of paper held down by a cup. Arnim scribbled something in his barely legible scrawl using a permanent marker. After nearly three years of living with him, I'm halfway able to decipher what he considers writing.

He writes that he's away on business. I mentally add the quotation marks around the word "business." No mention of approximately when he might return, but I'm supposed to take care of the animals. That was the agreement from the beginning. Sure, back then I thought I'd be living for free in a place where no one would get on my nerves. Feed a couple critters every now and then in exchange. No problem. But at the time, I didn't have the slightest clue what kind of animals he had.

"I guess I'm a full time zookeeper now," I say to the empty kitchen. No one there to laugh at my joke.

I wash out the coffee machine from who knows when—it's full of slime—dump some grounds into the filter, and smoke a cigarette while I wait for the morning's black milk. The back door isn't closed all the way . It was banging softly in the cool draft.

After going in the bathroom briefly to toss water on my face and notice how my stomach muscles are threatening to disappear under a thin layer of fat, I do various exercises in the living room for half an hour. I have them from a manual Kai gave me. It was written by a legendary inmate and street fighter from England who called himself Charles Bronson. Like the actor. It has instructions about how you can exercise your body without any equipment. Even if you're cooped up in a tiny prison cell. The best book I've ever read. Also pretty much the only one I've read, if you leave aside all the crap we were served up in school. But all you had to do was buy the CliffsNotes, with all the content and interpretation and stuff that was in it.

I slip into the boxer shorts from yesterday because I still haven't been to the laundromat. Doesn't matter. Don't want to go anywhere important today anyway. I pull on my rubber boots on the stoop behind the back door. The ground looks pretty soggy. I take on the dogs first.

Two Amstaffs that Arnim's probably had for at least two years. He got the white one, Poborsky, from a breeder of fighting dogs in Olomouc. At the time, Kai, Ulf, and me even went with him to Bohemia to pick it up. But we were along just to get drunk. Although Kai absolutely wanted to go see the breeder and check out the setup with the dogs, I was able to convince him not to. I told him he really didn't want to come along, and he should trust me.

Arnim had gotten the other one, a seven-year-old brown monster of a dog with the name Bigfoot, in exchange for a pit bull that had pulled in one win after another for Arnim. What his exchange partner didn't know was the pit bull had a heart defect and wouldn't last very long. The dog came from Russia. From beyond the Urals. From a place no one had ever heard of, not to mention the whole pronunciation thing. Which is why Bigfoot only understands Russian. Or as the previous owner said, "Beegfood."

I'm guessing it doesn't matter what language you speak to it. It's pumped so full of steroids it doesn't even notice when it has a massive flesh wound.

I thought it was all pretty exciting after moving in and recognizing what's going down here in Wunstorf. But that ended after I was at one of Arnim's events, which he puts on randomly from time to time. I mean sure, *we* slap each other around and sometimes something breaks. But this! Ulf asked me how I could tolerate it and square it with my conscience. How I could still live with Arnim. But I didn't even tell him everything I saw here. I didn't have a real answer for him either. I guess you get numb over time. Tune out some things. Fuck it. It is what it is.

Poborsky only notices me when I come out of the house. He starts to yap. Only then does Bigfoot catch on and start to yap too. Although yapping is probably the wrong word for the two of them. That sounds more like a dachshund or something. The two of them are like four-legged subwoofers. They throw themselves at their cages' fencing. Their cages are built together. Of course, there's a fence between the two of them. They'd tear each other to pieces in an instant otherwise. Sometimes they try to go at it even so, but dogs like that usually do catch on pretty fast when a fence can't be beat. Even these dogs. I walk past the cages and call out to them in a singsong voice: "All right already, I'm on my way."

The whole area behind the house is covered with multiple layers of camouflage netting from which water is dripping. The netting is draped over wooden posts and, along with the oak and the other trees on the property, offers perfect visual cover. Arnim is the most paranoid guy I've ever run into. But he has to be with his "hobby," as I like to call it, although he does earn money from it. One corner of the shed is still full of acoustic panels he's been meaning to attach to the cages since forever.

The shed is another one of Arnim's masterpieces of manic-paranoid underground architectural art. Everything here he's put together himself. Everything except the house. He inherited that ages ago. Even though the shed was already here, he completely redid the interior so his little arena would fit inside. Everything done by hand. He only has to close the shed doors and no one outside of a hundred-yard radius would have a clue what's going on in there. And no one just happens to come by either, because he owns the surrounding land. Inherited that too.

I push the huge shed door open wide enough to slip inside. It's not a joke like the one at my parents' place. But my grandpa had only had little tractors. There must have been some massive equipment in here. I fill the salad-sized bowls with food and water and set them outside. The dogs go crazy as soon as they pick up the scent. I pull two steaks as thick as my hand from the cooler in the kitchen and inject them with hell-if-I-know-what from the syringe in the "morning" box. Don't even want to know what the stuff is. Use the steaks to lure the dogs out of their kennels and into their cages. I toss the steaks through the window around head level. Then I can use a rope setup to close the doors to the fenced run area so I can safely go inside and change out the dishes. Also one of Arnim's DIY numbers. Everything in exactly that sequence. You don't go inside the cage to change out the bowls when the mutts are running around free in there. Otherwise you're short of at least two limbs in no time flat. After changing out the dishes, checking twice to see if the cage doors are really closed, and hastily rinsing out the used dishes, I reopen the doors. The two of them race out in tandem, broad muzzles straight to the food dishes, which they scrape across the floor against the mesh fence. They've already scarfed down the steaks.

After the second round of coffee and cigarettes, I go down into the basement, which extends beneath the entire house and stinks of moist mildew and rot. Down there I fill a bucket full of pig and cattle bones. I use the electric mortar and pestle to smash the bones into bite-sized pieces. I garnish the meal with a clutch of dead chicks and bring it all the way up to the second floor along with a deep bowl filled with fresh water. I knock on the first door on the left, saying, "Siegfried, are you awake yet? Yummy, yummy."

Something in the room rustles. I open the door. A narrow beam of light falls through the space between the window and the cloth hung in front of it, hitting me eye-level as I enter. I duck underneath it. Avoiding it.

"Siegfried?" I toss the question into the room. There's more rustling. The sound comes from the corner between the window and the slope of the roof. Siegfried's favorite spot. My eyes have readjusted to the darkness. I can see him now. He's sitting on the back of an ancient armchair completely covered in shit. It was already there before Arnim's time. Siegfried hardly moves. He still has his head hidden under a wing. Just peeks out a little to see who's talking and bringing him breakfast.

"It's me, old pal," I say, my voice like a refrigerator's monotone hum, "brought you some treats."

The floorboards are almost completely covered with newspapers where Siegfried can relieve himself. But he still prefers his armchair. Only a hint of its turquoise color remains after years of gathering dust and all that bird shit. I take a big step over the middle stretch of papers and dump the contents of the bucket in a pile in the far right corner of the room. Then he can pick out whatever he feels like. Then I step back, careful not to walk in the piles of crap, and approach the window. Taking care not to make any rash movements. I continue to reason with Siegfried. The meaningless chatter is more for my benefit. To be honest, I don't think the old bird gives a damn. I always lay out the papers so I have about one and a half feet of free space to the window. The whole time, my gaze stays glued to Siegfried, who shakes out his feathers. Maybe it's like when people yawn. Although I don't know if birds are able to yawn. At least I've never seen Siegfried do it.

"Sleep okay, old boy?" I ask and carefully lift the heavy blanket from the nails that keep it in front of the window. Thousands of dust particles float through the tilted rectangle of cloudy daylight. Siegfried pulls out his head and immediately has a closer look at me with his healthy, red-rimmed pupil while shaking out his wings, big as sails. I let the blanket slide to the ground and take a couple steps back. Keep my hands waist-high.

"Okay, everything's okay." We look at each other. "It's just me."

In the course of our acquaintance, Siegfried and I have tangled only once. It's certainly very different than with the silly pigeons. I was new here and hadn't worked out yet how to handle him. He probably viewed me as an intruder and thought what the hell does the dweeb want. He tried to snap at me. And that's no joke. When a huge, old bearded vulture grabs at you, then you shouldn't be surprised if your hand's gone. I was so startled I almost fell over. But I reflexively pulled back and whacked him with the back of my hand. Not everyone can claim they've bitch-slapped a fucking vulture. It's still one of Kai's favorite stories. For weeks I refused to set foot in the room. But because Arnim threatened to kick me out or make me pay rent, I did it again. And since then we've been cool with each other. What's more, I like the old buzzard.

He jumps from the back of the chair onto the floor with a thump and hops over to the pile of bones. When he's moving around on the ground, 'cause there's not much chance to fly in here, then he doesn't walk but hops instead. By getting up some momentum and jumping forward with both legs at once, but somehow he always stays slightly sideways. I stand still for a second. Smile. I like watching him when he moves around like that. Because his body is covered with thick, rusty feathers down to the talons, which are almost as large as human hands. It looks like he's wearing pants. Only the outside of the wings and his head have a different color. His face is black all the way to his beak, where there are the beard feathers he's named after. The underlying red tones shine through. He pokes with his beak among the pile of bones and starts with a chick.

"Tastes pretty good, right?" I say and begin pushing the papers together and balling them up so I can replace them.

When I'm done spreading them out, he's sitting up on the back of the chair again and looking out the window. I ask myself if birds—or animals in general—can feel bored. I hope not, because his life here is even more dreary than before. I decide I'll ask Arnim when I have the chance why he doesn't build him an aviary. Then he'd at least be able to fly a couple yards, assuming he hasn't completely forgotten how. It's probably like riding a bike. He's already had to spend fifteen years staring out this window. There's nothing interesting to look at. At least as far as the one eye can see. Arnim tells me he lost the other one to a monster of a raven that some Bulgarian brought over: "That was a brute, all right. I'd never seen anything like it, my boy. About this big." Then he spread his thick arms. "I had no clue they could get that big. Thought it just couldn't be, that it must be a Lilliput he stuck in a black costume."

The football-sized wad of paper sticks together pretty well with all the bird crap. I kick it out into the hallway, tell Siegfried to enjoy his meal and that he shouldn't take everything so seriously. As if he has a swivel stuck in his craw, he turns his head at an angle impossible for humans and looks at me. I give him a thumbs-up, who knows why exactly, and say, "Keep your head up, bud."

Then I close the door behind me.

———

A true football fan places great emphasis on tradition, on time-honored things. Nothing embodies this more than our local Hannover bar, the venerable Timpen in the old streets of the Calenberger Neustadt district. Surrounded by traffic-free cobblestone streets and half-timbered houses gussied up for the tourists, into which eye-wateringly expensive yuppie cafés had been dropped, the Skipper, with his, or rather our, Timpen, is one of the last bastions of true Hannover culture. And I swear, if it should ever cease to be, which isn't unrealistic, then we can just climb into the casket. From time to time, my uncle makes some pronouncement about taking over the place to keep it afloat, but seriously. Once in a while, he bugs Skipper about the liquor license and the whole nine yards. There've also been efforts by Axel to shift the focus of our "company" to his gym. But that was met with such resistance not even he could bring it off. I'm telling you: hooligans and our customs. Try to cut us off, and we'll hit the barricades. But Axel is basically just as much a traditionalist, and I don't think he'd trade Timpen for anything. The old farts are still the ones who tell the best stories. Hinkel, more than any other. When he's a little lit and starts to "spin," there's no holding back. About when all this was still a free country, which Kai, Ulf, Jojo, and me didn't ever really experience. None of this constant surveillance with cameras on every corner, battalions of policemen with helicopters for every pitiful match that's suddenly declared a problem game. And even outside the stadiums. Things must have been really hairy here. There were cases of bricks and benches flying through thick-barred windows.

Every time I sit here and nurse my pilsner, I feel a little like I'm in a museum. Listening to the talk of back when. Back when everything was better, la-di-da. But I did have some good times before Timpen. Back then we weren't really accepted and had to wait outside. Except in fall and winter. That was fucking hell. But it always paid off. Skipper sometimes even sent us a spiked pot of coffee. We couldn't have beer yet, but in a thermos like that you couldn't see something'd been added.

Today I feel like I'm a part of that story. Whether that means our "company" or the football club. Or even the city. It just feels good to sit here in the middle of all these idiots and lift one glass after another.

Ulf, Kai, and I are perched there like roosting chickens receiving our next freshly poured beverages into our parched throats. Because the weekend and match day are ahead of us, Jojo's doing an extra shift of coaching his youth squad.

"To you, Skipper"—Kai raises his glass—"and may the well never run dry!"

"Cheers!" We clink glasses with Skipper.

Axel, Tomek, and the rest of the crew are seated at the regulars' table at the end of the taproom. Behind them, the pennants of various Hannover-based sports teams hang thickly, partially overlapping on the dark, chocolate-colored wood paneling. Of course, every second one is from 96. The adjacent wall, which you follow to the shitter, is covered with pictures and photos. Besides the photos of him at sea, Skipper's particularly proud of the autographed team picture from the group that won the German Cup in '92. Hannover was the first second-league team to ever win the Cup.

Kai wants to start in with his Facebook spiel, but I get up and say, "Gotta take a leak."

"Think about it," he yells behind me. Startled, I glance quickly over at the regulars' table, but Axel's engrossed in a conversation. I go to the ladies' room. I can have peace there. Not that Kai would follow me to the crapper with his harebrained scheme. Since women never come into Timpen, Skipper summarily declared the ladies' room as his second storage room. The crapper still works, of course. You just have to make sure there's tp. Otherwise you can scoot your unwiped tush over to the other stall. And if both stalls are occupied, then cheers. The old farts here need ages to take a dump. Not to mention the stench of old-man shit. I luck out, and there's still half a roll next to the bowl. And because I'm not in a hurry, I choose a nice bottle of suds for the toilet. I can open the door to the stall and reach into a case and pull out a beer without lifting a cheek. Skipper's not opposed to people taking advantage in here. After finishing my business, I slip the bottle back into the case and tug my jogging pants back into place. In the hallway to the facilities, I hear a loud hubbub from the taproom and the sound of a chair or stool being knocked over. I open the door and see Kai in the middle of the room, holding a skinhead firmly by the scruff of his neck. The skin is slightly smaller than Kai, and his head has half disappeared into the collar of his Lonsdale jacket Kai's holding him by. Ulf is standing behind Kai. I know that face. It's his "you're in deep shit" face.

"What's goin' on here?" I ask, and several heads turn toward me.

"I just told that son of a bitch and his buddies they have no business here," Kai reported and pushed the skinhead away. The guy slips back a step and bumps against the table in the middle of the room, under which a chair lies on its side. Only now do I notice the other two Nazis. One of them is standing behind his buddy, the other next to the regulars' table.

The one Kai just manhandled says to me, "You're Heiko Kolbe, right?"

He clucks his tongue against his yellowed teeth.

"You wanna have my address, you cocksucker? You guys have no business here. So get lost already."

The Nazi at the regulars' table, the biggest of them, with a wrinkly, fat face and hamster cheeks, takes a hesitant step toward me and tries to put on a scary grimace. I just glance and blow some air through my lips. They make a *pfff* sound.

Kai's adversary says, "We for sure aren't getting lost, dude. We were invited."

"Then you must have gotten the wrong door, you idiots," Ulf said, his deep bass echoing in the beer glasses.

I nod. "Fo' sho'. I'm certain no one here invited you."

Then I walk toward Ratface with the yellow teeth, fists full of rage and all out of patience.

"Which isn't completely true," Axel says, loudly but completely relaxed.

I turn toward the regulars' table and look at him, dumbfounded, as he calmly sits there. One arm resting on the table. The other spread, his hand on his thigh.

"I invited them."

Ratface walks past me, knocking aside Kai's hand that halfheartedly tried to hold him back, and grins at me stupidly in a challenge. Then he pulls the chair from under the table, deposits it opposite Axel, and plants his dirty rat ass on it. The two other skins reveal teeth no less yellow. Hee, hee, hee. You dirty little bitches! Then I recognize them. They're the same ones who were sitting in Axel's office recently. And what's more, they're part of a group of Nazis from Hannover's Langenhagen district known for causing trouble.

"What do you have do to get a fuckin' beer around here?" Ratface said without turning around.

My feet are bolted to the floor. I look at Axel and simply can't close my jaw. He catches me with a stern look. Then he gradually releases the clamp of his stare and groans briefly. But not in a relieved way, more like he's annoyed. As if we were little boys who were annoying the shit out of their dad.

"Three beers, Skipper," Axel says soberly.

I feel the rage radiate out from my fists and temples, spreading across my body. I wouldn't have thought it possible to do what I do next: I extend my index finger and say, "Skipper, they don't get nothin' here!"

He takes his hand from the tap and mutters, "Too right."

Before the Nazis or Axel or anyone can react, I grab Ratface by the shoulders, yank him up from the chair, and throw him at the middle table. His back slams against the edge of the table, and the table slides sideways. It was all too fast for him, and before he's back on his feet I grab him again, pull him close to me, and give it to him. Straight to his crooked fucking nose, immediately producing a cut to the bridge. Falls over limply. I register chair and table legs scraping over the floor tiles through what feels like a down duvet wrapped around my head. Then Fatface is coming at me. Lumbering and uncertain what he even wants to do, I'm able to deftly step aside and smack him. He grunts in pain as my fist slams into the side of his belly. Ulf's already there and grabs his neck with both hands, pulls him away, and throws him to the floor as if he were made of marshmallow. The third Nazi runs at Kai, but Kai doesn't mess around. He takes his beer glass from the counter and knocks it over the dude's dome with a crash. He yells, and the blood flows down his forehead and over his face so he has to pinch his eyes shut. We grab the three assholes. Töller, who's standing close to the door, holds it open for us with a broad grin. We throw the Nazis from Langenhagen out on their ear. Stay in front of the door and watch how they check out all their individual parts and disappear with their tails tucked between their legs. However, Kai doesn't pass up the opportunity to hawk a loogie from way deep down.

"Yeah, fuck off, you fucktards!" I yell after them, middle finger extended.

We go back inside.

Kai jokingly slams his fist against my bicep and says, "Ah, man, what a beautiful thing. Now time for a beer."

I shake my head, don't say a word, and walk past him. Then I push the tables and chairs back in place and apologize to Skipper, who waves me off.

My uncle. Sitting there at the regulars' table. Still sitting there. Like Jesus on one of those paintings of the Last Supper. I just look at my uncle. My skull feels electric. My cheekbones are almost bursting out from the pressure. Then I grab my phone and wallet from the counter and leave Timpen without a word.

After spending the evening not answering my phone and stalking through Hannover, cursing to myself silently, I calmed down somewhat and was sitting with Kai on the roof of his house. We bought a chunk of hash from his roommate and smoked one doobie after another, and I was just venting to him, with him adding "exactly" and "hmm" and "fo' sho'" at precisely the right moment. He didn't have to do anything else. I didn't ask for anything more. Just being able to rant about what a crock of shit, and what the fuck was my uncle thinking when he decided he could invite in anyone and everyone he wanted, what was the point of the whole Sun King act, and why, of all people, this particular group of brown-assed Nazi sons of bitches, as if he wasn't aware of what kind of example that would set, as if he's from the fucking moon, as if he wants a situation like they have in Aachen or Rostock or even Braunschweig, and then I tell him we're gonna do that thing with Braunschweig, that we're gonna drive over there and really kick their asses, and if we do it, then we'll do it right, and do it my way, you're goddamn fucking right we are!

And Kai yells: "Damn right! Goddamn fucking hell!" from our roof down into the canyons of the buildings below. And Hannover is lit up from a thousand wounds in the darkness.

And from somewhere down below someone bellows, "Settle down! Can't a man drink a beer in peace anymore?!"

———

"Stupid idea, Heiko, just a fucking stupid idea," I say and examine myself in the rearview mirror of my car. The impression of the headrest can be seen clearly on my cheek. I don't even know why I do it to myself and keep coming back again and again. But I'm also not able to prevent myself.

A glance at the clock: it's just after 3 a.m. I've been hanging here for a good two hours. Should at least have grabbed something to drink at the gas station. I lean my seat back as far as it goes. It clicks, and I try stretching my tingling legs to find a more comfortable position. I look up at Yvonne's bedroom window. It's the only room on the street with the light still on. Here and there you can see the blue flicker from a television screen on the visible ceilings and walls. I shift the driver's seat lower so I don't have to move my head to have a direct view of Yvonne's window. I turn the spare key to her apartment over in my fingers, running my thumb over the teeth. Just like I did when I swiped it from the basket in the hallway. When we were still together, I was never allowed to have it. Of course, I always asked why, but the question soon became pointless. Maybe she already had the locks changed long ago.

"Fuck it," I groan and deposit the key in the glove compartment again. Then I lean back, room in view. No shadow or any indication in the part of the bedroom visible to me. Just white, blank ceiling.

While my eyes continue to watch, I stray mentally. Mie came into the kitchen as I was working with the pigeons and cleaning the feces from the boards. I only saw the rough silhouette of her head. Can't even say whether she saw me at all. Come on, of course. She has to have looked out into the fucking garden at least once while she was in the kitchen. Even if it was by accident. I nodded to her. Briefly. Not too friendly. Didn't want to give her the feeling she should come out now and we'd chat while I scrubbed the shit off the wooden roosts. I hadn't treated her very well when my father showed up with her and she moved in with us. I mean, I didn't do anything bad. I just acted like she was invisible, which isn't hard to do with her, because she already acts pretty much like a ghost. But I don't know, maybe that was unfair. Maybe not, either, but that's how it was.

My eyelids are gradually becoming heavy. The light's still on. I don't want to, but I wonder what she's doing right now. If she's doing anything at all. Who knows if she didn't already fall asleep hours ago. She always was so tired after shooting up. At least the couple of times I was along for it. When I didn't go, not wanting to leave her alone for a week till she came around by herself.

I'm tired. Exhausted. Axel and I mostly avoided crossing paths in the gym. I know he won't do it, but somehow I expect him to bring up the thing at Timpen. Explain himself and what he was thinking. He won't do it. I still don't have the right words. Can't do it without preparation, otherwise I'll go down without a whimper. I couldn't care less. But I do. I want for it to work. I want what he held out for me, even promised formally.

I nod off in the driver's seat.

———

Match against Karlruher SC. They were actually still in the Bundesliga then, like Hannover. You almost can't imagine that today. But they do sort of belong there somehow. Unlike Cottbus, especially, who were also in the top league then. 96 may have been meandering through the season, but we all agreed that regardless of where they ended up, the main thing was that Cottbus was below them. Even if that meant the Reds got relegated to the next league, coming in second to last. Fucking irrelevant if Cottbus came in last.

It's one of those things about seats in the stadium and affiliation. Generally. Sure, everyone has a seat number that's indicated on their ticket. Even in the North Curve, where the ultras own the stands. The oldest ultra groups are in the upper tiers. The younger groups are down below. Which is also probably some hierarchy thing. So the established groups can look down on the young mob. But we wouldn't have given a rat's ass anyway. Contrary to the so-called journalism produced by the media that always wants to lump us together with the ultras. What do they know?

It was the same with our allotted spots. Also because of hierarchy. So we were standing behind the fans in the North Curve stands, in the corridor behind the upper tiers. Axel, Tomek, and the other full members stood in the middle behind them. As young guns, we were a little farther back. Basically in the middle of the corridor with people on their way to the toilet, or the stands for food or beer, or returning. We don't go to the stadium very often. It's just not a place for our type. We move in other circles, but once in a while you just have to show up. Show that we're still here. In other words, for the ones that recognize us, which is just a fraction of the usual stadium-goers.

"But this is bullshit, man," Jojo complained. "Can't see anything from here. Karlsruhe nailed the penalty kick, right?"

"Jojo, would you get off my back? Right here is just our place."

"Yeah, they made it from the mark," said Ulf. At almost six foot six, he's always able to see more.

Kai pokes me and leans his head over and says: "Here they come again."

Plainclothes cops. Walking by for the second or third time. Axel and the old boys pointedly turned their backs to the cops walking by.

Kai stepped out from our group, started to curtsy, and grinned, saying: "G'day, dear sirs."

The cops move on, looking offended. No clue who they thought they were fooling with the show. Hastily pulling jerseys over their ironed shirts, still sticking out a little. Throwing scarves around their necks, like lipstick on pigs. And then clutching the alibi beer, which they can't even touch because they're on duty. Touch with their mouths, I mean. The piss they serve in the stadium couldn't get much flatter.

I told him, "You'd better be glad Axel didn't see that. You know what he thinks about making a scene."

Kai raised his hands in defense, pursed his lips, and said, "Oh, dangerous, super dangerous."

"Oh, cut the crap." I took a go at him but couldn't hold back a grin.

Then a group of ultras came up from the stands, probably just wanted to piss, and looked like they'd just come from the black bloc of disrepute. They walked past us and scanned us from head to toe.

I heard one of them say something like, "What kind of jokers are these?" Then the little fucker giggled.

Kai's mood flipped immediately. "Did you hear what that little shit just said?"

"Well?" I asked casually and tried to get a glimpse of the game, but people were constantly getting in the way.

"Didn't even know who we were. They don't have hair on their nads yet, those dickheads."

Jojo, who was still grumbling to himself in irritation and had ignored the ultras, said, "For real, Heiko, I laid out twenty bucks for the ticket and can't see a thing. It's fucking pointless. We could just as well have watched the game in the comfort of Timpen. Besides, the draft back here is murder. Could you ask your uncle if we can join them up front?"

I exhaled my annoyance and said, "You know how it works. *This* is our spot."

I pointed to the floor between us and looked at the group, which wasn't just the four of us but also a couple other young guns from back when. They've all left us by now.

"We just have to earn the spot over there. What do you wanna do?"

He looked at me. His tongue moved inside his cheek impatiently, back and forth.

"My god, then all right, I'll ask. Just knock it off."

"Excellent, Heiko, thanks," Jojo said.

I looked over at the group that had gathered around my uncle. It reminded me of the days when I was still a little twerp and my father brought me along every now and then. Back then it was exactly the same, except I was standing around with Hans somewhere instead of with the boys now, while people were gathered around Axel as if he was some kind of tiny solar system that only existed in the Curve. I looked at Jojo again and said, "Won't accomplish a thing."

And I was right, of course. I had barely stepped up to the group surrounding Axel and Tomek when my uncle snarled at me, wanting to know what I wanted. I tried to somehow acquaint him with the concept that we couldn't see anything and all that shit.

"Go back to your spot," Axel barked.

When I got back to the boys, Jojo asked, "Well?"

"Shove it, Jojo," I said and drained my beer in silence.

———

"Manuela, please don't bust my balls. I'll find him already! Yeah. Sure, bye."

I chuck my phone on the passenger seat. It bounces off like a rubber ball and lands on the floor.

My father's caregiver wasn't able to give me any useful clues about where he might be when I'd spoke with her. Just said he must have disappeared sometime around lunch and moans something like, It's so awful, we've never had anything like this happen before. Thanks, a lotta help you are, you old hag, I thought and turned the key. Then my sister had to bitch me out. As if it was my fault he wanted to step out of the rehab clinic. I mean, here I am, and all this craps lands on me, typical. She couldn't leave. Because of classes, and all that.

The car's running, and I'm steering from the clinic parking lot onto the street. Trying to make my way to the middle of town.

It's windy. I pull the zipper up on my windbreaker. Then I shove my fists into my jacket pockets and walk randomly down an unfamiliar street. Hans doesn't have a phone. Even though Manuela bought him one once, as far as I know he never used it. My dad's just old-school. Real old-school.

I arrive at a square paved with cobblestones, a kind of a market square. Maybe it's the middle of town. Clueless, making the rounds. Mostly there are pensioners sitting outside in front of the cafés, holding down their napkins against the wind. Deep, snow-white tumors of clouds stream over the rooftops. The aroma of fresh cake and pastries seems to emanate from everywhere. It's making me slightly nauseous. That and how perfectly arranged everything is here. Like a typical spa town. The old farts watch me walk by, mouths agape. Probably asking themselves what kind of shady customer I am, decked out in a black jogging suit. And in a place like this, I truly do feel as out of place as a right-wing extremist at a gypsy wedding. I go down a narrow, one-lane shopping street leading away from the square. A couple of teenagers are sitting in front of the supermarket and sucking energy drinks. They're laughing, kidding around. Calling each other "son of a bitch" and that sort of thing. Acting like they're Turkish or something. Even though they're just stupid nobodies. I walk past the driveway to the parking lot belonging to the supermarket, which is located behind the row of residential buildings. A ruined, elderly guy with a gray flowing beard is sitting against the wall. His facial hair has taken on the typical color of tobacco-yellow above the lip. He's wearing a dirty sweater that basically screams the 90s. A gray threadbare denim vest on top of that. His blue cap, which he wears loosely over a wide mop of hair, has attained a kind of batik pattern from years of sweat. The cap is labeled MODERN DRUNKARD – EST. 1986. I approach him and he looks up at me with a tired gaze. The bags under his eyes look like washrags.

"Hey pal. Maybe you have a little spare change?"

I pull out my wallet, say, "Sure," and give him a two-euro coin.

He holds it up for a second, depositing it in his breast pocket of his vest and says, "The company expresses its gratitude."

I crouch down next to him, silently offering him a cigarette, which he also raises in thanks. Then I pass him my lighter, but just for him to give back to me. He offers his hand. His fingers are rough and rutted like the bark of an oak tree. The fingertips have long gone beyond tobacco yellow to take on the color of morning urine.

"Heiko," I introduce myself.

"Pit, but my friends call me Osaka Pit."

We smoke a while in silence. Then the next cigarettes. At some point I say, "Let's assume I'm treating you to a beer, straight from the tap. Where would we go?"

He strokes his invisible chin with his fingers, making a rustling sound. He's pondering as if I'd asked him the meaning of life.

"There's not a lot around here. We'd probably go to Schüssler's. It's right around the corner."

I stand up, pat down my butt, and say, "Let's go then."

Schüssler's reminds me a lot of Timpen back home. A typically rustic, old-time tavern that, from the outside, during the day and when none of the lights are on, gives the impression it's closed. Hans isn't there. Doesn't show up either while I pay for a couple rounds of draft with Pit, who everyone seems to know, and we chat. Better than running around without a plan.

"Hannover 96, right?" Pit says, and the suds he's licked off fizz in his beard. "I don't know much about football. Was more interested in cricket. Seemed more complex. But you don't get very far with that in German-speaking countries. My dream was to watch a top Indian match. But that probably doesn't interest you." He tapped against the bill of his cap and turned toward the barkeeper. "Gisbert, which one of those Hannover 96 players came from here, from Bad Zwischenahn?"

Without having to think very long, Gisbert, whose left eyelid twitches incessantly, answers, "Carsten Linke."

"What do you know," I say, astonished, "our defensive rock. What a coincidence! Well, then, at least now I can claim that I was once in Carsten Linke's hometown."

Pit nods, satisfied he was able to gratify me with that bit of information, and looks into his glass. Preparing for the next sip. He has yet to ask what brought me to Bad Zwischenahn in the first place, and I don't really feel like talking about it.

We move from straight beer to a couple rounds of boilermakers, which reminds me of the liters of black beer and vodka mix at the Marksmen's Fair. We clink the shot glasses. Down them and say, "Ahhh," as if we were drinking an isotonic beverage after running a marathon. Gisbert flips the light switch on. I glance at the clock. It's getting close to evening. One more, I say, and order another round.

"Hey, why do they call you Osaka Pit, anyway?"

"Well," Pit waves me off, chuckling, "old story. I smuggled opium for a couple years. I was around your age. Far East, to make a long story short. Then they nabbed me in Osaka. Was trying to sail to Taipei. I was sentenced to four years in Japan. Then it took me two more to get back to Europe." He chuckles again, as if he was telling a joke. "Got lucky. If they'd grabbed me somewhere else—like Singapore or Taiwan, for example—I wouldn't be sitting here today. Even if you're just courier, they send you into the sunset before you know it. They don't fool around."

We empty our glasses. I gradually remember why I'm here in the first place.

"I have to keep moving," I say and ask where there's another bar around here.

Pit directs me to the Twüschenkahn, a bar that's closer to Zwischenahn Lake, the local pond. I pay and get up. There's still one last generous splash of backwash.

"Pit, if you're still thirsty, I'll buy you another." He waves me off, saying, "Nah, my body's had enough for today. Your finances have already suffered enough for good old Pit. I thank you much for that."

"Sure?"

"Absolutely. Otherwise my lady will bitch at me." He laughs with his mouth open, throwing his head back. I didn't see a ring on his finger. If that's supposed be a joke, I don't get it.

"All right," I say, and we shake hands good-bye.

"Keep your chin up, boy. You'll find what you're looking for."

I thank him and leave.

As the door falls shut behind me and seals out the clinking of glasses and rush of table talk, the thought crosses my mind that after all maybe I did tell Pit what I was doing here. That I drove here just to look for my father. Pit would nod approvingly, and raise his glass toward the bar in a gesture. Then I'd assemble everything I could say about Hans. Like the first time he took me to the stadium. How everyone looked up to him and shook his hand respectfully and gathered around him. How I was always allowed to help feed the pigeons, and how we kicked the ball around afterward. For Pit, all of that would be true of my father. He didn't know my father, after all. And it wouldn't make any difference to Pit. Then we'd raise our glasses one last time. And then there would be, at least in Bad Zwischenahn and only if it lasts for just a couple of drunken nights, someone who's heard the name Hans Kolbe and raised his glass. But instead of all that, I just turn my back to the wind to light another cig and then try to find my way to the next bar.

I don't like Twüschenkahn as much as Schüsslers. Large, open windows allow a view of the water. Overall, the bar seems significantly cleaner and more orderly. There appear to be people here who still have to drink their way into advanced age and an advanced stage in life in order to feel comfortable in Schüsslers. Besides, there's something to eat here. I order the local specialty, a sausage with kale. It tastes good, but the kale leaves an aftertaste of iron in my mouth, making me nauseous. I try to eliminate the taste with another beer and a cup of coffee, combined with a saucer of sprats. I grab the sprats by the heads, hiding their eye sockets with my fingers, and slide them into my mouth, tail and all, and bite down. They taste pleasantly salty.

And then, when it's almost already ten in the evening, something happens I no longer expected. My father comes through the door. I instantly put down my phone and delete the fourth draft of a message I'd started writing Manuela. He sits down two chairs over without noticing me. Maybe I should be furious. Or relieved. I am neither. The various rounds of beer and boilermakers have packed my head in comfy cushions. I look over. Hans orders his beer. Even from the side, I can see his hollow gaze. He appears to not have shaved in the clinic. The good old stache is coming on. I get up, push my beer one seat over, and sit down.

Without looking to the side, I say: "Hey, Dad. Finally come on in?"

He looks at me. Needs a second. Then he recognizes me after all. His face opens.

"Man, Heiko. What're you doin' here?"

He slaps his bare hands on the counter. I explain everything. Why I'm here and not Manuela. Tell him what the people at the clinic had said, that he'd simply run off, and he acts completely surprised. As if he had been unaware you couldn't just go on a bender when you've been sent to rehab precisely because of your drinking. I don't bother to give him a lecture, just say I'm going to take him back and I'm not going to come back here to catch him again. To my own surprise, this comes out slightly less judgmental than intended. I blamed it on the alcohol.

We pass most of the time just drinking next to one another. Once in a while we exchange a couple sentences. Out of the blue he asks if I'm still in touch with Mom, which I deny. I say I don't want to talk about it.

"Hmm," he says and somehow sounds disappointed. Then he looks away again.

"Why do you wanna know?" I ask anyway, and it comes across just as randomly.

"It's okay," is all he says, and drinks.

It's late. Actually, it's not that late. Just before midnight. But considering I've been driving around half the day and spent the other half in bars, it's already late.

"Come on, finish up. I'll take you back to the clinic."

He does what I tell him, without any back talk.

When we find a spot in the clinic parking lot, I wait for him to get out, walk to the illuminated entrance, apologize for going missing, and go to bed so I can drive back to Wunstorf. But he makes no move to do so.

"All right then," I say, and knead my thighs to help the circulation.

He turns toward me slightly in his seat, saying, "Here's a suggestion, Heiko."

I'm tired, say, "I'm not even thinking of taking you home with me."

"I don't want you to either." He sounds as if he was keeping a hiccup down. "Your sister would wring my neck."

"And mine with it."

"No, what I wanted to say—" He draws up his legs. "I've been watching matches again since I've been in here. Goin' pretty well for the Reds, right?"

He looks up at me.

"Decent," I say and lay my head against my extended finger. I have the elbow supported against the bottom of the window.

"Away game tomorrow against Werder Bremen."

"I know."

"What do you think? The two of us? Like we used to. That'd be something. Against Bremen, Heiko."

I feel the pressure rising behind my eyeballs. Don't know where that's coming from.

"I don't think that—"

"Oh, come on. Don't be a wuss. Go to the game again with your old man. You can buy yourself a Coke. Just for you."

He winks at me, but a little too slowly, making it seem like one side of his face was nodding off.

"Man, Dad," I groan.

"Do you have something planned? A fight? Gonna hit the field tomorrow, right?" he asks.

"No, that's not it. Come on, let it drop."

"Heiko. Please. One match."

Instead of looking for a hotel room somewhere, I spend the night in the clinic parking lot. Surrounded by thickening fog that makes the interior of the hatchback very damp. Luckily, I find a couple of blankets in the trunk, so I'm able to wrap myself in them. Around three in the morning, I finally send a message to Manuela, telling her I've found Hans and everything's fine, but that I'm going to stay another day because it's so late. Then I sack out.

I spend most of the next day at Mickey D's and bakeries, charging my battery and waiting to be able to pick Hans up from the clinic. Then we drive to Bremen together.

I'm not interested in knowing and don't ask whether he got official leave or just vanished again. We spend the drive talking about football, even though I notice his knowledge basically stopped around the end of the last century. He can't believe it when I tell him about the appalling millions of euros thrown around for players, some very young, by teams like Barcelona, Real, or English Premiere League clubs run by Arabic sheiks.

"So much money," he repeats, "so much money. Imagine that." And "Where the hell is Dubai again?"

The fact the Ajax Amsterdam and Steaua Bucharest haven't been top European clubs for ages appears to be news to him.

We bypass Bremen, which seems enclosed in a single massive cloud bank, only exiting the autobahn at the Arsten interchange. Then we cross Werder Lake, the choppy Weser River, and drive to the familiar Osterdeich Avenue. Weser Stadium protrudes before the gray sky like a gigantic petri dish from biology class. It's fairly quiet in the open space in front of the stadium entrance. The cops standing around in protective vests and with their hands near their batons cause a nervous shiver to run down my spine, and we disappear into the crowd. It lasts even when I buy our black-market tickets from a guy who seems too friendly for a scalper, but anyway I don't have a choice .

Weser Stadium is full, every last seat. There's a tifo being pre-pared on the East Curve, where the Werder ultras are located. They're unrolling a banner that covers almost the entire corner. On the opposite side, the Hannover fans are making a racket, yell-ing insults in the direction of the Bremen fans. I'm glad we're in neutral seats and aren't sitting in the visitors' section. Wouldn't have been too keen to cross paths with certain familiar ultras. One of the Capos, the oldest ultra group in Hannover, is probably still a little sore at me since we tangled by the urinals at the traditional Marksmen's Fair, which ended with him getting a black eye and his face shoved in the trough. Not that he could do anything to me. But it wouldn't be a chill stadium experience.

"What, did they run out of Coke?" Hans jokes when I return to our seats with two cups of beer. Before taking a seat next to him, I have a view of his old man's receding hair line through his thin-ning, brown hair. Soon it will meet up with the increasingly large spot on the back of his head and merge.

The game is fucking disgusting. No goals. The Reds, along with Bremen, all lose a handle on balls somewhere in the mid-field because no one can make a decent pass. Or someone sends it long and they go for it like in amateur league—one bungled header after another. Because the Bremen defense has a tradition of being a pile of incompetents, several chances for 96 do materialize during the course of the match, but they're all wasted, as commented on by my father with a throaty "crooked foot!" He also keeps bringing up the Cup-winning team's finals in '92, when Hannover's first-round draw was Werder Bremen, of all teams, which meant their European adventure was over before it started.

"Still hurts, you know. Still hurts, I'm telling you."

Then he pats me on the knee with his fist if I can't pull it away fast enough.

"Are you taking good care of the critters?" he asks, and I confirm it monosyllabically and swallow the stadium beer.

"How's Mie doing?"

"Yeah, good, I think," I say, and he says: "She's a good woman, Mie is. Good woman."

"Aha."

"And the boys? What are they up to? Kai, Ulf, and the two brothers?"

Something goes down the wrong way and I start hacking. Hans is about to pound me on my back when he notices how deeply he's put his foot in his own mouth and withdraws his hand.

Several errant passes and botched headers, and I say out of the blue, "Was at the psychiatric clinic with Axel. We visited one of his old friends. Somehow seemed familiar to me." I keep watching the game, occasionally catching Hans numbly staring straight ahead. "Must have been a huge guy."

My father mumbles something indefinable into his beer while taking a sip.

"Sat in a wheelchair. Dirk was his name." Now I notice Hans is rocking back and forth, barely perceptibly. I have no clue if he's been doing it the whole time and I only noticed now. "You remember him?"

Hans coughs into his cupped fist, and I have the feeling he hasn't blinked for several minutes. Then he says, "Hey, let's watch the game, okay?"

Without another word spoken, a miserable North German rivalry comes to a close.

Just before Bad Zwischenahn, Hans tries to apologize while the rain begins to beat down hard on the windshield. I say he should forget about it and that it didn't matter.

"Thanks, my boy. Really had fun. Horrible match . . . but, oh well."

I nod and turn the key in the ignition. "Gotta go."

"Yep," he says, "take it easy. Drive safe and give them my regards back home."

He closes the door, turns, and stops for a second. He looks over at the clinic, and I can hear his deep sigh even through the car door.

———

Something was banging against my door like crazy, making me sit almost bolt upright in bed.

"Heiko! Heiko! Fucking hell, you open up now!"

The wooden door is just barely hanging on its hinges. It vibrates with each of Arnim's blows. When he hears me turn the key, he stops the pounding.

"What's up? How late is it?" I ask.

Arnim is covered with drops of sweat. From his medicine-ball-sized head down to his old man chest, which must have been muscular once. His much too deeply cut wifebeater sticks to his paunch.

"The time has come! I'm getting it. I'm finally getting it!"

"What, huh?" I ask and rub a hand over the stubble on my head.

"Man, the tiger, my boy. The tiger!" But he pronounces "tiger" like "tigger." Because I'm still busy rubbing my eyes and not really registering things, all I can think to say is a meager "Huh."

"My dear boy," he booms, "you're sure slow on the uptake today."

"Yeah, I understood: Tiger. You're getting a tiger."

"Oh, knock it off. It's finally happening. I'm getting it next month!"

Gradually, I grasp the significance of what's he's been jabbering, and I peer at him through my fingers.

"Holy shit! For real? Don't jerk me around!"

"Nope. Not shitting you, my boy. An honest-to-God fucking Bengal tiger! Here in our house."

I drop my hands from my face. "What, that's it? Is it here? Where'd you put the beast? You didn't put it in with Poborsky or Bigfoot, right?"

He flips me off, pushing his flabby skin up on his forehead.

"Did they take a shit in your skull, my boy? Naw, the month after next. Then it'll be time. I can pick it up."

He turns around, almost skipping down the hallway like the fattest kid in the world, calling out to me, "Come on, pull yourself together, it's time to pack!"

After I've gathered my wits and figured out that I slept late into the afternoon, I go down to the kitchen. The dogs are barking their asses off at each other and don't stop. Arnim's yelling at them that they should shut up only spurs then on. I bend over the sink filled with weeks' worth of dirty dishes and look outside. In the back of the yard, which seems unusually well lit, there's a small yellow backhoe. I move through the door. The yard really is getting more light than usual, though the sky is cloud-covered. The camouflage netting is rolled up in front of the shed. Arnim swings himself up behind the backhoe's controls, spots me, and waves with a grin. Which once again makes him look like the fattest, sweatiest, most heavily tattooed kid over fifty. He starts the motor and all at once you can hardly hear Poborsky and Bigfoot.

"Arnim!" I shout. "Arnim!"

He stares at me, eyebrows raised, and turns it off again.

"What?"

"What are you doing? Where'd you get the backhoe?"

"Don't scream your head off like that. Borrowed it from a buddy."

Ah, okay, borrowed. I ask ironically if he's planning to dig a tiger's pit.

"Whadda you think? Sure, that's gonna be a tiger pit. Top-notch tiger pit, my boy."

"I-I can't believe it," I stammer.

"What?!" He calls, "Come and lend me a hand!"

Using the scoop of the backhoe, Arnim had done most of the dirty work of clearing the earth out of the planned pit, whose edges he'd marked beforehand with an X and wooden stakes. All the while I'm standing in the increasingly deep hole and going at it with a shovel. Shove it into the earth, which luckily isn't too hard, scoop, and toss it over my head and out of the hole like a no-look pass. After a couple hours, the arm of the backhoe doesn't reach deep enough. It's raining. The soil is soft and soggy. I'm covered with a thin film of mud, but it's only drizzling. I pray it stays that way. Or it really starts pouring and we have to stop. Though Arnim wouldn't hear of it anyway. Arnim joins me, jumping into the pit, and the slurry splashes. Together we shovel out the remaining pile in the middle, because the arm of the backhoe was too short to come that far. Arnim had estimated about fifteen square meters and a depth of four meters. After leveling off the inside of the pit, we start to work toward the desired depth. The whole dirty job drags on into the evening. My hands have blisters despite the work gloves.

I come back from the shitter and gulp down a gallon of tap water when a voice calls out from the pit: "Heiko! Heiko! You there?"

I step over to the edge of the pit. Arnim takes a step back from the earth wall so he can see me better.

"Can't get out of here!"

I laugh at him, which he doesn't think is very cool, and he bellows up at me, "Come on and hand me the ladder! I have to piss."

For a minute I consider leaving him in the tiger pit, just to give him hell, but he'd given me a leg up so I could reach to top edge. So I get the aluminum extension ladder from the shed and let it slide down. When he steps on the lowest rung, it slides farther down, and under his monstrous weight the bottom sinks into the soggy earth.

"What'd you have planned for the walls?" I ask and hold the ladder tight.

"What d'ya mean?" he wheezes.

"Well, did you ever see one of those tigers for real? I mean in the zoo or a TV nature show? In the end, they're still cats. Fucking huge cats, but cats. You probably don't think it could scramble up a dirt wall with its claws."

Arnim gets off the ladder and stands still, with his hands resting on his knees, breathing deeply. Then he snorts and says, "Sure did cross my mind, my boy. Everything's lined up. It'll get fine accommodations with walls of aluminum siding."

By now it's late in the evening. Arnim had set up extra floodlights after taking a piss and pointed them into the pit. We need another two hours to reach the depth of four meters.

I chuck the shovel out of the pit in a high arc and sigh, "Finally," and start to climb up the ladder when Arnim holds me back.

"Not so fast, my boy. The lid's going on before we knock off."

There are tons of aluminum studs and wooden boards stacked in front of the shed. I pass Arnim one after the other. He temporarily spreads them out next to the pit while I bring over screwdriver, square, and other tools, and then we put this monstrous fifteen-square-meter lid together, drilling, screwing, and nailing it under the shine of the floodlights.

"So, tomorrow the walls, and then you're released for the time being," he says, and tosses two big-ass steaks into the sizzling skillet.

I stuff myself full of meat till the meat in my throat hits other meat, and Arnim tells me the old story for the nth time while I keep on nodding off at the table: "My boss offered me 10,000 marks. That was a real stack of cash at the time. I hadn't even earned that much in a year as a butcher. Maybe earned, but I didn't get it." He shakes with laughter at his own joke. "Well, I thought, can't be that hard. Knocking someone off. You see it on TV all the time. In all the movies. People are constantly being offed. I can hack it, I told myself. So one day I went over to the farm of my boss's neighbor. With a gun. Double barrel. In case one bullet wasn't enough, y'know? Went over there. Ski mask, you say! Why would you need it? A dead person can't identify you, I thought. The thing might slide in front of my eyes and I'd end up blasting away at my own foot. Which would be pretty stupid. Nope. So I head over. Looked around and didn't see no one in the yard. I went into the loafing shed. It was already evening. Not so light anymore. And there, standing between his cows, I see him bending over a cow's ass. Snuck up, but he probably heard me. Doesn't matter because he'll be dead in a sec, I thought to myself. Gets up and makes to turn around, and I cock it. But I don't shoot from the hip. Could go who the hell knows where. I might even shoot a cow in the ass. I cocked, and pulled the trigger right away. Boom! Right in his face. Did a top-notch pirouette, the dumbass. Well. And then he lay there, arms all twisted under his body and the legs cockeyed, like he's climbing a steep staircase. Wouldn't recognize him. Sure did take care of his face. That's where the bullet came out, 'cause I shot him in the side of his head and it came out front. I'm telling you, it looked all messed up. A hole about"—he used the thumbs and fingers of both hands to form a big hole—"about yea-big in his kisser. I split from there as fast as I could. Yeah, and I got into really deep shit, you know? Because that wasn't him. It was the vet. The actual target, the dumb fucker, was on the latrine. Shittin' away. The vet was there to look at the cow because it was supposed to drop one soon. Then it all got out, and less than two days later the marshals came and popped me at my place. Locked, cocked. Yep, that's what happened. Went to Hainholz, in the slammer. Sat there for ten years. Never saw the cash either. But I'd wasted the wrong guy, after all. Fucking vet."

I'd finally fell asleep at the "boom" part, but I'd already heard the story a dozen times, so I knew it in my sleep.

———

My second week in the Neustadt hospital. But even after one day, they'd shown me unmistakably that, as someone doing voluntary service, I was just their slave. Go there and mop up the puke! Come here and scrub the blood off the walls! Dig the pieces out of the bone saw blade! Not that the tasks themselves were annoying. After all, someone had to do the dirty work, and if I'd been the doctor or nurse, I'd have made the volunteer do it too. It was the way they talked to us. As if we were the worst of the tards. It wasn't much help either that at twenty-one I already looked like I could pound all of the head physicians into the ground. I almost regretted not having listened to my father's bitching and moaning and just done the mandatory military service. Almost, but didn't. 'Cause first of all, then I'd have been doing far worse, and second, I would've had to put up with all the fatherland patriots, and third, I'd have done anything to avoid giving Hans the satisfaction of heeding his sniping. Like, what a little fag you are, doing voluntary service. Go to the army, they'll make a real man outta ya. What a pushover! I'd already had to hear it when I got kicked outta school for the second time and could forget about getting a normal degree. My teachers were a bunch of snobbish assholes and frigid old cunts. All of them! And the worst was our principal, the old jerk-off. Put 'em in a sack and beat 'em. You won't hit anyone who doesn't deserve it. But the fact that I didn't even go into the army, which was what was expected for a straight-shooting young guy, that really made Hans even more livid. Such bullshit. Whatever. At any rate, all that changed in week two, when I was called to the room of some senile geriatric who was only clinging on the threshold of death with his little toe. He'd almost croaked three times during my first week, but then he came around every time. So I went into the room and heard the doctors and nurses yelling at each other. Saw everyone fussing over him. I wanted to scream they should let him die in peace. Then I noticed her. She was standing at the edge of the group. She seemed completely uninvolved, as if she'd done this a thousand times before. But Yvonne was still in training, as I later found out. So she couldn't have done it that often yet. If at all. She was holding something. I don't even want to know exactly what. It was obscured by the back of a doctor and a chubby male nurse. But it was more about her face. So fucking beautiful! Her cheeks were so smooth your hand would slip if you stroked them. They narrowed as they approached her mouth. A cute, small mouth. Not one of those big old frog mouths like so many others. Her nose was so narrow and delicate. Hardly had nostrils. Everything about her is slender in the first place. Seems so delicate. And then when she opened her mouth, I was left gaping and just thought, kudos, girl, I wouldn't have had the balls to say that. And her little eyes, those blue eyes. Like ice cubes with a fly frozen in the middle. So sharp and precise, but at the same time so open and free-floating. But the best thing about her, I noticed in that moment, was her brow. Free of eyebrows. Two perfectly formed crests I immediately wanted to kiss, one after the other. Or wanted to trace with the tip of my tongue. Simply smooth skin, without pores.

All at once, the whole group around the bed jumped back. When the old man started hacking. He had one of those thumb-sized tubes sticking out of or into a hole in his throat. For breathing and all, I think. They'd pulled out the tube because of complications, and now he started rattling and squirting bile and puke and even some blood. And after the first big torrent, all of them went back to the man, and the resident there cracked some kind of joke. I didn't understand it because of the acoustics, glued as I was to the doorway and ogling Yvonne, and then she started laughing. Her laughter sounded like one of those wind chimes or whatever they're called. Like a rainstorm in summer, sprinkling down on my exposed brain, calming me and giving the feeling that this miserable life was somehow bearable. As long as I could listen to her laughter. Yvonne's laugh is actually more like a choppy cackle if you take a sober look at it, yet I'd never heard anything more beautiful. In that moment I wished *I'd* made the joke and not the asshole resident, and she was laughing at *my* joke.

Nobody there called out for me to help. No one even noticed I was there because they were so busy with the bag of bones in the bed. The geezer died. The doctor recorded the time of death, and they joked they'd all have to change their clothes now. I'd snuck out into the corridor. By the door. I didn't want to stand there completely useless. Later that day, smoking outside, I saw Yvonne again and I talked to her.

————

"Here it is. In there," Kai says, following the Google Maps route on his display.

Everything had to go superfast. Kai called me right after he spotted the Braunschweig son of a bitch's Facebook post. I was sitting on the crapper, and as always when you have to take a dump in a hurry, the shit turns out messy and horrible, not one of those nice, slick turds that glide out your anus just like that, so all you have to do is wipe and you're good. Nope, of course, first I had to rip off what felt like fifty sheets' worth of paper from the roll. Then I got up to speed. Packed my mouth guard, jumped into a comfortable jogging suit. While I was doing that, Kai called Jojo and Ulf. Ulf had to cancel because he was eating with Saskia and her parents. Jojo immediately said yes. I picked him up and we drove over to Kai in Hannover. Only then did I realize that under no circumstance did I want to drive into Braunschweig with my own beater. Hannover tags. We might as well have sprayed a big fat 96 on the hood. So I went back and forth on it. Taxis are too expensive and unreliable. Trains unreliable and have set departure times. Stealing a car would have taken too long because none of us knew how to get into one of those new things with electronic locks. And then I thought of the VW van from my uncle's gym, which we also use to drive to the battles. A simple, black thing. Can't be pegged. Besides, it didn't have Hannover plates because Axel had it registered with some loser stooge because of some illegal shit he'd done with it. So we go to the gym and thank God the van was parked there. Grabbed the keys and race off.

We're on the west expressway from the Braunschweig North interchange, and now take a left from the highway into an industrial area. A garden allotment area emerges behind the yellow glow of the streetlights.

"Still can't believe you stole the van from the gym," Jojo says and grabs my backrest again.

"Jojo, man, get your paw off right now before I hack it off. I just told you it makes me nervous"—he pulls his hand back— "and I didn't steal it, of course. Just borrowed it."

Kai giggles. "Yeah, for extra-ordinary off-duty activities."

"So to speak."

"Shouldn't we at least let him know we—"

"Are you nuts, Jojo?! Then we should just climb right into the casket. Axel can't know anything about it. At least not right away."

"Okay, okay, drive a little slower," Kai says and licks his upper lip. "We should be there any minute. Over on the left."

I take my foot off the gas, letting us putter along without being too slow. After all, we aren't here for some damn drive-by shooting. We look anxiously out the side window. There's a small gap on the sidewalk where the pink neon light of a sign between two long factory or storage buildings reflects in the puddles on the street. It slowly glides into view. The neon sign shines in cursive writing: *Lucky Luke.*

"What do you want to bet they didn't get permission from the copyright holders?" Kai whispers.

I say, "Shhhh!"

There are only a couple of cars in the gravel lot, which is also covered in puddles. A bouncer is standing under an aluminum awning. Next to him is a group of girls in miniskirts and little leather jackets, huddled together. I ask myself what kind of ho you have to be to wear a miniskirt in this weather. There's a broad window in the wall behind the bouncer that's covered from the inside.

"They must already be inside," Kai whispered when we rolled past Lucky Luke, and the wall of a warehouse pushes into our field of vision. The weakly illuminated street opens onto a three-way stop. I turn the bus around and park on the side of the street. Luckily, the streetlamps overhead don't work, and we're sitting fairly safe in the dark.

"I feel like one of those private eyes from a black-and-white movie," Jojo says and pokes his head into the front.

"What now?" Kai asks and tosses his phone in the air. It does a few flips and he casually catches it. The next time he throws it, I grab it out of the air.

"Hey!"

"Wait a sec. Let me look at the post again."

He reaches over and fingers the Braunschweig profile on the display. I set the brightness to the lowest level.

The fucker had posted: "Pre-game waaaarm-up at Lucky Luke!!!" Then linked a couple of names that told me nothing.

"You wanna take a look inside?"

"Shut it, please."

There's even a link to Lucky Luke. I tap on it and the bar's profile appears. I scroll down through stupid party pictures from random theme nights, ladies' nights, and all-you-can-drink vodka parties. Then I find what I was looking for: in one of the posts the owner announces a separate smoking lounge.

"Aha," I say triumphantly and not entirely unsatisfied with myself and show the post to Kai and Jojo.

"What's that supposed to tell us?" Jojo asks.

"It tells us, dear Joachim, that the curmudgeon to my left is a damn Columbo," Kai replies.

"Sure, but why exactly?"

"They have a smoking lounge, Jojo. That meeeeans: the only chance we have to catch those sons of bitches is when they come out from their pre-game"—I point over the bar—"to go to some random club. But that could take some time because the post from that guy is only two hours old."

"I get it, because there's a smoking lounge they won't come outside to smoke."

I tap the tip of my nose and grin at Jojo and Kai.

"Shit, fuck. If only I'd brought along my hemorrhoid cushion," Kai jokes.

"Naw, you know what? I have better things to do than hang out here in the dark the whole night." I quickly brush aside the thought of how I sat all night in my car in front of Yvonne's apartment. "Much less in Braunschweig. Here, I've got an idea."

"You're full of surprises, buddy," Kai says and flashes his pearl-white teeth.

I pull two thin rubber gloves out of the driver-side door that Tomek and I had stuffed in there at some point. Kai's facial expression vanishes and his mouth became a straight line.

"Let me rephrase that: you're full of shit!" he yells at me. "What do you need those for? You want to tell me? You want to do a prostate on the motherfucker?"

"With the tip of my shoe at most. Kidding aside, buddy. There's a smoking lounge."

I nod at him encouragingly.

"Yeah," he says and nods along.

"And we can't hang out here in the van for hours on end. At some point someone will notice the black rape van. Not an option. So . . ."

"So?"

"So the only chance for us to catch those fags is if they come out to take a piss."

Kai nods, attempting to follow my line of thinking. I continue: "Which won't happen if the toilets in there are in working order. Understand now?"

A grin slowly slides over his face, becoming wider and wider.

"Yeah, fucking hell, look at you, you old mastermind!"

I hiss at him and look around, but there's no one close to the vehicle that could have heard anything.

"You don't really want to march in there and clog the toilets, right? What if they recognize you?" Jojo asks skeptically.

"Bullshit, they're sitting around at some random table and drinking themselves blind. It'll take five minutes tops. Maybe ten. In, stuff 'em, and out."

"Guerilla style."

I don't know if Kai's comparison really fits, but I let it slide because it sounds damn cool to me.

"It's their turn, boys. When they come out and they're holding their tiny dicks in their hands, then they'll catch it."

I stuff the gloves in my jacket pockets and place my hand on the door handle. And because Kai can be convincing with his nonsense, I add: "If I don't come back in twenty, call Steven Seagal."

"He's not available, but Michael fucking Dudikoff is on call," Kai says, pushing his hand against my back as I get out. I close the door and flip him off through the window. Then I put on a poker face, stuff my hands in my pocket, and walk away. Hundreds of questions shoot through my brain, slam against the sides of my skull, and wedge against each other. What if he recognizes me after all? If he just happens to be in the restroom when I come in? What if the bouncer doesn't even let me into the bar because I don't fit the desired dress code with black windbreaker, black jogging pants, and jogging shoes to top it off? What if there's someone in the restroom the whole time, so I don't have a chance to carry out my plan?

I take a first step onto the gravel in front of Lucky Luke and suddenly all those questions vanish. My hands calmly remain in their pockets, the thin rubber of the gloves between my fingers. The nervous eye twitch feeling I'd just had has disappeared. Peace and calm descend over my face like a Buddha mask. The group of bitches just walks past the bouncer, who holds the door open with a smile. Then he sees me coming and the corners of his mouth head south. A wide puddle blocks my path. Plywood has been placed over it as a makeshift gangplank. I walk carefully over it. Water seeps over the boards on the sides.

"Evening," I say as I approach the entrance. The bouncer had the typical standard black rain jacket, with SECURITY probably printed on the back. His carefully shaved boxer cut rises toward his forehead like the peak of a roof. He has a slim face and chubby, coarse-pored cheeks. Lousy roids, I'm guessing. He holds his hands in front of his nads. Rocks his shoulders slightly back and forth.

"Evening," he answers.

I ask if things had been calm this evening. He's still busy checking me out. Come on, pal, you're not guarding an exclusive club here, just wave the jogging shoes and sweatpants through!

"Yep. Till now," he says.

His voice is oddly high pitched. His nose squeaks a little when he talks. Just get outta my way, you asshole! But he doesn't move. So plan B. Buddy strategy. I pull out my cigarettes and stand next to him. Shoulder to shoulder. As if I were a colleague who'd just gotten back from his rounds. I offer him one. He hesitates briefly and I tap the bottom of the pack so that a couple of cigarettes slide up. He takes one and thanks me.

"Light?" he says.

I pull out my Zippo, work the wheel, and hold out the gas-scented flame. He bends over with the cig in his mouth, takes a drag, and thanks me again. I light one up and am just about to put the lighter away again when he says, "Wait a sec."

"Huh?"

"What kinda lighter you got? Show it to me."

Fuck! I'm such a damn idiot.

"Why?" I ask, and he says I should just show him.

There's a skyline engraved on the Zippo and "Hannover" in old German script underneath. I'm a fucking idiot!

I show it to him. Hold it up, the side with the letters toward him. He's already seen it, after all. I have to resist the urge to thrust the corner of the Zippo into his eye.

"What's this? Why d'you have this?"

"Oh, that? 'Cause of the picture? That . . ."—now think for once, Heiko—"I swiped it off a super fanboy prick from Peine-West after a match between the U23 reserve teams"—using the derogatory nickname Braunschweig has given Hannover—"a kind of war trophy."

I smile stupidly and try to scowl, though I'd like to barf because I'm denying my hometown. He looks at me, probably checking to see if he can really believe me.

I double down: "He got on my nerves. I smacked him one and pocketed this here."

"Right on," he finally says and can't hold back his shit-eating grin.

I put the Zippo away and shrug my shoulders. Like it was pretty damn easy. Nothing special.

We smoke a while next to each other. I flick the cig into the huge puddle and say, "I'll go then."

He steps aside so I can pass. Got lucky, worst case I'd have had to knock out the fucker or something.

"Have fun," he wishes me, "and thanks for the cigarette."

"No problem," I say and push open the door.

There's amped-up pop music booming from the loudspeakers in the bar. On the left is the counter lined with imitation bamboo, with two greasy barkeepers standing behind the bar and mixing cocktails in the neon light. Probably made up purely of knock-off products from big box stores. Gallon canisters and such. At any rate, the bottles with the good stuff are lined up behind them on the mirrored shelves. None of these cocktail bars can offer drinks on the cheap without using lower-quality ingredients. Straight through the room. Low round tables with wooden chairs spread around like groups of islands. Most of them are taken. In the back and to the left, I can see the glassed-in smoking lounge, which is full of people willing to put up with smoking while packed in like sardines instead of just stepping outside. I can't see the guy with the wart. I look around some more and to the right, on the wall covered with thick, black fabric, I spot an arrow pointing to the toilets. There's a guy washing his hands just as I enter the men's room. He leaves, and I'm left alone. Finally get lucky for once. There's just a single stall. There are three urinals attached to the wall behind it. I slip the gloves on, grab the back-up roll of toilet paper from the stall, rip off a wad of paper, and stuff it into the drains of the urinals as fast and as deep as I can. Then I flush repeatedly so the urinals are full to the brim. Go into the stall and lock up. Lift the lid off the tank and try to remember how exactly Ulf and I always ruined the toilets at school. Just about to flush when the music gets louder for a second. Quickly check if I really locked up. Okay. I hear footfalls heading for the urinals. Then hear a "Shit, what the hell is this?" The footfalls come closer, and he knocks on the door. Faster than I can think, I'm bending over the open toilet bowl, pulling off a glove, accidently ripping it, and sticking two fingers down my throat. My gagging echoes in the bowl.

"Finish puking already, man. Need to piss," I hear from outside. Come on! I stick my finger as deep as it'll go down my throat. Dry gagging. He knocks again.

Past my spit-covered fingers, I say he should fuck off and I'm gonna need a while. I try to sound as trashed and wasted as possible. Then a torrent of bile finally shoots out of my mouth and splashes into the toilet bowl. The guy laughs gleefully. I have half a mind to throw the door open and stuff the idiot's face into the toilet, but then you could hear the music again and the door to the men's room falls shut. I listen briefly. Then I peer underneath the stall. No feet visible. He gave up. I let myself close my eyes for a second. Give myself a breather. Spit sour left-over bile into the bowl. A trail of drool sticks to my lower lip, which I wipe with my bare arm. Come on! I encourage myself. I press down on the lever. The water circles down from the tank and into the bowl. Using my hand with the glove, I reach for the stopper in the tank and hold it up. Use my other hand to unroll some paper and quickly stuff it into the opening under the stopper. I press it down with two fingers. Calcium slime clings to the fingers. Have a sniff. Let go of the stopper. While the tank is filling, I yank at the bobber with all my strength. I drop it and kick it away. Then I put the lid back on the tank and wipe my hands with the remaining toilet paper, and throw that into the bowl.

"Oh man, you smell like a mix of urinal deodorizer and crotch cheese," Kai says as I climb back into the van and toss the gloves into the door pocket.

Jojo asks impatiently how it went.

"How do you think it went? Because I'm such a fucking idiot, I almost already gave myself away at the door, and I had to stick a finger down my throat in the men's room, just to deliver an Oscar-worthy acting performance."

"I don't understand a word," Jojo says.

So I give them all the details, the way it went down. Then we wait.

Kai's constantly lighting up his phone to check the time, till I tell him to knock it off.

"What kind of steel-lined bladder does that dog have? Has to take a piss at some point."

"Maybe they've already fixed the toilets," Jojo says.

"I did a bang-up job. That'll never happen—"

Kai taps me on the shoulder, and I follow his gaze through the windshield.

"Well, fuck my shit—is it him?" I ask.

Kai and I slide down a little farther in our seat, and the trio just leaving the bar staggers onto the street and into view. My eyes have narrowed to slits. The three guys step into the glow of a light on the other side of the street.

"It's him," Kai says and pounds on his thighs. "That's the cocksucker."

I thought I spotted the wart on his cheek for a second. And the blond part.

"Yeah," I say, and my mouth starts to water, "okay. We'll wait until they've finished pissing. Calmly get out. Don't slam the doors, and then jump 'em."

Jojo and Kai nod. We lie in wait for our fucking prey. They walk up the street a bit so that they're almost level with our van. Then they take position, close together and legs apart, next to the fence that separates off the factory grounds behind it. They appear to be conversing. Their heads move slightly up and down.

"Let's go," I say and carefully open my door. Kai and Jojo follow my lead. I keep the handle cocked and close the door as quietly as possible. The click of the lock still feels like a hammer blow. The three guys are pinching it off.

"Hey, you cunts!" I call out.

We're standing in the middle of the street. They turn around. No chance to react. Kai, of course, is the first there and jumps toward wart-face with his foot extended. The guy flies back against the fence, exactly where he'd just pissed. The two others have no idea what's going on when Jojo and me run at them. I reach out with my left hand and grab the dude's shirt, following it with a swinging right that lands full-force under his nose. I feel his rows of teeth through the skin and my fingers supposedly hurt. I pull my hand back. He pukes. Maybe from shock. Maybe from pain. I've split his upper lip and the thick scent of blood flowing wafts in my direction. The guy howls. Holds his face and goes down. He catches the blood in his palm and even in the dusky glow of the streetlamps, I can see that his hand quickly fills. I glance to the side. Kai's pulled wart-face up and is pushing him against the fence. Landing one punch after another to his gut. Jojo's having a harder time. His opponent has grabbed his arm and pulls him around. Jojo starts to stumble and runs right into his elbow. I run over and pull the guy off Jojo. Put him in a headlock and make my knee slam up like a spring, Muay Thai–style. He tries to raise his arms. But my knee still lands in his solar plexus and he releases air like a beanbag you've jumped on.

"What's going on?!" yells a loud voice.

I push the guy away and look around for the source of the voice. There are two cars in the middle of the street between us and Lucky Luke. All the doors are wide open. Eight guys are coming our way. At first I can't make out anything except their silhouettes. Till they come into the light cone from the street-lamp. I immediately recognize two of them as hooligans from Braunschweig. At least three have telescopic batons in their hands, snapping them out.

"Shit," I whisper and then say out loud to Kai and Jojo, "get outta here!"

Kai and Jojo take a left at the T-intersection, I take a quick detour to the van. Keys already in hand. Somehow I manage to get it into the lock on my first try, and lock the doors. Then I pull it out and run off. The electric whoosh of a baton very close by. It grazes my jacket but doesn't hit my back. I run. Look back. They're right behind me. Gather momentum from my arms. I pump the air out in bursts and see the outlines of Jojo and Kai in front of me. Another glance back. Created some space. They yell at us, try to stay close. Kai's the first who has the idea of running across the field and jumping over a barbed-wire fence. We follow him. Across an industrial ruin. Crumbling concrete under our feet. Don't bite it now! We move away from the streetlights, running past loading ramps and under conveyer belts. My lungs are burning. I could puke. Keep on running. Until we can't hear another sound. We collapse in exhaustion on the grounds of a trucking company and wheeze our guts out.

Jojo, who's splayed out on the cold concrete next to me, asks if we think it'd be safe now to go back to the car.

"What do you think, Jojo? They'll just leave the car alone? How stupid are you?! They'll bash in a window, at least. If not with the telescopic batons, then they'll get a couple of bats. They're just waiting for us to come back."

"Kai's right," I say.

"What're we gonna do then?" Jojo asks and lifts his head.

I breathe the cool night air through my nose, in and out. Ponder. My skull is throbbing, as if it was stuck in a vice. I can feel my lungs so distinctly under my ribs, it's as if they're foreign objects implanted by someone.

"Ain't no use," I say in the end, "we have to call Ulf, have him come and pick us up."

Kai screams a long, extended "Fuuuuuuuuck!" into the night sky.

We'd just gotten in deep shit in more than the metaphoric sense. I dial Ulf's number.

———

Back then, we spent a lot of time at the Seidels' house. Had given up on forcing Jojo to do something with us. He actually only left the house to go to work or go shopping with his mother at the discount supermarket. So we were constantly hanging out at his place. But it wasn't cool, and we were relieved every time Jojo closed the front door behind us in the evening. This day, we were sitting as so often in Joel's old room, which meanwhile had half-way become Jojo's room. I thought it was spooky and somehow sick that he slept in his little brother's bed. Of course, I'd have never said that to his face, and if it did something for him or made him feel better, well then he should do it anyway. We watched as he constantly sorted through photos and organized the reports of Joel's games in folders. He hadn't been to the barber in ages, and with his mop of curls he was beginning to look like the German version of the great midfielder Carlos Valderrama.

We went into Jojo's room to smoke and leaned out the window. Jojo didn't want us to smoke up his little brother's room because it would yellow the football posters Joel had covered the slanted ceiling with. And Joel had never smoked. In contrast to us. Hadn't even tried it. Never. We didn't put any pressure on him. Knew why he did it. And he didn't touch alcohol either. Except on birthdays or something. He couldn't hold his liquor and was smashed after just one and a half beers.

So we spent the day hanging out on the sofa bed that had once been Joel's bed, leafing through old issues of *Kicker* magazine, and watching action movies, the American Ninja stuff, or old Jackie Chan Easterns, from back when they were still cool. Joel's jerseys hung on the clothes hangers next to the door. Jojo wanted to have them framed at some point. His father was constantly walking past the open doorway. I still remember he seemed vaguely busy without giving the impression he was doing anything in particular. He had really come unglued in the months following Joel's death. Even more than Jojo and his mother. Hardly said a word, and within months Dieter looked like he'd aged years. Face fallen in. And even though he'd stopped smoking after the funeral. If he ever uttered a sound, his voice was as rough as it always had been. Comes from all those years of inhaling cigarillos. Gives you a voice like the vocal cords have been put through a cheese grater. So he wandered the corridors in his long, gray work coat like the resident ghost and occasionally glanced in the room while floating past.

Mrs. Seidel was down in the kitchen. That was her place. One of those real traditional housewives. Hair pulled up into a tennis-ball-sized knot at the back of her neck and always wearing an apron. She prepared coffee and cake. It was a firm tradition at the Seidel house. Nice in a way, I guess. I'd never really known it myself. I mean at my house. On the other hand, it also seemed really annoying you had to gather at the kitchen table at three thirty in the afternoon. Whether you wanted coffee and cake or not. The same thing applied for us visitors. The rule simply transferred to us. Besides myself, no one seemed to think it was strange, so I never said anything. Different house, different rules, I guess.

I think I was out smoking with Kai. We were debating where we should go drinking that evening, and with our phlegm we were spitting yellow holes in the thick layer of snow covering the Seidels' garden and everywhere. It was already cold by early autumn, and snow soon followed. We closed the window. When we opened the door to Jojo's room, the warm, sugary smell of cake was floating up the narrow staircase. Despite it all. I was looking forward to having my own place. Even though I was still in school, if you could even call it that with my infrequent attendance, I had moved out once already two years earlier. Simply hadn't been able to take it anymore, just the three of us with my father and Mie. Manuela had left to study in Göttingen long before. At any rate, even if my place in the Barne residential tower was no bigger than a shoe box, living alone was a thousand times better than some pragmatic living accommodation with my family. You can't pick your family, unlike your friends. And when it's fucked up, then you just move out. Regardless of how old you are.

"Coffee is ready!" Mrs. Seidel called from below. Ulf and Jojo came out of Joel's old room. Jojo's mother was waiting down below on the landing and asked if we'd seen Dieter.

"He was walking around earlier," Jojo said. "Maybe he's taking a nap. I'll go look."

The rest of us followed his mother to the kitchen and took our seats at the table. There was steaming hot black coffee in our cups. A piece of poppy seed cake was waiting on each plate.

"You boys go ahead and start," Mrs. Seidel said. "Otherwise it'll get cold."

We thanked her like nice, pleasant boys. Kai and Ulf relished these cake sessions considerably more than I did. Ulf most of all, that icebreaker. The way he shoveled it in obviously pleased Jojo's mother and confirmed her in her housewifely pride.

There was a bang from outside. Mrs. Seidel got up and closed the kitchen window.

"Those neighbor boys with their fireworks again. But it's still a ways until New Year's Eve."

"Probably left over from last year," Ulf said, and had poppy seed cake crumble out of his mouth.

"They're desecrating the beautiful, white snow with their explosions."

Kai gave me a light kick to the shins, leaned over to me, and whispered: "You remember? The dead rat?"

He threw back his head and laughed diabolically.

One fall, I'd just left grade school, and we were shooting off the leftover fireworks from the previous New Year's. We had found a rat carcass in a construction pit close to the main train station in Hannover, and we shoved a thin, powerful firecracker from Poland into its asshole and lit the fuse. Had underestimated the explosion radius and hadn't moved far enough away.

"Pssst," I said and whispered out of the corner of my mouth, "sure. That was a huge mess."

Mie had been scared to death when she found the innards still stuck to my clothes in the laundry basket. The memory made me grin.

Jojo came into the kitchen.

"He's not in the bedroom, but I looked out the window and the footprints go across the lawn to the garden shed."

Mrs. Seidel wiped her hands on the kitchen towel and went to the window.

"He can't be tinkering again. Dieter knows when coffee's served."

"Let him be," Jojo said, pulling on his rubber boots and heading out into the garden.

"Eat. Eat," his mother encouraged us. Ulf didn't have to be told twice and pushed another brick-sized piece of cake onto his plate.

The coffee and cigarettes from before were already having a little brown fiesta in my abdomen, and I was preparing for a nice round of fecal bobsledding.

Jojo came back into the kitchen through the living room, leaving tracks.

"Joachim, take your boots off!"

"You guys have to help. The door to the shed isn't locked, but something's pushed against it from the inside.

The three of us fetched our shoes, putting them on in front of the patio door, and followed Jojo through the snow to the pitiful garden shed his father had repurposed as his personal carving shop.

"Look." Jojo pushed against the door, which gave way slightly, but couldn't be opened completely. "Doesn't open."

We helped him, pressing our hands and shoulders against the wooden door.

"You smell that too?" Kai asked, face twisted.

Something inside gave way, and something could be heard crashing down. A cupboard fell over and spilled tools onto the floor. Screwdrivers and bits rolled against the rifle lying there and the foot belonging to Jojo's father.

———

Ulf and I meet up in Ricklingen. Amid all the look-alike housing projects, nail salons, drug dealer hangouts, and shabby internet cafés, this is where our favorite betting parlor, Wanna Bet?, struggles to stay afloat.

We used to hang out in betting offices nearly every day. After all, football's being played almost constantly somewhere. And someone's betting on it. That's why I used to have the teams from the top leagues in Azerbaijan and Kazakhstan memorized. On weekends, our first stop was at the bookies before we went over to Timpen to watch football and get shitfaced. Over the years, that changed when betting went online and things like SureBets emerged. But also because the betting offices are always changing hands, became increasingly impersonal and standardized. But the ownership usually just moved within a family, for example from father to son, then to the cousin, and back again. Wanna Bet? is a century-old oak in a forest full of Tipicos and Bet-and-Wins. Then, around five years ago, the owner, Kallhein, turned his back on football gambling exclusively and has been showing horse races from all over the world ever since. Mainly from Great Britain, of course. That was always his specialty. And the old fart still has fabulous connections to famous bookies from the island. Here everything works like way back when. There aren't any electronics aside from the televisions, the kind with tubes, and the coffee machine. The whole nine yards along with the counter, behind which Kallhein is always seated, and the paper betting slips. There are brochures and magazines on the big horse races circulating around. And the clientele hasn't changed over the years either. Except maybe more and more walkers have taken their place at the tables. At some point, Kallhein had to build a ramp over the front steps for that reason.

Accompanying all this are the best fried pastries in all of Lower Saxony. Every couple of hours, his wife, who runs the bakery next door, brings over a tray of warm, fresh pastries. The old farts aren't the only fans around here. Once in a while we come by and without any real expertise place bets on random horses, most of which fail fabulously and are the last to crawl over the finish line. Then Kallhein shakes his head and his chin flaps, and he grouses about how clueless kids are these days. Besides us, he probably doesn't know anyone under forty. We only do it to make our contribution to Kallhein and keep his gambling den alive until he's lying dead and cold behind his counter.

Ulf is already seated at one of the round tables when I come in. Two tickets in hand.

I was just in the neighborhood visiting Gaul and had him give me a new tat. He does it at his kitchen table in his place in the projects. Right next to the 96 in the circle over my heart, I had a full-size jungle knife inked over my sternum. I had recently seen something similar in a movie Kai lent me. All about the Vory gangsters, which is kind of like the Russian version of the mafia. They basically have the coolest tats. If I were to land in a Siberian prison for some reason, I'd regret it a little less because of the tattoos.

"Heiko." Ulf gets up when he sees me.

The cling wrap under my clothes rustles. We shake hands.

"You doin' okay?" I ask him and sit down. "Why'd you want to chat with me?"

He folds his tickets, then unfolds them, then smooths them flat with his fingers. Breathes out through pursed lips, his cheeks puffing slightly. Old boozers saunter past our table, greeting us with curt nods, as was the custom in the good old days. Ulf shifts the words around in his mouth.

"Spit it out already," I urge him.

"It's just . . ." He places his open hands, the sides parallel, on the tabletop between us, "after I picked you guys up in Braunschweig . . ."

"Yeah, thanks again, man. Don't know how we would've handled it without you. How we'd have gotten out in one piece."

The pressure spreading in my chest reminds me of my short encounter with my uncle in the gym, when he asked if I knew what happened to the van. I'd pretended I was clueless, no idea. I couldn't think of anything better on the spot.

"No problem," Ulf says and clears his throat. "When I came home, Saskia was sitting in the kitchen. Had stayed up for me. Couldn't sleep anymore after I'd driven off."

A misgiving arose in me, but I kept listening.

"I'd told her from the beginning the way we roll. Had tried to explain it to her so she could understand a little, even though she wasn't familiar at all. Or at least accept it. And she did. But now our little one is almost ready for preschool, and of course he picks up more and more and understands more."

"Ulf—"

"Hear me out, Heiko. She said it's enough. I've done it for years and she's tried to ignore it, because of course she didn't think it was all that great when I came home with injuries and everything. But at some point, it's enough, she said. And before it gets even worse, she'd like for me to quit."

"She'd like that?" I press him. "And what would you like?"

"That's not what this is about right now."

Before I'd even realized it, I was standing and planting my fists on the table.

"It's not about that?! Fucking hell, Ulf! It's about what you want! This is our life. Why doesn't she get it? Maybe I should—"

"Heiko," he booms. Then his voice relaxes again slightly. "It's simple. If I keep it up, she'll leave me. With the little one. I'm out."

"I don't fucking believe it!" I yell and get a tongue-lashing from Kallhein behind the counter.

"I'll still come around Timpen once in a while, and we can go to the stadium regularly. As a kind of compensation. I just won't be along on the road trips. Come on, Heiko. We'll still be friends. This doesn't change anything."

But all I caught was a wild whooshing sound that went through my ear canals like steel wool, glowing white hot.

I say, "Everything changes, Ulf. Constantly! What the hell?! And that thing about staying friends? I'm not too sure."

I kick my chair aside. It falls over and slides a bit. I step over it, fling open the door, and storm out.

———

I close the door to the coop behind me with wobbly knees, listen to the cooing from countless bird throats one last time. The grass is wet from the day's rain and licks up my pant legs like long, thin chameleon tongues. Using the water faucet on the side of the house, I wash out the feed troughs I'd swapped out and lean them against the wall, upside down. When I was in the coop, I hadn't noticed the patio light was turned on. She comes out. Must have been watching from the kitchen. Mie is wearing a thick wool sweater she risks disappearing in. Even though it's size S at most. Her long, black hair is tied in a knot at the back of her neck. In one hand she's carrying a deep bowl with noodles that are steaming in the cold evening air. In the other, she carries a full glass of wheat beer. She sets both on the table. Then she pulls the garden chair back from the table. There's already a cushion on it. She motions to me, offering the chair. I hesitate. Feel like a deer or rabbit someone's trying to lure into a trap with food.

"Have you already eaten?" she asks.

I shake my head, but then I think, damn, just say yes, thank her, and go. Too late. So I go over, thank her, and take a seat at the table. She disappears into the kitchen. I hope she won't go and get a dessert or something, and I start to roll the noodles on the fork. The diameter increases by threefold, and I stuff it into my mouth. Then I dump a sip of beer behind it. Because I'm scarfing, I only notice from the aftertaste how good the food is. It's nothing but ordinary fried noodles with egg, so she must've done something with it. Maybe a special spice mix. It tastes like ten things all at once, but in a good way, and not as if they'd all overlap. Mie comes back from the kitchen. This time with a cereal bowl full of noodles and a glass of water. Sits down next to me and begins to eat as well. She sucks the noodles hanging off her fork. Not like I did, rolling it up like a spool of cable only to shove it down the hatch.

She looks up from her bowl. Her chin very close over it.

"You cold?"

I say, "Hmm." Which is to say no.

"You take very good care."

I feel my eyebrows shoot up and say, "What?"

"You take good care. Of pigeons. Of father."

For a second I think she's pulling my leg, and all these years I hadn't picked up on her subtle, cutting humor. Then I get that she's actually serious.

"No, no," I say and feel my cheeks go very hot, which simultaneously makes me furious. This is how a man without arms must feel when his nads itch. A half-plate later she's already done with her mouse-sized portion and watches me eat, which makes me terribly nervous. But I can't really tell her she should look somewhere else.

"Hans is difficult."

I look at her blankly and finish the beer. She's about to jump up and reach for my glass, but I say I've had enough, thanks.

She eases back again and continues: "Difficult, your father. Has many problems. But very, very nice man. You too."

I cough up half a noodle onto my plate, quickly excuse myself, and shovel it back into my mouth. I don't have the slightest idea how I should answer. Which is why I force my eyes to the rim of the plate and only give polite little glances. She continues to stare at me.

"My parents long dead. My . . . um . . . aunt. Grow up with her. In Bangkok. Big and bright and loud. But also lots of fun there.

You must go there once. Very different from Hannover. Not so gray and cold."

"I like Hannover." It spilled out of me, and I think to myself, What kind of blockhead are you?!

"When you went away, your father was sad. I could see. He not say. But see. Thought maybe you go to your mother and—"

I'm finished with the noodles, let the fork clatter in the plate, and thank her for the delicious food. Mie whispers a "Thanks," and together we bring the dishes into the kitchen.

"Let me," I say, and wash the dishes and glasses, and place them on the drying rack. I ask Mie if it's okay if I look for something in my old room. She nods and smiles.

I flip the switch. The bare lightbulb hanging from the ceiling hums and flickers and slowly becomes brighter, as if it were waking up from a deep sleep.

"What a room full of junk," I say to myself. "Nothing changed."

I doubt Hans has set foot in here since I moved out. The air is harder to breathe, as if it had an expiration date that's long passed. I open the double window to let in some fresh air. A whopper of a moth immediately flies past me and aims for the light bulb. The moth flings itself against the light like crazy, bangs surprisingly loud. All that's lacking is the moth saying, "Ouch!"

I put my hands on my hips and look around, clueless where I should start searching. I look under my bed, but the small space between the slats and the carpet is covered with such a thick layer of dust and cobwebs I don't want to make the effort to pull out the boxes from underneath. The bulky duvet is just as crumpled as when I left it the morning I moved out. In the middle of the pillow the impression of the back of my head, stamped like a memory. I'd better leave the wardrobe alone, for starters. I still remember that back then I first took out all the clothes and casually tossed the ones I didn't want anymore back inside and quickly closed the doors. If I opened them now, everything would tumble out onto me. So I pull the stacked shoe boxes from under the sawhorses and the sheetrock slab that formed something like a desk. A butt-load of unsorted pictures. From our legendary trip to the away match in Cottbus, where we were fighting for the chance to move up to a higher league. In one of them, Kai is holding up a blood-covered cup and making a face. In another, you can see me and my uncle from behind. I'd climbed onto the fence to the field, stretching my arms straight out to be able to see better. I'm wearing some kind of training jacket. Can't remember where I had it from. It's one of those classic jackets from the eighties and nineties in impossible colors: pink, turquoise, yellow. The sleeves are rolled back because otherwise they'd have slipped over my hands, but it looks like I had exaggeratedly puffed-up biceps. Axel stands next to me, his arms crossed, and is able to look over the fence effortlessly.

Then photos of Kai, Ulf, Jojo, and me in front of Timpen. We pose, acting cool. Relaxed expressions. Like we're modeling for an album cover. On another we're with Joel. He's in the middle of us. With his pitch-black hair. Side part, as usual. His hair always looked like one of those Playmobil figures. As if you'd be able to click it off his scalp and attach other hair. He's holding up his 96 jersey. It had to be number seven. We're lined up behind him. Everyone has one hand on the jersey and one raised fist. Faces fixed in shouts of joy. Naturally, Jojo blinked the very second the picture was taken and looks like a slightly retarded stoner. I put it in my inside jacket pocket.

Unfortunately, the drills Jojo and I had sketched in pencil for Joel's private training can't be found. But my first Bundesliga sticker album from the '95/'96 season, completely full. It'd felt like Hannover 96 had never been farther from playing in Germany's top league. I leaf through it. Many old names, hairstyles, and mustaches that I'd already forgotten: Mirko Votava, Tom Dooley, Vladimir Beschastnych, Manni Bender, Heiko Scholz, Alain Sutter, and whatstheirname.

I toss all that stuff into the boxes and push them back in place. Suddenly, I feel wiped out and tired. At the same time, I feel a need to spend the night in my car in front of Yvonne's place. I'd like to distract myself and go lifting with Kai but don't think I'd survive a ride to Hannover tonight.

I say good-bye to Mie. She locks the door behind me. Then I climb into the VW and drive to the Midas gambling hall, which doesn't close till six in the morning for an hour so they can tidy up with the vacuum.

I take a seat at the bar, ordering one coffee after another, not playing with any of the machines, and if I nodded off on my forearm from time to time, it felt like a decade had passed and we'd all grown old and gray and could finally look back at our lives and say: we don't regret a thing. Would do everything exactly the same way.

———

Four figures stuffed in black suits stood on the field and were making their patent leather shoes dirty. The deep blue sky above us, transected by power lines and occasional clouds that floated above us like chalk penalty mark and sidelines. Joel's football shoes, black and yellow Adidas Predator, were hanging from the crook of my arm. The knotted laces were rubbing brown marks into my suit while I needed my one hand to drink the warm can of beer and the other to smoke. Jojo stood a couple yards away from me. Ulf behind us. Kai twenty yards in front of us and talking on the phone. In position. Jojo and me the man-to-man markers who took care of everything that might come our way. Ulf, the big man, the last line of defense. Keeps it clean at the back. Kai dodges the opposing defense and only has to sink the thing. Someone was missing. Sonic the dribbling hedgehog. The young genius talent. The free kick prince of Westaue township. There were to be no more genius passes. No Roberto Carlos–style free kicks curled around the wall of defenders. No more dribbling solos.

Kai came over to us, yelling, "Now toss those things over! I'm shriveling up out here."

Jojo looked at his watch.

"It's probably about to start. Give 'em here." I handed him the Predators. The beer went down like brackish peat mud. Jojo placed his can on the soil. Then he trained his sights on the power lines, pulled back, and threw. The shoes didn't even get close to the lines. He walked over to where they'd landed. Tried again. This time almost straight up. He had to take cover when they came back down.

"Oh, shit, man, that looks really pitiful," Kai murmured, having come over to me. We watched Jojo as he threw, failed, ran, threw, failed. Unflagging. Without a break. He became worse with each throw. His lips wobbled when he ran, and he made dust rise. Throw, run, pick them up, throw, run, pick them up.

Kai rested his arm on my shoulder, groaning. "Goddamn fucking hell, please let him finally nail it."

Ulf forced himself between us and stomped over to Jojo, who gave him the shoes. Ulf flicked his cigarette, took a broad stance, swung the shoes, and then let them slip free at the right moment. They rotated through the air in a high arc, as if someone was still in the shoes and walking with them, and then caught in the lines. We had expected sparks. A little fireworks in Joel's honor. As a symbol. For Joel. And also for us. Because we were a team. Even if we would all bite the dust at some point, we hoped the shoes at least would remain. Then the church bells rang out loud and clear from over in the village. The service was beginning. We downed the cans of beer. It wasn't my first that day. We walked four in a row with our heads bowed, like after a defeat.

Later we sat in the church during the service. Kai, Ulf, and me in the second row. Directly behind Jojo and his parents. I stared at the back of a curly brown mop of hair that was rocking uncontrollably next to Dieter's shoulder, his head buried in his hands. Jojo and Joel's mother patted his bent back to comfort him. The pastor gave a generic eulogy, which I complained about in a low voice because it had nothing at all to do with Joel and the cans of beer had gone to my sun-struck head. After which men with unfamiliar, serious faces came to escort me out of the church. A small scuffle ensued, which wouldn't have drawn the slightest shrug in a bar but in a church immediately caused a fucking hubbub. Ulf and Kai supported me and yelled at the men, telling them to let me go. Kai led me outside, to be on the safe side. I followed the rest of the ceremony from outside, through the closed church doors. Then Ulf brought me back inside for the public viewing. The unfamiliar men and the pastor spoke to the Seidels. Ulf whispered they wouldn't press charges. I stepped in between Kai and Ulf in the row of mourners. Before the open coffin, Joel's father faltered. Jojo helped him up, and after making sure he was standing halfway safely, he pulled the jersey with number 7 from his back pocket and placed it over his little brother's chest. The collar on his neck, the sleeves over his arms. So that he'd be able to play any second now. Then he broke into tears. It was Kai's turn. Once again, he found unbelievably encouraging words—where, I asked myself, where had he gotten them from? Unfortunately I can't remember what he said. Then it was my turn. I looked at Joel for a long time. And wanted to look at him far longer. So long he decayed in front of my eyes and then turned to dust or something like that, and then I would inhale him. Not like you sniff coke, but just as naturally as you breathe, and then somehow he would live on with me. Of course, that didn't happen, and it also sounds really perverted, but that's what went through my head in that moment. I squeezed my eyelids shut to hold back the tears, and when I opened them again, and when I saw Joel's quiet, narrow, face in front of me, I said to him: "I'll see you on Tonga." Ulf, Jojo, Kai, and me played the role of pallbearers. I rejected the cushion for my shoulder that Ulf offered me. Out of pride or the weird feeling that tolerating a little pain would help Joel in some way. What nonsense! We all started sweating. The shirts clung to our upper bodies. The team was waiting for Joel outside, dressed in their game clothes. That's what Jojo wanted, because he thought Joel would have wanted it that way. Including shin guards and cleats. The red jerseys shimmered like candlelight in the sun. As we laid him to rest, I asked myself if that was really rest or just complete, all-encompassing oblivion. We let the coffin sink evenly into the hole. Then dirt was trickled down. We would stand there till the next summer. Hands folded, gaze directed into the hole in the ground. In reality, it was only a half an hour. Then there was coffee and cake at Joel and Jojo's house.

———

This morning I took the fast train from Hannover to Braunschweig. In the industrial area on the west side, I expected trucks or at least a couple of construction workers at some sausage stand around noon or generally during the day. It must have been the coldest day so far this fall. The wind blew the rain diagonally through a fog. The moisture crept under my clothes like a sexual assault.

The Lucky Luke parking lot is completely washed out. The sign isn't lit up and looks pale and pitiful. Roaring streams are shooting out of the gutter over the awning, forming a bead curtain of water in front of the entrance. The van is down the street. Even from a distance, I lose interest in getting closer. The van is resting on its rims. The tires are slashed with long gashes. They'd bashed in all of the windows with their telescopic batons or baseball bats. It's completely sprayed with yellow and blue colors. The fragmented remnants of the busted side mirror and the roof, which was completely cut off, were lying next to the van's corpse. The roof is upside down. A puddle has formed inside, reflecting not only my pitiful face, but also the fear. What should I tell Axel about this whole fucking mess? On the battered hood, which clearly shows dents from blunt objects, they've also sprayed in yellow and blue: PEINE-WEST SONS OF BITCHES. I glance inside the vehicle but immediately regret it. The mustard-yellow stuffing spills out of the slashed seats. The steering wheel's been ripped out. No sign of it anywhere. The radio stolen or also thrown somewhere. The footwells are filled with liquid that can't be rainwater, based on its color. The red, semitransparent dildo that was attached to the gear shift with duct tape was also very creative. In addition, dark brown piles of shit are towering on the driver and passenger seats. I take a picture of the vehicle for Kai and the boys. Otherwise they wouldn't believe me.

I kick against the driver-side door. One dent more won't make much of a difference. Then I make my way back to the train station. Just get out of this shit town.

———

We'd been riding a fucking wave of success since Joel had taken the offer from Hannover. At the time, everything we did seemed to succeed. We couldn't do anything wrong. Well, if you don't count flaming out in school, but who cares about that?

It was perfect weather that day. Hazy and gray. Visibility of less than five hundred meters. It was the second-to-last match of the season, and 96 was hosting Borussia Mönchengladbach. Jiri Stajner, our lucky Czech ace, equalized for the Reds in injury time with a shot on the turn in the penalty area. It was perfect. There was no way Hannover could be relegated to a lower league again. Uncle Axel had placed a lot of calls that day and had managed to organize a spontaneous match with a group from Gladbach. The whole thing was supposed to take place on the grounds of the trade fair. Where Hannover had had its fifteen minutes of international fame with the Expo in 2000.

The men were waiting on the west side of the broad parking lot. It was my job to coordinate the guys. Axel wanted to finish the season with a bang and gave me free reign positioning the scouts after I'd worked hours to convince him.

We were firmly expecting the Gladbach gang to come from the Trade Fair/Laatzen train station. My uncle had given the station as a final orientation point for the rumble. Ulf was waiting in the hall that stretches across the tracks like a bridge. He was supposed to watch the incoming trains. Anyway, you wouldn't be able to miss a group of muscle-bound meatheads. When they arrived, he calmly strolled to the entrance and gave a sign to Kai, who was waiting in the pedestrian tunnel leading from the station to the fairgrounds. Me and Kai had already taken the entry doors off their hinges. Even back then, Kai was the fastest of us by far, maybe aside from Joel. He sprinted down the long glass corridor. Jojo was supposed to be hidden with his Airsoft gun at the corner to Nuremberg Street, where the tunnel ends, and make sure not to miss Kai when he ran past and waved at him as went by. Axel impressed this on him.

"If you're picking your fucking nose and miss Kai, then I will personally kick your nads back into your torso."

"Take it easy, Heiko, don't piss yourself. I'll pay attention."

I was waiting at the end of the tunnel and could see Kai running toward me through the long, straight glass tube.

He was yelling something like: "They're coming! The cocksuckers from Gladbach! They're here!"

I took the stairs down to street level in a couple leaps, twisting my ankle, and ran against the pain. Over to the parking lot, where the whole gang was already waiting and rubbing their hands.

"All right. Good job, Heiko," and then Axel turned to Tomek, who was supposed to lead the splinter group. "You'll come out in front of Kaufland supermarket."

Tomek and the others ran across some company's grounds to position themselves in an alleyway that came out at about where the corridor did, in order to attack the flanks of the Gladbach group. Axel and the larger group of men followed me back to the end of the sidewalk. Until we arrived, Jojo was supposed to try to pin down some of the Gladbach bastards from the hiding spot he'd taken up on the roof, in typical sniper fashion. He was our best marksman with the Airsoft. A true fucking ace with the gun. His rifle packed a punch, but nothing that could really harm anyone from that distance. It was just supposed to provide some distraction. It was such an awesome feeling, I can still remember how the phalanx of hooligans was running behind me. I kept on looking back and felt like the leader of a horde of rhinos or something. Even if I once heard, I think, that they're loners. Regardless. It's all about that feeling. All of them on the double. And I'm out in front of them. Even if I wasn't allowed to participate in the actual clash. At any rate, we turned onto the sidewalk and could already see the group from Gladbach bellowing, and heard the dull shots of Jojo's air rifle. Then Axel resumed the leadership. Like in fucking *Jumanji*, when Robin Williams yells, "It's a stampede!" Galloping toward the guys from Gladbach, who are still totally preoccupied with dodging Jojo's BBs. Just before Axel and the others reached them, Tomek and his group came out of the alleyway between Kaufland and the factory grounds and had just knocked a couple of them over. Then Axel and Hinkel, who was a little more fit than he is today, and Töller and the rest of them reached the opponents. Unfortunately, the four of us had to watch from a safe distance, but I still felt like I was in the middle of it and would catch some punches, but dodge even more, and dish it out myself. My heart nearly jumped out of my chest. That's how much it was thumping inside me.

———

I almost feel like a salt-of-the-earth working man when the alarm makes me roll out of bed at four thirty in the morning, to knock back a quick cup of coffee and then roll down the highway, half asleep, to my construction job. But that's where the comparison breaks down. I don't work in construction but rather a knuckle-head gym, and it was my uncle calling, not the alarm, that yanked me out of my hammock.

"Heiko, get up. You need to come to the gym right now. You have to give me a hand with something. Get your ass up and don't fall back asleep!"

He personally meets me up at the driver-side door and pulls on my arm, tugging me inside. There's a pile of cigarette butts next to the back door, smoked down to the filter.

"What's going on?" I ask, and notice that the thing that had been scratching my neck the whole way was the label of my sweatshirt. It's on backwards. While I slip out of the sleeves and rotate it around my body till it's right, Axel explains the situation: "Check it out, it's like this. One of the Angels called me earlier. Said he had a tip from a friend in the drug squad—"

"The rockers have pals in the police department?" I ask.

"Pals, friends, informants. Doesn't make a fucking difference right now. Listen to me, for fuck's sake! Anyway, they're really worked up right now. Reason for existence or some sort of bullshit. There'll be raids conducted all over the state today. Don't know who they have it from. Maybe it has something to do with the van. Fuck!" My legs suddenly start to tingle. As if they're telling me to run. "Anyway. We're on the list too. You have to help me get rid of a couple things before they come over."

"And when is that?" I look at the clock on the wall. Five twenty.

"He couldn't say exactly, but before eight for sure. Come on!"

He pulls stacks of paper from the file cabinet, and just when I think that's all of it, he goes somewhere else and gets just as much paper as before. And plastic bags full of vials and pills.

"Fuck, where was all that?"

"Stop asking retarded questions. Run that shredder!" He points to the big office shredder, a massive white block, as big as a copy machine that dominates a corner of the office. I'd always asked myself why he needed such a huge paper shredder. Well, there you have it, I think to myself, and start pushing stacks of paper through. The machine is running at top speed. Rattling like a tractor or a mower whose blades kept hitting rocks. I don't have much time to look over the contents of the papers. Seems more like scratch paper. Bullshit scrawled all over. Most of it looks like some sort of lists of names and corresponding numbers or sums of money. Some of them, this much I could gather, not peanuts. Once a bucket is full, I take it to the showers and dump it out on the tiles there, sloped down toward the drain in the middle. Then I douse it with lighter fluid and light it up. When the scraps of paper have burned down, I turn on the showers. My uncle says we don't have to worry about clogging the drain right now, but the drain is nothing more than a big pipe in the ground with a large grill attached. It's not going to clog that fast.

"They'll smell it," I say and wipe the sweat from my forehead.

"Smell what?"

"Well, that someone was playing with fire. Know right away what went down."

"So what," he yells from the office, "does that give them any evidence? Nope! So shut up and keep at it!"

Because the shredder is the hardest working employee this morning, I've soon destroyed all the paperwork. While I'm at it, my uncle's busy using all the toilets in the building to dump bags of drugs and flush them down.

The whole time he's babbling away: "Fuck, fuck, fuck. Break my neck. Break my bones."

Once in a while, I see him pause, pick out certain pills from the bag, and throw them down the hatch. I help him flush. A rainbow of pills swirls down the drain. Even after he's stopped talking to himself, I think about his words. All these years, I've never asked what actually goes on in here or what I may be missing. I wasn't tremendously interested or just thought it was okay. My god, letting the bikers hawk their wares here. But I wouldn't have done it differently if I was the boss. But that's exactly it! Who's actually the boss? Or bosses? Then for some odd reason, I think of an old TV series with a similar name. I think it was *Who's the Boss?* Fuck if I know why I thought of that. Just occurred to me.

And then we're done with all the shit and Axel has collapsed against the wall next to his private throne. I think it was less from exhaustion. More from panic. Or dread. Not necessarily because of the fucking cops that were about to show up here. They didn't have anything on him anymore. But maybe frightened of other people.

We're sitting in the space behind the back door and treating ourselves to a coffee, accompanied by a good morning beer. I look at my uncle. He's on a folding chair that's dangerously close to splitting because of the mass of muscle it has to bear. Axel's sitting so bowlegged, it's as if he has bull's gonads as big as bowling balls. He's wearing a pair of black jogging pants with snaps open halfway up his calves. Almost like he's wearing bell bottoms. His salmon-colored shirt, which clearly needs ironing, is also unbuttoned. Two rivulets of sweat run along the open collar, down to below his chest. He has his elbows propped on his knees. His forehead resting on the palm of one hand. Somewhere beneath there's still eyes in his sockets and maybe they're already seeing rather unpleasant things coming his way. His neck is so red. How can it be so red? As if someone had skinned a baboon's butt and refashioned it as his neck brace.

And then I just say it: "I have the van."

Any second I expect to catch his fist with my face. But all he does is slowly lift his head.

"Say that again."

Something has to happen now. Hit me! Then it's over.

"Say that again." He repeats himself.

I keep the others out of it. "There was this opportunity that presented itself. Looked like a sure thing. There were . . . complications."

"What kind of opportunity?" he asked. His voice was as calm as a storm behind a mountain ridge.

"Some guy from Braunschweig wasn't careful. Posted all kinds of shit on the web. Open to everyone. I just had to do something. I mean . . . they're from Braunschweig. You only get an opportunity like that once in life—" My rib cage blocked. Tightened. Breathing was hard. "I fucked it up. But it wasn't just my fault! I couldn't have known that two cars full would suddenly roll up!"

His gaze pierced me. It's a miracle his head didn't fall back. Like with a shotgun that kicks.

"And the van?"

"We had to run. Couldn't save it, and had to leave it there. Went back a couple days ago. Couldn't do nothin'."

I show him the picture of the VW on my phone. Any second I expect it to melt away in his hand or be crushed like a can of beer, but he just hands it back.

He sighs loudly. Then he says, "The vehicle is registered with a guy in Hildesheim. A junky. You know that. Right?"

"Yeah."

"I sent people around to his place. I sent Tomek over there. To find out if he'd sold the car for cash."

He doesn't need to say anything else. Don't even want to know what Tomek and whoever else was along did to the guy. A long silence follows. I can see the hairs on my forearm standing on end.

Then my uncle says, "You'd better go now, Heiko."

I do as I'm told. Get up slowly and retreat. No sudden movements. I'm afraid he could attack me, like a puma with rabies.

"One more thing," he says and I stop.

"Why the van? Why not your own car?"

"No Hannover plates."

He closes his eyes, nods, and his mouth even makes a tiny motion upward. "Okay, sure, understand. Smart." The moment passes. "Go." And I go.

After turning from the side street where Wotan is located, I see several police cars and a van in my rearview mirror, coming down the street without their lights on. They turn off toward the gym.

———

The driveway to Arnim's house is full of dark, boxy transport vans. Plates from Russia, Ukraine, Poland, Serbia, Lithuania, hell if I know. The cocksuckers have boxed me in. Arnim should hire a fucking valet service. The smell of zoo, animal shit and urine, penetrates the house and coats everything. I climb the narrow, creaking stairs. Brought the bucket I always use to bring Siegfried his bones. I hear people speaking Russian in the kitchen. Arnim has tried to teach me some over the years. But it never amounted to any more than standard stuff like "hello," "thanks," and various insults and curse words. Never really wanted to learn Russian. Think it's better if I don't understand what Arnim's visitors are saying every year or half year. The conversation falls silent when I come into the kitchen. The three guys with typical Russian canister-shaped skulls and cruel faces stare at me. I'd like to tell them that they can keep on talking shit because I don't understand a word. But they don't speak any German, either. Probably not even English. They blink at me from underneath their Neanderthal-like foreheads. One of them has a harelip beneath his mustache, splitting his upper lip. It looks like someone's tied a thread from his gums, out his mouth, and over his head, pulling it back. He's wearing a baby-blue Camp David shirt, unbuttoned. I can recognize horizontal stab scars on his small pot belly. The next one is wearing an army-gray vest covered with pockets. His bare arms make it look as though he's wearing a fucking tight, patterned long-sleeve shirt. All of it tattoos. Tanks, howitzers, those Russian churches with onion-shaped towers, ornamented crosses, and countless broads with big racks. The third guy, who's supporting himself on the sink with his seven remaining fingers, has a goatee. Splotches on his face that look like burns and a scar along his throat like a tight necklace.

"Privyet," I say.

They only nod grimly. I walk into the yard. The camouflage netting is back up. Arnim is standing with a couple of other people around the pit where his fucking tiger is supposed to live soon. The oversized wooden cover is pushed to the side. He explains something in Russian, fat chest extra swollen with pride. Really cleaned up today, even putting on a shirt to match his stained cargo shorts and the flip-flops. He'd set up industrial-strength construction floodlights pointed toward the ground, providing indirect lighting that reached the faces of those present but left their eye sockets with shadows. Makes these figures seem even more dodgy than they already were. *This* is the true dregs of society. Yet the press is always picking on us. If they only knew. At least we smash each other's faces in and don't have it done by some poor shitty animals who have no choice. Nights like these, I sometimes wish the cops would roll in and lock up all these thugs. But that never happens. Arnim is just too careful. He organizes these fights here too infrequently. Precisely because it's so risky in Germany. The scene mostly happens in the former East Bloc states, the Balkans, and over toward Turkey. It's much easier to grease the police's palms there. If they're not already standing in the arena in the first place with some banana republic's funny money clutched in their hands. He told me once there're only two other guys in the whole country who hold animal fights on this scale. One behind Hamburg. The other near Frankfurt, by the Polish border. But they just do dogs, he said, it's boring, my boy, you have to offer people something, my boy. It makes me think of my first year living with Arnim. All of it was completely new to me, so I looked in as it was going on, behind the shed. Thought I was imagining when they had a fucking brown bear fight against two pit bulls. Even tag-teaming, the dogs didn't have a snowball's chance. After they'd tranquilized the victorious bear and pulled out the tattered carcasses, and I popped behind the shed to barf, I just wanted out. I haven't let myself be drawn into that shit ever since. All the fucking creatures we've had here. That bear, sure. But we've also had wolves. And a fucking steer! And then two years ago there was that old, feral male chimpanzee. It'd been brought here by some Armenian who stank of drug and weapons money. He'd showed up with a bevy of bodyguards and had Arnim doing his bidding. He even had an arsenal of weapons for the fucking ape! I saw how he presented the animal to Arnim. Razor blades attached to leather arm cuffs and twisted shit like that. Couldn't keep my eyes shut that night. Till they left with the chimp. But before that. Lay in my darkened room and had to listen to the monkey howling nonstop. Fucking hell! But that was the good thing: toward morning, just before it got light, the whole filthy squad of gangsters packed up their animals and fucked off. At least there was that. That morning I had half a mind to sneak down into the living room and wrap my hands around Arnim's neck, while he was down there sawing logs. Squeeze tight till all the air had slipped from his lungs and his eyeballs were bulging from their sockets. But I just buried my head under my pillow. Things like that pass. And then you just skip out for a night or turn up the music in your headphones till they're ready to bust.

There's a travel cage with thick bars against the wall of the shed that Arnim cleared out during the day. The dogs are slowly waking up. They're pumped full of tranquilizers for the long trips from all those banana republics. Looks like things could get started soon. I walk over to Arnim, who's pulling the lid over the pit again. Then one of his guests tests how much weight it can support by bouncing on it and gives a thumb's up.

"Hey, Arnim, I'm about to head out. Just so you're not looking for me."

"What?! But things are about to get wild here, my boy!"

"Yeah, no, forget about it. I don't need that."

"Oh well, then get lost. Can't make anything off you anyway."

When I come back through the kitchen, the harelip and titty-arms are still sitting there. Harelip yells something. Doesn't seem to be directed at me. I walk past him. Goatee man is in the living room and is bent over, probing the sofa cushions and the spaces between them. His shirt's slipped up. The butt of a pistol pokes out of his waistband. He looks around, sees me, and pushes himself away from the sofa. We're standing face to face. He smiles at me. Clearly trying to provoke.

"Me nothing," he says with a shaky accent and holds up his hands.

Maybe to show me he doesn't have anything or wasn't looking for anything. Then he places his pointer in front of that nasty kisser and says, "Shhhh," winking at me. I go upstairs. Then I toss a couple things into my duffel bag, call Kai, and ask if he can pick me up with his car from the train station in Wunstorf. There haven't been any trains running for hours. I say he shouldn't ask such stupid questions, and whether he'll fucking pick me up or not. We agree to meet there in an hour. I leave the room, lock the door, and add the two padlocks I've installed extra for nights like these. Inside there are two more that you just have to click. On the outside you need keys, otherwise they don't lock. I'm not so retarded that I'd let myself be locked inside my own room. Goatee man is back at it when I go down the stairs. Don't give a fuck. And he could care less that I see him. I slam the porch door shut, but it immediately swings open again. Then I find my way to the country road with my flashlight and from there, on to the station.

———

"Just moved in and there's already a ruckus! Unbelievable!"

"Shut your trap!" Kai bellowed at my new neighbor in the pre-fab high-rise, one door down, and called him an old geezer or something like that. I pulled him back into my place and yelled at him, wanting to know what it was about. He'd probably call the cops and they'd kick me out, but then I had to laugh anyway, and we laughed our asses off, cracking up about the old fucker with a stick up his ass. Kai had been nice enough to bring along some-thing to celebrate with, and I'd already knocked back two ecstasy and blazed three blunts thick as my thumb. The whole apartment stank of weed and skunky beer. Ulf was rolling the next one. On my new couch, which we had found on the side of the street on the way here. We all pitched in, and it went in the elevator to the sixth floor. Everything was perfect. Just the way it was supposed to be. Summer vacation in my sights. But I hadn't gone to school for a couple weeks anyway. Since I'd moved out. Just had to celebrate finally escaping Hans's stinking cottage.

"Now put down the fucking phone for a sec and finish rolling that thing!" Kai bellowed at Ulf, who'd been exchanging messages the whole time with Saskia, his new flame. "It's about time we listened to some nice Rotterdam tunes."

Kai cranked up the volume on my stereo and ear-blasting Gabba techno boomed out of the speakers, which were having trouble dealing with the racket and were noticeably humming.

We were yelling over each other, and I flopped down on the couch next to Ulf, who had the grass fall out of his paper. His furious face protested, but I couldn't understand a word through the hardcore noise. Then I saw my phone light up. The light from the display glistened through a page from an open porn mag. It was Jojo. I jumped over to the stereo and turned it down. Kai threw everything at me he could find. I fended off coins and cigarette butts with one hand and picked up.

"Jojo, where you at? We've already almost killed everything we have."

"Heiko? Heiko, don't yell so loud. We're on the road. My dad is driving us. Me and the man of the day."

His voice cracked a couple times.

I said, "Huh?" or something like that.

"You'll see in a bit. We just turned onto Barne Street."

The doorbell rang a couple minutes later and I pressed the buzzer on the intercom. Jojo, Joel, and their dad came into the apartment.

"Hey, Dieter! How's it hanging?!" Kai shouted, sitting on the windowsill, and knocked back a can. One leg in the room, the other dangling out the sixth floor.

"Hello, boys. How's it look in here?" Dieter laughed. As always, he was wearing his gray work coat, which almost reached the slight man's feet.

"Tip top, right?" I asked.

"I don't know. But to each his own, right?"

"Come in, get something to drink. There's still some in the fridge," I said and pushed everything off the table. Including the overflowing ashtrays. I didn't care.

"That's all right, I have to leave right away. Just wanted to drop off these two. Joel has something to tell you all."

"Dad," Jojo said, "I wanted to do it."

"Well," Dieter waved him off.

"What's up, dude?" Kai asked and jumped from the window and into the room, staggering and only barely catching himself on the wall.

"Spit it out already," I pressed Joel, who once again was standing there with his shoulders turned in, making himself seem even skinnier, shaking the part out of his hair. Maybe he just looked that way because of the two ecstasy pills, but I thought he would disappear into thin air any second.

"Got a call from Hannover two days ago. Yesterday we went there to look everything over and—"

"Guys, you should have seen it," Jojo interrupted his little brother, "the best equipment, great setup, top league standards!"

Dieter pushed Jojo aside and said, "Let him tell it himself, Joachim."

Joel continued. Squeakily. He was still in the middle of his voice change. Zits everywhere, the poor guy.

"We talked to the head coach. Didn't need much time to think about it. This morning we were back and signed the contract."

"Contract?" Ulf asked. I think he was trying to hide the grass from Dieter under the porno.

"Joel, out with it!" Jojo yelled.

And Joel reached into the tote bag he'd brought along and pulled out a red Hannover 96 home jersey and, holding it by the shoulders, turned it around. The back was covered with the team name, a big number seven, and finally the name Seidel underneath.

"I'm on the B-team," he said.

I think it took Kai and Ulf just as long as it did me to process what we were seeing. When the realization wound its way through our drug-affected brains and arrived, we jumped up together and ran over to the three Seidels, screaming with joy and yelling, "96!" We gave each other high fives and fist bumps and grabbed our heads because we simply couldn't believe it. One of us, a true Red. A player for Hannover 96. That's the last thing I can remember about that day. And the two-day hangover that followed.

————

I think about going home but put it off till evening. Arnim can clean up all that crap himself. I don't need to deal with wiping up animal blood. Besides, I'm honestly a little afraid of coming home and finding Poborsky or Bigfoot's cage empty. Not that either of those killers is near and dear to me or anything. But I don't want them to pass into the sweet hereafter either. At least not that way. I take the next bus to Luthe. Jojo called us in the morning and asked if we'd like to finally visit him at practice. Kai declined. He'd made a date with some girl from class to do a study group for the upcoming test. Of course, study group is just personal code for fuck buddy. But she doesn't know that yet. Visiting Jojo is clearly the better alternative for me. The other would be having to listen to Arnim recount last night's events.

The field belonging to the TSV Luthe field team is located behind the village elementary school, where Jojo and Joel went. It's bordered by tall, thin trees that I can already see from far away. The tips of their crowns, bare by now, bend from the gusts. Then a high kicked ball appears in front of them. It flies straight up, remains almost motionless in the air for a second, and is blown away by the wind. I can already see Jojo as I step onto the checkered border surrounding the field. Hands forming a megaphone around his mouth and shouting, "On the ground! Try to keep it on the ground!"

He's watching over a training match. Jerseys against vests. Jojo's wearing his black-and-blue coaching outfit. He's letting his hair grow again. Dressed in his gear, from the back you could almost mistake him for the coaching legend Klaus Toppmöller. If the hair was a little longer and gray at some point, the illusion would be perfect. But, when it comes to facial feature, he more resembles Peter Neururer, without the stache. He also has such a good-natured face with a funny beak. I position myself slightly behind the coaching bench and watch a bit. Fathers and mothers are leaning against the barrier that separates the spectators from the field. Mostly fathers. Two of them are standing not too far away. Just the sight of them gives me the creeps. Outdoorsy jackets. Khaki trousers, and breathable middle-age sneakers. I don't care much about appearances, but here it's the connection between the, well, you could almost call it a uniform, and what the douchebags trash talk. While their progeny hump it across the field, they just lean back and play a round of "who's more successful." Whose paycheck is plumper, whose vacations are more luxurious, who was able to negotiate a better price with the contractor, raise the roof on the garage so the new, unnecessary family SUV fits even if the old station wagon would have done the job. I'd like to go over there right now and give both of them one helluva bitch slap. Not that either has the slightest clue about football. It's all just about your own brat's an undiscovered Lionel Messi and, oh, of course, so fantastic in school, straight As in math. What a bunch of hypocrites! And wondering why that uppity little Turk doesn't pass the ball, and Junior could have done it with his eyes closed. But he's already expending all his energy running straight ahead. And then Sonny was even fouled! That was a foul! Coach! Why didn't he see that?! And did you know that little daughter started dressage? A true talent when it comes to riding, the teacher says. I'd like to go up to that prick and say, "Boy, are you sure the teacher meant horse skills and isn't just playing grab-ass with your daughter in the stables?"

That'd be a little harsh. But I'd sure like to give those uptight weekend warriors a bitch slap.

"Hey, you old motherfucker!" I yell, and cup my hands around my mouth like Jojo.

Irritated, he turns around. I wink and smile. He hustles over to me.

"Heiko, dude. Are you smashed?! You can't yell stuff like that around here."

I make a dismissive gesture.

"Don't get your knickers in a twist 'cause of those fags over there." We shake hands. "How's it going? Are you bossing around the little shits?"

I must have busted some dam, 'cause Jojo immediately let loose a flood of words. Tomorrow's an important match, the boys are really making an effort, just have to keep the balls down, a couple talents here. Blah blah blah.

"Yeah," I say, and point to the field, "that little guy there. The Turk— "

"Kurd," Jojo corrects me.

"Kurd. Sorry. He's really got something. Tight dribbling. Uses his body well, and seems to have a good eye for the other players."

As if to confirm what I just said, the kid gets past the fullback down the outside with an expert stepover and crosses low into the area, so that all his teammate has to do is stick a foot out and it's in the back of the net.

"Yeah, I think Erbil might be able to make something of himself," Jojo says and crosses his arms like a pundit.

"Great this is going well, man," I say and pat Jojo on the back. He looks attentively at his boys.

"By the way. National team's on Tuesday. Friendly against Slovakia."

"Yeah?"

No one gives a fuck about the Mannschaft. Except when the Euros or World Cup is on. Then the daddies pull their German flags out of the closet and those motherfuckers clip them onto their windshields.

"Was at Kai's last night—"

"Didn't sleep much, huh?"

"Right. Can you see it?"

"You look like you crawled out of an asshole," Jojo whispers to me.

"Sure, fuck it. At any rate. Kai'd heard something from the boys in Hamburg. Rumor has it that the Slovakians floated a trial balloon, see if anything might work out."

"Where?" he asks.

"Leipzig. Tickets have already been ordered."

"You serious?"

"Four tickets. You and Ulf, and me, of course."

Jojo's eyes bug: "Ulf?"

"Yep. Even him. Talked to him on the phone. But he said he'd look for a bar after the match and wait for us there."

"Didn't you have a blow-up with him? He told me you really flew off the handle when he said Saskia didn't want him to go to the matches anymore and all that."

I offer him a cigarette. He declines, waving the hand poking out from under his crossed arms. I light one.

"Yeah, my God. It's completely understandable. But no way it's serious. He'll feel the itch soon enough."

"If that's what you think."

"I do. Okay. You're coming, right? Just a short-notice match. At least toss around a couple chairs or something. Also depends on how heavy the cop presence is."

"Well, if you've already ordered tickets, then I can't really say no, right?"

"Good man," I say. "Besides . . ."—I think about what I actually want to say—"maybe it'll do some good. I mean. Getting out of here for once. And we've never been to Leipzig either. Maybe we could make some connections with the people at Lok or Chemie. That'd be something. They're supposed to have some really good people, those retards in the fan bloc."

Jojo runs over to the touchline and screams, "Diagonal! Diagonal!"

Then he comes back and asks me if something's up with me.

"Huh, something up? Don't know what you're getting at."

"That thing in Braunschweig and all. Maybe that?"

I exhale the smoke, pick off some flakes of paint from the barrier, and say: "Hell if I know. Told Axel. Went horrible. Either he'll come around . . . well, or he'll leave it be. Who knows? By the way, kept you guys out of it. So not a word about that to Axel. Was all me. Wanna knock some back tonight?"

"Man, Heiko! You didn't have to do that. We all fucked it up. We should at least all take responsibility for it."

"Is what it is. Are you gonna be there tonight?"

"Can't."

"Why's that?"

"The game tomorrow. I have to be in shape."

"Are you a player-manager now? With a fake badge and everything?"

He laughs nervously.

"No, seriously now. I . . . With this coaching job," he points toward the field, as if he had to show me again what it's about, "it's important to be a good role model. That's why I don't smoke here either. In front of the boys. And the boozing . . . Heiko, man, I just have to take it down a notch."

"You're shitting me, right? Those rug rats don't know it if you drink something somewhere at night."

"That's not the point, dude. Hey, I have to get back now. Want to go over the strategy with the boys again. Then practice free kicks. Stick around and watch."

I flip my cigarette away, blowing out the last cloud of smoke, which is immediately blown away, and say, "I'm gonna head out."

We shake hands good-bye. He presses tight. My hand lies on his like a dead flounder. Then he goes back to the coaching bench and whistles at the players. I leave, mumbling, "Role model. For fuck's sake, Jojo."

I look around the parking lot and kick the side mirror of a white, highly polished X5 BMW. Feels good.

———

Leipzig is colder than the crotch of a one-legged, high-priced hooker. The night sky over Red Bull arena is still illuminated by the floodlights. We fall in line with the stream of people made up of families, groups of blond girls wearing Podolski and Hummels jerseys, and other fair-weather fans. The boys from Hamburg we'd spent the match drinking with had already left for the city center even before the end of the match to see whether anything might still happen with the Slovakians. We're waiting for the streetcar.

"Fuck, it's cold," Jojo says, rubbing his paws and blowing into them.

If only he'd joined in the drinking, he wouldn't be freezing his ass off like a fucking pussy right now. But no, instead he just alternated back and forth between shandy and Coke.

"I gotta piss this place full again," Kai says and mentions to Jojo, "In case they're selling hot chocolate somewhere, I'll bring your faggy ass one, okay?"

Jojo laughs ironically and flips off Kai, who moves away from us toward the river. Ulf is just standing there passively in our group, checking his phone and looking for the city center bar where he'll be waiting for us. Can't resist throwing him a blatantly disapproving look, but he doesn't even notice.

The minutes till the next streetcar arrives fly past and Kai still hasn't shown up. The doors open.

"Where the fuck's that tard?"

"Maybe he got the runs or fell in the river drunk," Ulf says and positions himself in the door of the streetcar. "I'm going to go ahead. Let me know when you're done."

Yeah, sure, we say. A bell rings. The doors close, and the street car drives off.

"Later," I mumble.

"What?" Jojo asks.

"It's okay."

My ears gradually start to feel like they're wrapped in ice packs, and I pull up my hood. Of course, I don't say I'm feeling cold. The next streetcar toward the city center slowly moves down the digital clock.

"What's going on? Where's he at?"

Jojo shrugs. My neck's starting to hurt from looking around. Kai is nowhere to be seen.

"Maybe something's happened," says Jojo.

"Come on, what can have happened?" I answer, remove my phone from my pocket, and call Kai.

It rings until the answering machine beeps. I hang up and try it again. Same exact thing.

"Fuck. Okay, let's go find him."

We go across the street and reach the wide bridge over the river. A park along the water on the other side makes a dark shadow reflected on the river's surface. There are groups of people in German national team paraphernalia where the sidewalk widens in front of the bridge, sitting around cases of beer they've brought and half-blocking the bike lane, making the bicycles ride slalom. They're singing *"Deutschland, Deutschland über alles!"* I yell that they should shut up. They look over and fall silent. They start singing again once we've moved past. Jojo was on the other side of the bridge and now returns, shaking his head at me. I'm standing at the railing and looking down at the footpath that runs parallel to the river and is only slightly lit. No sign.

"Maybe he went into the park and got lost," Jojo says.

I press the red End Call button on my phone when just Kai's answering machine picks up, and say, "The hell if I know, man." The next streetcar rumbles by. "Okay, I'll try it one more time. When he doesn't pick up, I'll yell at him so bad his ears'll fall off when he listens to the message."

My fingertips are cold. I can hardly feel the smooth surface of the display beneath them. It rings again. Nothing. I get ready to yell into the phone when the beep comes, but Jojo grabs my arm and says, "Listen." I hang up and ask what I'm supposed to hear.

Jojo looks at the street. There aren't any cars coming at the moment. He says I should call again because he thinks he heard Kai's ring tone. "Fix Up, Look Sharp" by Dizzee Rascal. I press to repeat the call. After I've made sure it was ringing, I take the phone off my ear and bend my torso over the massive stone railing and listen down into the cold. Jojo, next to me, does the same.

"There," he whispers, "do you hear it?"

And now I actually do hear it. The normally pounding base of the "Fix Up" beat, very low.

"Sounds like it's echoing," Jojo says.

"What the . . . ?"

I scan the path and the bank below, meter for meter, till I'm staring straight down. The answering machine kicks in again and

I immediately press Repeat Call. Then I bend even further, making my crotch rub on the cold, rough stone. The base and the bark of the grime rapper disappears briefly under the roar of passing cars. I have to concentrate to grab the sound. Yes, definitely!

"The underpass!" I say and run around the railing. A wide, stone staircase leads down to the riverbank. I take it in several leaps and am by the river when Jojo's still only halfway down the stairs. The tunnel is a black frame where only the rounded silhouette of the other side is visible. Jojo bumps into me from behind when he rushes down the stairs. He bends past me.

"There's nothing there," he says, but I hold my hand up to tell him he should wait a sec. Then my index finger goes taut and I point into the tunnel.

"There's something," I say. My cheeks suddenly feel really flushed. Without looking, I press Repeat once again. A couple seconds later, the connection is made and something blinks in the middle of the tunnel. Accompanied by the rhythmic, pounding beat. I'm about to put my first steps into the tunnel when someone yells the Braunschweig chant: "BTSV! BTSV!"

I instinctively look up. The silhouette of a person can be recognized above the railing. He looks like he's cut out of black paper, with the glow of the streetlamps behind him. The figure grabs at his head and pulls something down. Then something falls to our feet. Jojo bends over to pick it up. It's a coarse balaclava. Mouth and eye holes are outlined in red. The mask is half blue and half yellow. Jojo holds it out to me. I look back up, but the shadow has disappeared. I look up at the dark blue, almost black starry sky. My brain seems to have dissolved into hot wax and run down my throat into my stomach. I sprint into the darkness. Something in front of me glows. Kai's phone. There's something next to it, leaning against the wall. Crumpled. I crouch down and reach for it. Feel clothing that gives way under my fingers till they hit against the resistance of an arm. I grab it and provoke a weak groan. I yell at Jojo he should move his ass. He slips out of his frozen state and together we pull Kai out of the tunnel. Into the light.

Jojo immediately inhales sharply. What lies at our feet looks very different from my best friend. The pants dirty and slipped down to his thighs. High-riding boxer shorts peek out. The Stone Island jacket hangs on only one arm. His shirt is ripped his undershirt visible. Bruises have formed on his collarbone, sticking out darkly against the white fabric like bullet holes. His eyes are closed. His eyelids shine blackly, as if a horde of Goths had forcibly applied makeup. His face is covered with bruises and deep rivulets. From wound to wound. They overflow, and the blood runs down the side of his head in tiger's stripes, coagulating around his eyes, nostrils, and mouth. The tip of his nose has taken on the color and form of a swollen cock head and seems terribly out of place under the bridge of his nose, split by a horizontal cut. His lips look shredded. We roll him on his side. I open his mouth. Blood immediately flows out of the lower corner of his mouth. I push two fingers into his mouth cavity. Feel where his tongue is at. I come across loose teeth that feel like pebbles. I scrape them out of his mouth. Thick cords of blood and mucus stick to my fingers like cheese spread. Then I reach inside again and shift his tongue so it's straight and can't slip back into his throat. Jojo crouches next to me and stammers to himself, "Oh shit, oh shit."

Annoyed, I blurt out, "Knock that shit off! Call an ambulance, damn it!"

My whole skull is glowing, and for a moment I picture how it steams in the cold night air. As if I'd just completed a long-distance race. I bend down over Kai's mouth. He's still breathing. Even if it's so shallow I can't even hear it when I hold my ear directly to his lips, but I can still feel the light draft against my skin.

I kneel down in front of Kai's stomach, which he still has protected with crossed arms. The sleeves have slipped over his hands. I can see that his fingers are moving. My hands are on his hips. I watch as they stroke him. As if he were an amped-up ox you need to speak soothing words to. I force my hands to stay calm. Then I look back up. The sky is brighter than before. The clouds have faded and are illuminated by the lights of the city. Their answer is that they slowly close their shutters. Drops of rain fall straight down on me. More and more. Till they can be heard splatting down against the stones and asphalt by the hundreds. Separated by milliseconds. It seems to me like the drops are actually small bubbles floating in the air that only come toward me because I'm flying swiftly toward the sky. Jojo's panicked voice, yelling to the emergency response that he doesn't know exactly where we're at, just at the stadium, down by the riverbank, feels like it's miles away for a split second. Kai suddenly coughs, spitting blood against my pant legs, and pulls me back.

"Kai! Kai!"

I grab his forehead and chin and turn his face slightly back toward me. As carefully as possible with shaking fingers, I pull his eyelids open. They're also drenched in blood and swollen, making me immediately release them. I jump up and leap over Kai and Jojo. Run up the stairs. Two at a time. A streetcar rolls by. Illuminated faces from the inside stare fleetingly. The gang around the case of beer next to me is still singing their stupid victory songs. Otherwise no one else can be seen. No one I can give a flying kick to in the face. No one I can slam my pounding fists against. No one against whose teeth I could cut my finger open, only to keep on hitting till they were separated from the roots and the gums. And no one I could keep on beating till he choked on his own teeth. Instead, the rain is pounding against my shoulders and the crown of my skull and hammers the rage into every fiber of my body.

———

Kai wolf-whistled at a group of women walking past Timpen with their designer handbags in the crook of their arms.

"Dude, they were at least thirty or so," Jojo said, laughing and bracing himself against the brick wall.

"So what? Climbing into the saddle on an old horse is the best way to learn how to ride. I only hope you two'll learn that lesson too."

Kai still swore he'd done it with the hot MILF who lived next to his parents and him. And we still didn't believe him. Next time I'll take pictures, he always said, but the next time never came. And once, when I'd skipped class again to visit him at his school in Hannover and we went to his place afterward, we met her on the stairs. She didn't even give Kai the time of day when he said hello, but when we'd gone inside he claimed it'd been my fault. Because I'd always make such a face, so I shouldn't be surprised. Also, that I was still a virgin at the age of sixteen. Which wasn't true, either, because I'd already done it with Lisa in the school bathroom stalls the year before. But I hadn't told anyone. Not even Kai. Wanted to wait and see if things would get serious with Lisa, because I really liked her. And then just a week later I'd gone to the bathroom during biology to smoke, and I heard her in the stall next to mine, heard her moaning. That sounded just like with me, and then I'd stood on the toilet and looked over the wall and saw she was screwing some son of a bitch from the parallel class. And then I knew she was just another fucking slut.

A goal celebration burst out of Timpen's slanted window and immediately after that the sound of beer glasses clinking.

Jojo couldn't control himself. He ran to the door and pushed it open.

"What? Who?" he yelled inside.

The answer came in the form of a chorus of loud curses and that he should close the blinds again, otherwise something else would happen. I asked Jojo what he'd seen.

"Couldn't see the television because all the old farts were standing in the way," he said and pulled the pack out of Ulf's hand so he could light a cigarette.

"I mean inside. Not the game."

It was clear enough that Hannover had scored a goal. Why else would Axel and the rest cheer? Not for the opponent.

"What? Um, no clue. They're just sitting there. Or standing. Drinking. Watching the game."

"And my uncle?" I asked and slapped Jojo's shoulder with the back of my hand.

"Yeah, him too. What's your deal, Heiko? He's sitting there and drinking," he said, rolling his eyes in annoyance and taking a seat on the cobblestones, "like all the others. It's just *we* have to stand out here like bouncers and not see anything."

He rested his face in his hands, pushing up his cheeks and making his eyes into slits. All at once, the door opened and Töller burst out. He was still holding onto the door with one hand and bending his upper body over. He was pale as a corpse. His back bent over and he took a couple loud breaths. I'd already seen the neighbor's cat do that before barfing up a wet hairball. Töller's blond hair fell in his eyes, and he spewed directly in front of the main entrance.

Jojo, who'd been sitting right next to it, jumped up and yelled, "Fucking hell, dude!"

"Well, Töller," Kai said loudly and cracked up, "couple pints of horse piss too many, right?"

Töller had already been knocking back beer when we'd arrived at noon. I'd seen him at the bar when I'd tentatively poked my head into the barroom, being careful not to let the tips of my toes go beyond the doorframe, and ordered four Cokes from the boss. So we at least had something to drink out in front of the door.

"Come on over here, you," Töller slurred and tried to grab Kai, but he was standing too far away. Töller swung his arm around and lost what little balance he had left. If Ulf hadn't have been in the right spot and held him tight, he'd have fallen face-first in his own barf. Tomek came out of Timpen to help and pulled Töller back inside, depositing him on the chair next to him like a trophy and tugging at him over and over till Töller sat there on his own with a dead gaze, without his arm slipping from the edge of the table. We choked down our laughter when Axel came and stood in the doorway, Tomek behind him, holding open the door so it wouldn't hit my uncle's ass. Axel was holding out a mop and pressed it in Jojo's hands because he was unlucky enough to be standing closest.

"Here, wipe up the mess," he hissed through his fangs and went back inside without another word.

Jojo tried to fob the task off on us, but Ulf and I politely declined.

"Hey, come on, I'll do it already," Kai said and was already grinning so I knew what he was planning. He wiped around in the puddle of vomit, whistling away. I took a couple steps back in prudent foresight. Kai looked to the side over to us and grinned like a shark that'd discovered a surfer who'd fallen off his board. Then he cocked back the mop, dragged it through the puddle, and swung it around and whipped the vomit toward us, laughing like a maniac. I was able to dodge away in time, but I think Ulf or at least Jojo caught a couple of drops and screamed like little girls. And Kai loudly laughed his ass off, and Jojo and Ulf ran at him to disarm him. I stood by, hands on my hips, and laughed and watched as the three of them fought and pushed each other into the remaining barf. Then Axel poked his head out the door one last time. His brows covered his eyes and his chin was mostly out of the door. He glanced briefly at the tussling rug rats. Then he turned his head to me and said, "Make sure you get a grip on the dipshits, okay, Heiko?"

I nodded. Well, I think I did. Still remember that somehow it felt more like I was drawing back my head and then pressing it forward. Like I was trying to swallow a whole sausage all at once.

"I will," I said.

———

They kept Kai in the hospital in Leipzig for two days. While he lay hardly responsive in his room, I occupied the row of chairs in the hallway. It was almost impossible to sleep, but I didn't let the doctors and nurses get rid of me either. Jojo and Ulf went ahead, leaving the next day because they had to work. I simply didn't let Axel know. He didn't call me to ask where I was at either. On the third day, Kai was transferred to Hannover, to the medical school. I wasn't allowed to ride along. I'd made a ruckus in the ambulance on the way to the hospital, so the EMTs had stopped halfway there and kicked me out, despite the flashing lights and the whole nine yards. So I took the fast train to Hannover.

Kai's parents completely ignored me when they brought over some clothes. Shooting recriminations at me. I went to the clinic's cafeteria and waited till they left again. I didn't go home once. No show. Always the same clothes. I could already smell myself. My greasy clothes gradually fused with my skin. Kai had made progress the last few days. By now, he was able to eat some things that weren't poured into him from a tube. Just stuff that had been through a blender, but still. He couldn't even get his injured mouth open an inch. When he talked, it sounded like his teeth were glued together.

I help him with all the motions he goes through with monotone groans. I stabilize his head. Pay attention so he doesn't bump it climbing in. He muffles a groan, and I lift his legs into the car. He closes his eyes in pain. His face looks like he played with two ADD kids who couldn't decide whether they wanted to play doctor or paint his face. The physicians insisted he should be kept there for several more days, if not a week. We ignored them and packed up his stuff. I close the trunk and climb in on the driver's side. The chemical smell of his various bandages, Band-Aids, salves, and the general hospital stench—which by itself is enough to make you sick—spreads through the car. He rolls down his window a crack. Then he rolls his head toward me, past the headrest, while I'm backing out of the parking spot, and says, "You stink, pal."

I laugh, saying not everyone's lucky enough to be bathed and washed by a hot nurse. He laughs too, then coughs and groans. Squints and groans even more because his eyes hurt so much.

"The eyes are the worst," he wheezes, "everything is so bright. A little like you're looking into the sun, but instead of going away, it just stays that way. But keeping them shut almost hurts as much."

I say, "Hmm," because I'd already run out of fitting comments to stuff like that in Leipzig. Instead, I look down at him and crank up the heat despite the open window. He's still wearing his hospital gown. He would never have done that otherwise. Normally he'd have insisted, despite the pain, on getting dressed up before going out in public. But at least he kept the backside open during our short, sluggish walks down the hall. He wanted to offer the nurses something. No one can beat that out of him.

We're silent during the drive into the city. He has his face turned to the side window, and I don't know if he's looking out or sleeping. My phone rings in my pocket. I reach inside. Press End Call without looking. The city seems unusually calm. Cars, trains, street cars. Everything rolls past muffled by the windows. The sky looks like it's covered in smoke. Gray streets below and people in colorless raincoats who silently push past each other.

When I park in front of Kai's house, I see his parents' car. They get out and walk toward us. Must have spent the whole time waiting in the car. I get out quickly so I can be at the passenger side before them and help Kai out.

"Bag's in the trunk," I say to his father, who walks around the car and takes it out. The single step before the front door is already a barrier, and I almost have to lift Kai so he makes it. The shaking of his legs is so severe it transfers to me.

"Thanks," he whispers while his mother holds the elevator door behind him.

"Sure I shouldn't come up with you?"

"Go take a shower. You stink like a tiger cage."

I grin at him. The flushed corners of his mouth twitch like the wings of a dying bee.

"I'll be in touch," he whispers.

I wait in the doorway till the elevator door closes and swallows his parents, who are still looking grimly at me. We used to get along. I go back to my VW hatchback and yell at the meter cop who's hard at it on the other side of the street that I'm on my way. My phone rings again. The meter cop bitch waves excitedly. As if there was nothing worse in her sad shitty life than a car that stops for a minute, double parked. I drive off and take my phone out of my pocket. No number. Without giving it much thought, I pick up.

"Yeah?"

"Heiko?"

"Who's there?"

"Heiko?"

"Yeah."

"Hans is here. Very drunk." The barely audible female voice at the other end draws out the *u* unusually long. "Out of rehab. Is very drunk. Angry."

"Mie?" I ask.

"Please come," is the only answer I get, then she hangs up.

I turn onto the driveway to my father's house when Axel calls. Fuck! When it rains it pours, of course.

"Hello?"

"Heiko, come to the gym. We have to have a little talk."

I can't produce an answer.

"Heiko?"

"Yeah. But I can't right now. Something's going on with Hans. Can't leave," I say.

A pause follows. I look around. Manuela's car is by the sidewalk in front.

"Tomorrow," my uncle says, and it sounds like a threat.

I hang up, go to the front door, and ring the bell. The door is immediately ripped open. Mie is standing there. She's wearing pajamas with a teddy bear pattern. Her long hair isn't flowing down her back as usual but has formed a crazy nest on her head.

"Please come. Your father. He is completely furious."

"What's he doing here?" I ask, but she silently points past me. To the stairs.

My foot bumps against a suitcase in the hallway. The commotion can be heard from above. Accompanied by some sort of incomprehensible swearing that rises and falls. I walk past the kitchen. In the corner of my eye, I see someone inside. I stop and turn around. Manuela had pulled a chair away from the table and is sitting on it. Face buried in her hands. Crumpled tissues on the kitchen table.

"What's going on here?" I ask.

Above us, something heavy is pushed over and slams onto the floor with a thud. My sister doesn't look up.

"Manuela?"

"Please leave me alone," she says, sounding like she has a cold. "I can't take it anymore."

Confused, I look to Mie, who pushes past me and sits down at the table behind Manuela, wrapping her toothpick arms around her upper body. I walk up the stairs. Every stair squeaks like I'm stepping on a pile of cats. The white glazed door of the bedroom at the top of the stairs is ajar. Even when I come closer, I still can't understand a single word of the mumbling. I push open the door, saying my father's name. The bedroom is very small. There's hardly any space to really move around next to the king-size bed that's right behind the door. An armchair is lying on its side in front of the wardrobe. I step on the rug, which is as thick as a bear's pelt, and every step is padded. I look around the door and close it. My father is sitting on the edge of the bed. Head thrown back. Urine-colored rivulets of beer flow out of the can, past his mouth and down his neck. They stain his wifebeater yellow. He lowers the can and lets loose a loud "Ahhh," as if the long swig had been infinitely refreshing. There are empty cans spread over the rug in front of the bed, leaking backwash that soaks into the fabric of the rug. It smells like a recycling bin with flatulence. The nightstand has also been knocked over. The contents of the drawers dumped out. The sheets are covered with beer stains.

"What's going on? What are you doing here?" I ask Hans. He lifts his head. Searches the room for the source of my voice. The hairs of his mustache are standing up like wires. His pupils floating in a milky whiteness.

"Pa?" I say and lift the chair onto its stubby wooden legs. Push it back onto its indentations in the carpet.

"Yes. Heiko. My boy." He belches.

"Why are you here and not in rehab?"

"Don't give a shit anymore. All those fags! Was supposed to put my dreams in a wish box. Supposed to build something myself. Out of a shoe box. Fucking fairies. They'll read through the scraps of paper when we're off at lunch. Laugh their asses off."

I say I don't understand a word of what he's rambling on about. He makes a sweeping gesture with his free hand.

"They're fucking each other up the ass!" he screams. "Couldn't take that shit. Who here has a problem? Huh?" He looks in my direction, but isn't really looking at me. It seems like he's arguing with some imaginary person. "*They* have the problem! Fucking fags! Can't kick me out. I'll leave on my own free will, if I want to. Don't need it!"

I crouch down in front of him. His gaze follows me, staggering. I reach for the can in his hand and say it's enough. He reacts immediately. When his beer's in danger. He pulls his hand back. Shakes his head. Like a sulky kid when you want to take away the scissors because he can't handle it yet.

"No. Nooooo!" he screams, drawing it out.

I grab his forearms.

"Pull yourself together now, man!"

He pushes away from me. Scoots backward across the sheets and bumps up against the wall with his back and head.

"Everyone thinks they need to tell me what I should and shouldn't do. Not a kid, damn it!"

I get up again, righting the nightstand, and say, "Then stop acting like one." He looks away, taking another sip. "Seriously. Have you completely drunk your brain to smithereens or what?"

"Just stop it," he says, without looking at me, rubbing his hand over his mouth and chin. "Now you're starting in on it too. Why don't you all just leave me alone?"

"At the Bremen match, you didn't act like the biggest asshole around," I say, "but as soon as you're back here, there's only trouble."

"Huh?" he says and looks at me, flaring his right nostril and making his nose hairs stick out.

"Don't remember anymore, do you?" I smile ironically and can only shake my head. I drop down onto the chair. "You're such a loser, Hans." Somewhere inside a switch has been flipped. The give-a-fuck switch. No way back. "Manuela's sitting downstairs in the kitchen bawling. And why? Because she can't handle it anymore, with a father like this! Who never gets his shit together! Who was never there. Who was always hanging out at the local bar with all the other losers instead and getting blind drunk!" I had to pause for a second because I was irritated by the beating of my own heart and the way my fingernails were digging into the covers of the armchair. "No wonder mom fucked off!"

Hans is instantly on his feet. Is swaying, but on his feet. He didn't even expect it himself.

He straightens up in front of me so his knees are almost bumping into mine. That intimidation shit might have worked when I was still a twerp, but that's been over with at least since I turned fifteen.

"She just ran off and left me all alone!" he yells and sprays a shower of spittle at me, which I take without moving an inch.

"*You*. She left *you* alone?" I hiss through gritted teeth.

"What was I supposed to do?" He holds his right arm as if it didn't belong to his body. "You think I wanted it that way? That I fell off the roof on purpose?! Unemployed. What's a man then? All you can do is start to drink. She left me behind, the old bitch!"

I take a step forward and before I can control anything or pull myself together, I've smacked him one. He staggers back and crumbles. Something red streams through his fingers, covering his nose, falling drip by drip onto the sheets. I look down at him. He's shaking. My father's crying.

I go down the stairs and stomp past the kitchen. Someone yells something. I don't listen. Slam the front door behind me, shakily remove the keys from my pocket, start the car, scream curses against the windshield because I can't take it anymore, and just get the hell out of there. Just leave.

––––––

I come into the gym and the first thing I do is go to the lavatory to hold my face under the cold water faucet and lap it up like a dog. I still haven't showered. I stink of old sweat, and the alc seeps out of my pores. After I'd locked myself in my room with two cases of beer and didn't respond to Arnim's calls from downstairs, I staggered to my car. The firm conviction that it was impossible to arrive in Hannover without an accident. And yet, here I am now. Because if my uncle says jump, then I jump. Fuck it! I sit on the toilet and take a couple deep breaths.

"Pull yourself together," I tell myself several times, and then I propel myself up from the toilet seat. I knock on Axel's door.

"Come in!"

I take a seat on the chair without being bidden because I can hardly stand for more than a couple seconds. The lamps on the ceiling seem like floodlights directed at me. I try to blink away the splotches of light in my vision. Somewhere behind them Axel is staring at me and spinning a pen between his fingers.

"Looks like someone vomited you out, Heiko," he says with an indifferent voice.

I take a pass and say he'd wanted to talk to me. He leans over and folds his hands on the desktop.

"We have problems."

Instead of posing a question, I simply wait for him to continue speaking.

"Your collective tomfoolery in Braunschweig makes us look really shitty. You know that?"

"Just my own stupidity," I try to correct him.

Axel's head swerves to the side, as if he has a spastic twitch. "Stop blowing smoke, Heiko. I know that Kai and Joachim were along. And that Ulf got you out of there."

Fuck, that idiot! But maybe it's my fault. Like everything is my fault. Should have told Ulf he should keep his trap shut about Kai and Jojo's participation in the Braunschweig action.

"We can't count on Ulf anymore"—he sniffs impatiently and continues to stare at me—"and it can't be put any other way than that's also your fault."

"Was his decision," I say. But there's something to that. We should've. Could've. If I hadn't fucked it up so bad, then Ulf wouldn't have had to get us and Saskia wouldn't have been forced to choose.

"By the way, the thing with the VW van has been fixed," he says and shuffles some kind of papers on the desk. It sounds like he's talking about something dry like balance sheets or something. "Gave the guy from Hildesheim some compensation for the . . . unpleasantness that Tomek showed him based on the incorrect assumptions. And because the whole thing is mostly your fault, you can forget about a couple months' pay."

"But I never claimed he had anything to do with it," I burst out.

"Be quiet!" he barks at me, and I sink a bit deeper in my chair. "Next item. The day after tomorrow we're going to Frankfurt. Eight against eight. Because of the stack of shit that's piled up under your name, I wanted you to come along and just take pictures at most. But because we happen to have the absence of Ulf and Kai to compensate for"— my eyes go wide and my mouth opens, but I can't produce a sound—"yep, I also heard about the thing with Kai. Because of the casualties, I have no other option than to bring you along. On probation, so to speak."

"When did you intend to tell me? Since when has the match been planned?" I ask.

"I'm telling you *now*," emphasizing the word "now." "That's got to be good enough for you. I really had to bend over backwards to even round up eight men. Do you actually know how stupid I'd look if I had to call off the Frankfurt match again?"

I want to rub my face because it's itching unpleasantly, but I keep my hands still. Someone knocks on the door. The hint of a smile flits over Axel's otherwise chiseled stone mouth.

"We're done here. You'll be waiting here at ten in the morning the day after tomorrow. Come in."

I get up. A woman with blond hair and brunette roots enters the office. She has a bulky leather bag and underneath her matching leather jacket she's wearing a halter top. Accompanied by skin-tight pants.

"Lock up behind yourself," Axel says.

I'm briefly irritated. Turn around. Then I see he'd been speaking to the broad. She stood still, wrinkling her nose at the sight of me. Or perhaps my smell. She waits for me to leave the room. Then the professional closes the door behind me and turns the key. I go into the locker-room, change clothes, and pull my MP3 player from my locker. I pound the punching bags for an hour without taking a break for a drink. Then I go under the showers, lock the door with my key from the inside, let myself soak, and hope that past days and weeks wash off me and everything is like it used to be when I come back out. Bullshit.

Two days later I'm back in the space behind the gym, waiting like the others for Axel to give the sign to go. The usual suspects, like Tomek, Töller, and Hinkel, are there. And—I can hardly believe my eyes—two of the Nazis we kicked out of Timpen. I stay away from the group and smoke, but the skins keep their distance too. Just glance at me occasionally. Don't want blow it with my uncle by starting something with me again. Too bad. I gave up trying to reach Jojo. He texted: "Sorry. Can't pick up now. On way to practice. Best, jojo."

Instead of writing back something like why the fuck I'm left hanging, I write Kai a message: "How are you feeling today? When I get back from FFM I'll tell u how it was. PS not even Jojo's along. really promising . . ."

Uncle Axel comes out wearing jogging pants and a sweater. He locks the gym door and say, "Let's go, men!"

He'd gotten some new vehicles, and we spread out into two groups of four. I get shotgun next to Hinkel. Tomek and Töller are on the seat in back. No trace of anticipation inside me. I can only hope the adrenaline starts pumping soon because otherwise I'll jump out of the car while it's going full speed.

The three are talking some pointless shit. I don't participate in the conversation. Just look out the window and pick at the rubber seal around the glass. The autobahn's endless dark green noise barriers obscure the view of the landscape. If someone asks me something, I answer in monosyllables. Say yes. Say no. Say don't know.

"Can you give me something from the toiletries bag?" Hinkel asks me at some point.

I take his bag out of the glove compartment and open the zipper.

"Waddaya want?" I ask and poke around in it. The bag has an old man smell and is full of strips of tablet blister packs.

"One of the big yellow ones and a little white one." I press the pills out of the packaging and into Hinkel's palm, which he's holding out in my direction. He tosses them back, grabs for the water bottle in the middle console and washes them down. I pack the toiletry bag back away.

"What're they for?" I ask, more out of boredom than true interest.

"For my old pumper. So that I don't collapse behind the wheel," Hinkel says and starts to laugh, which ends with him hacking into his fist and having to take a sip of water. His face is red as a beet. Probably almost choked, the way he looks. He pounds his chest. His eyes are bugging out. Shiny and watery. He stops coughing, wheezes, and says, "Man, man, man."

I play with the lever that adjusts the side mirror. I use it to watch Töller and Tomek, one after the other. Töller's sunken cheeks that don't quite fit with his fairly muscular body. Broad, dark rings under his eyes. Tomek's Adam's apple bobs up and down with every breath. As if he needs to swallow air instead of breathing it. His mouth stays open, and I can hear his panting all the way from where I'm sitting. His ears are scrunched down to little cauliflower buds. I think how the long scar on the edge of his right cheek sticks out in particular, and it looks like someone's taken a buzz saw to his face. I immediately feel really sick and weak and imagine how somehow we're all just old stock bulls in an animal transport, on their way to some kind of animal sanctuary before we cross the Jordan in a couple weeks or days.

―――

We meet outside Darmstadt on a race track for remote-control cars. I'm totally zoned out. Clueless, I climb out of the car like anyone else. Shove the mouth guard into my mouth and check out the opponents. It's like back in the day. Axel meets with the leader to the Frankfurt group. They briefly discuss the procedures, and the rest of us get ready. At least I can forget everything else for the few minutes that the match lasts. It rains without interruption, and the miniature track is fucking slick and makes us slide into each other like huge Godzilla monsters. We go down in flames. I'm able to take down a guy from Frankfurt but slip and catch a knee to the head. In the end, Axel and Tomek are the only ones on our side left standing, even though our opponents are able to keep at least five people on their feet. I inspect myself in a side mirror. There's already a large bump from the knee forming on my head. On the skin above my cheekbone, but the rain immediately washed away all the blood from my face. My forearms and the heels of my hands are scraped, and my pants are ripped at the knees. The bare lower layer of skin shimmers red through the holes. I need better protection in rainy weather. Despite everything. Despite the defeat. Despite the ride back before us and the bad-tempered thoughts of what you could have done better. And despite my burning knee. Despite everything, I feel significantly better than after my half-hour shower at the gym.

———

It'd been that way all day. Actually the whole week. The closer Manuela's moving day came. And now the time had simply come. She was supposed to start studying to become a teacher at the university in Göttingen. I'd even come along once when she was looking for an apartment. Just to get out of the house.

Hans yelled at Manuela that she could just commute. That she didn't have to move away. She could always take the train to the university. About a month ago she'd worked out the math for him, that it was complete bullshit, and how she'd have to get up before six every morning to get to class on time. But he hadn't been listening at all again, said it was pure chicanery, whatever he meant by that, and slammed her bedroom door behind him, mumbling to himself as he went past me. Barged into me. Pulled on his jacket. Opened the front door so he could finally go to the Olle Deele dive bar, but then immediately closed it again. Took off his jacket and tossed it in the darkest corner of the hallway and marched back into Manuela's room.

"Dad, I'll come every weekend to visit, if I can!"

"Sure, to visit your friends. Might as well stay over at their place, too! Don't need to show up around here anymore."

She started crying again. I was sitting in my doorway, Indian style, ball between my legs, and listening to the two of them. I'd probably be way too late to kick around. The others had probably been waiting for me for ages in Luthe, but I couldn't just up and leave now. I flicked boogers and must have retied my cleats ten times. Each time a little tighter. Then I loosened the laces and tied them again, this time a little less tight. Earlier, I'd thought it was halfway funny the way Hans got upset and screamed. He did it all the time. But normally things settled down once he'd finally gone off to his local dive bar again.

"I have my own life, Dad! I want to make something of myself," I heard Manuela's squeaky voice protesting from her room. Then a wardrobe door was slammed shut.

"Sure, great, the lady wants to have a career! And what about me? You'll leave me behind!"

I rolled my eyes and shook my head. Hans came back out, yelling loudly into the hallway, "Fucking hell!" and stopped in front of me. Little bubbles of spittle had caught on his porn stache.

"And you? What are you doing sitting here and staring around?"

Before I could think of a good answer, he turns on his heel and whips open Manuela's door, disappearing behind it.

"Dad, would you leave me alone for once? I'll be back in a couple days already."

"The hell you will, young lady. You don't need to think that you're welcome back here!"

In the corner of my eye, I saw something move and when I looked over, I was barely able to recognize Mie scampering into the kitchen and quietly pulling the door closed.

"Stupid slit-eye slut," I mumbled and in that very moment I meant it that way, because I couldn't stand the intruder. And I only said the thing with the slit-eyed slut to make the insult more powerful. I would never have said it to her face, or whoever. At least I hope.

"Could you knock it off once and for all!" Manuela screeched.

"Then take your shit out of your bag and stay here!"

Then my sister'd had enough. "Why? So that I can keep playing the role of the cheap cleaning lady?! You have Mie for that now!"

The unmistakable sound of a loud slap echoed across the tall walls of the hallway. Accompanied by a muffled scream. I was immediately on my feet, ran over, and pushed the door open. I only needed a fraction of a second to register that Manuela, holding her hands in front of her face, was lying with her upper body sprawled over her bed. I ran inside and pushed both hands against Hans's back. His head whipped back. He wasn't ready for it and completely lost his balance. He fell over, stumbling over Manuela's desk, and slammed into the table, which broke in the middle. Our father groaned and grabbed his head.

He looked at me and whispered, "You little piece of shit."

I stood up, taking a wide stance, clenching my fists, and waiting. I'd already caught up to him physically. What little he had on me had already dissipated after he'd gone on disability and even more with the hardcore boozing, and I'd quickly made progress because I had my uncle as the best example of what you can get done with a little power.

"Come on," I said to Manuela. "Let's wait for your taxi outside. I'll get your suitcase."

I took her hand and pulled her up. She wiped the tears from her cheekbones and fled past me, out of the room. I kept an eye on Hans and grabbed the suitcase. He just looked at me sulkily but didn't get up. If he'd wanted to, he surely could've still beat me up. But he didn't make the effort. At all. Except when it came to blowing his disability check at the bar. Walking backwards, I pulled the suitcase out of the room. Hans wiped the spots of enraged spittle from his mustache with the collar of his work sweater that bore the logo of his former employer. I turned around once I was sure he wouldn't jump up and grab my throat from behind. I still remember that I slammed a fist against the kitchen door in passing. Probably scared Mie half to death. Was in the heat of the moment, I guess. Manuela sat on the stoop before the front door and was blowing her nose. I dropped the suitcase and sat next to her and stared at the cobblestones.

"Thanks, Heiko," she said and tried to regain her composure.

I nodded and said, "Have fun at college."

Then the taxi came. The driver got out and stowed the suitcase in the trunk of his cream-colored car. I was glad Hans stayed inside and didn't come outside and make another scene. I raised my hand, said, see you soon, or something like that, but Manuela came over and hugged me. I don't know why, but somehow I sank into the embrace of my older sister. She pressed herself against me, and I felt her cheek on my shoulder. Her warm breath against the 96 logo of my jersey with the name Dworschak and the number 22 on the back. My gaze connected with that of the taxi driver, who leaned against the driver-side door with arms crossed and waited for our farewell to end. I didn't care if he saw me like that. Some stranger.

Then something slipped out of me: "I miss Mom too."

Manuela pushed me away, looked at me aghast, as if I'd just held out a dead rat.

She said, "What? No. I didn't mean that at all!"

Then the taxi driver looked away because it was none of his business. He climbed inside. Manuela opened the door, but then came back after all. I must have been standing there like a fucking idiot.

"Heiko, I'm sorry. I didn't want to—"

She didn't finish the sentence, looking past me. I turned around. The light in the hallway was on. And when I turned back toward her, she climbed into the taxi and waved. Then she drove off. Left me all alone. In the driveway. In this house with the cold, dark hallway. With the door to my room that I always locked, never left open. With Mie. And with our father.

———

Kai didn't have to beg me very long to join in the celebration, and I agreed to go clubbing with him. Even though I'd hoped a little that he'd take it easy at first. After all, he's still pretty worse for the wear, but of course that wasn't even a question for Kai. Goes whole hog. I wasn't allowed to help him with anything. For example, climbing stairs or getting up. Even though he pressed his lips together and held his breath in pain, he wouldn't accept help at all. He walked like he was walking on eggshells, and as if his upper legs had been replaced by tree trunks. But who cares, if one evening going out and drinking eases all that, then I'm definitely for it.

"I can ask if they have a bag for you here," I say. We sidle up to the bar and I order two beers. "We'll just cut out two holes for your eyes and that'll do."

He laughs derisively and says, "True beauty cannot be tarnished, dude."

He adjusts the bandage across the bridge of his nose. His battered face still has the color mixture of a fruit basket. The Band-Aids and the bandages don't make it much better, even if they cover the bulk of his face. He looks like he's escaped from a horror film, and I tell him he shouldn't get his hopes up too much he'll find something to screw right away, and that, first and foremost, today we're raising our glasses to the beginning of his recovery and his speedy return to the field.

"Ulf sends his greetings," he mentions in passing, and lifts his glass of beer to his mouth with a slight tremor.

The bass beats of a Eurodance mix boom across the dance floor, still sparsely occupied behind us.

I say, "Hmm," while the first sip is still running down my throat. I put it down, lick the suds from my upper lip, and ask when he saw him.

"He called this afternoon. They're in Cuxhaven for a couple days. Wanted to hear if my face was slowly growing together."

Kai turns around, leaning against the bar with his elbows, and briefly closes his eyes in pain. I also lean back, and together we watch the dancing dots of light on the waxed dance floor.

"You still hurt all over?" I ask without looking at him.

"Mhmmm," he hums in confirmation, "compressions, contusion. Busted rib. At some point I stopped listening."

He squints, looking at his glass from above and clucks, "Whatever. How was the match?"

I tell him about the Frankfurt tour. That the two skins from Langenhagen went along but didn't cause any trouble. That we may have had to concede a clear defeat, but nothing else was in the bag. And that I'm thinking of getting a pair of hiking boots with tread for rainy weather and wet footing, so I don't slip all the time and fall on my face.

"And anyway, it wasn't the same at all. Without you guys, it just doesn't rock. Just make sure that you get back in line soon, you fart."

He nods to himself, nipping at his beer, and, lost in thought, watches the DJ on the stage who's turning knobs on his mixing console as though bored. I look at him, and suddenly have to laugh.

Irritated, he looks at me and asks, "What's wrong?"

"You have your undershirt on wrong, boy."

Kai pulls his chin into his throat, looking down at himself. He reaches into his open shirt and pulls the label of the undershirt from the collar.

"Oh, crap. I was asking myself the whole time why my throat was itching so much."

He puts down his glass and say he's going to pop over to the toilet to pull the thing around right.

I order us two more overpriced kiddie beers and look at my smartphone to see when the draw is for the next round of the German Cup. Then I check my emails. Tomek had sent me a temporary link to the pics from the Frankfurt match. I download it and scroll through. Terrible quality. Shaky. Raindrops on the lens. You couldn't recognize next to nothing. I roll my eyes, drink the beer, and order myself one more. At some point, I look at the clock. Kai's been in the bathroom for almost fifteen minutes. I can't help thinking of Leipzig and how Jojo and I waited and Kai didn't come back, and an uncomfortable feeling gathers inside me. Such bullshit. We're here in Hannover. What could happen to him here? It's completely ridiculous to think stuff like that now. My phone rings. Kai's number.

"Dude, what's up? Did you fall in?"

I immediately notice from his voice that something's not right. It has such a disturbing tone: "Almost. But. Can you just come?"

I cross the dance floor and dodge a couple people jumping around who are clearly tripping and have their heads pointed toward the ceiling.

"Kai?" I call as I come into the bathroom.

The smell of piss is already pungent, even though it's still pretty early in the evening.

"Here," a voice responds, "second stall."

I want to push it open, but the door is locked.

"What's up?"

"Wait," he says, and I hear how his hand rubs over the surface of the door. "Wait a sec. Shit." Then the lock clicks open. "So, it's open."

He sits on the closed lid. Holds his iPhone with both hands and fidgets with his legs.

"Close the door, all right?"

I do it and ask, "What's up? Should I call a nurse who helps you wipe your ass?"

"Knock that shit off for a sec," he says and sucks the snot up his nose. Had he'd already done some blow?

Then he looks up at me. I can immediately see that something's not right. His eyes are tear-stained. The pupils dart from left to right but don't appear to look anywhere really, don't respond to my gaze although I'm standing right in front of him.

"I . . ." He swallows, his shoes tapping a fast rhythm on the tiles. "I can't see anything."

"What, you can't see anything?"

"Heiko! I. Can. Not. See."

His voice is unsteady, as if he'd just cried.

"What happened?"

I crouch down in front of him. His gaze briefly stays up. Then he appears to notice that I've changed my position, and sinks his head slightly. I wave my palm in front of his eyes.

"Knock that shit off," he says.

"So you do see something."

"Yeah." He exhales. Stutters. Searches for the right words. "No. A little. Changed my clothes, and then. First there was some kind of spark. From outside my field of vision. Thought at first I'd accidentally looked at the light too long. Went over to the sink and washed my eyes. Then I went over here because it didn't get any better." His throat produces gurgling sounds. "Then the curtain closed."

"The curtain?"

Because his jittering was also driving me completely crazy, I placed my hands on his knee and he finally went still.

"Dude!" he exclaims, and the moisture of tears spills over his cheeks. He wipes it away. "Just black. Like a black curtain. I can see almost nothing anymore. You get it now?"

"Fuck. Okay. Wait. I'll call an ambulance. Should I call an ambulance?"

I get up and open the door.

"Heiko?"

I turn around again. He looks to the ground, turning his smartphone in his hands and once more tapping with his feet.

"I'm fucking scared."

We waited in front of the club for the ambulance. He insisted I check if anyone was hanging around in the foyer because he didn't want anyone to see him that way. When the coast was clear, he walked arm in arm with me, and I led him to the door with small, retired-people steps. Then I placed him by the street on a box for road salt and went back inside to fetch our jackets.

After we'd explained as well as possible what was wrong and Kai lay down, the EMTs started dabbing at his eyes. Bandages were placed over them while we drove to the hospital. They had no idea what it could be, and said we should wait for what the doctors would say.

All of that took forever. I spent half the night waiting in front of various examination rooms. Every time a doctor went by, I jumped up expectantly, but most of them stared at me with a mix of boredom and exasperation and passed on. I planted myself back on my ass.

The double doors open. Kai is led out, a doctor and a nurse on either side. I explode out of the chair, go to them. Kai has two round white flaps of fabric over his eyes, attached with transparent adhesive strips. He looks like an enormous fly.

"Well? What's he got?"

The doctor, a blond guy, at most a couple years older than us, takes Kai's arm and says with a Dutch accent, "Are you a member of the family or a friend?"

"Bud," I answer.

He considers briefly, but then he remembers the meaning of the word. "Ah, okay. It looks like a detached retina. Caused by a rhegmatogene amotio retinae." I look at him with incomprehension. "Retinal tear. He's not just had it since today."

"Hell if I know?" I say and throw up my arms, "And what does that mean? Does he have to stay here?"

The doctor sighs and looks like he was forced to talk to a kid who's slow on the uptake, and says: "Take a look at your friend. Of course he has to stay here. Additional tests tomorrow. But I can tell you this much: because it was protracted and apparently not diagnosed or not diagnosed thoroughly enough, there's some danger of an irreparable loss of function for the areas affected. And in this case we're talking about damage on both sides. How could this not be recognized? I'm going to take another look in his file and perhaps speak with the colleagues who are responsible. A serious talk."

"And irreparable, that means . . ." I start, but for some reason my mouth just stays open instead of continuing talking.

"Heiko," Kai says wearily, "that means that I might stay blind."

His head hangs low, as if someone had shot a tranquilizing dart into his neck.

"Partially," the Dutch doctor chimes in once again. "At least there's the partial danger."

They lead him past me. I stand there. Have to process it first. When they reach the elevator and it opens up with a *ding*, I follow them.

"Irresponsible," the doctor mumbles when he hands Kai's arm over to me and remains in the hallway, "irresponsible."

———

"Heiko, you're getting on my nerves! No. All right. For real. Go home. I'll fend for myself. Thanks for everything you've taken care of and all, but hey, I really need some peace and quiet. You're driving yourself crazy. And me too."

That's how Kai sent me home. His parents sat on the other side of the room on two chairs a nurse had brought in. They'd been pretty restrained toward me recently, then took it up a notch and didn't look at me anymore. For them, I'm probably the embodiment of what happened to Kai. That's the only way I can explain it. When we were still small, and my parents and I still lived in Hannover, they lived right next door. Just as my mother often watched over me and Kai, they frequently took me in. They were something like my replacement parents those first years. Before we moved to Wunstorf. And now they ignored me like a piece of shit. But somehow I can't blame them. I should have never gone for Kai's stupid idea. Then we wouldn't have gone to Braunschweig. He wouldn't be sinking in a paper hospital bed like the picture of misery. Half-blind. Ulf would still be one of ours. I mean really. I wouldn't be out of favor with my uncle. All this fucked-up shit wouldn't have ever happened if I'd just said no.

I throw the tennis ball I'd found outside in the backyard and washed in the sink against the wall in my room. It bounces off and flies back to me in a precise arc. I throw it again. It bounces off. I catch it. Throw.

Arnim bellows up the staircase, "What the hell is all that noise?! I'm trying to call someone here!"

The dogs start barking.

He yells, "Shut up, you curs!"

They keep on barking. This time I didn't aim good enough. I don't catch it and it ricochets right into the ashtray beside me on the mattress. Cigarette butts and ashes made soggy by the still-moist tennis ball scattered over the sheet.

"Oh, shit!"

Arnim comes rumbling into the room. He has his phone in one hand and covers it with the other.

"Heiko. What's the ruckus about?! Trying to sort something out right now." He looks at my dirty bed. "You spilled something."

What, you don't say! He disappears back into the hallway. I can hear that he's speaking an odd mishmash out of German and English. Instead of scraping up the mess and putting it back in the ashtray, I pull the sheet off the mattress. Then I pull up on the four corners so that the ashes slip into the middle of the resulting bag and stuff the whole thing into the trash can.

I go downstairs. A stack of old papers that are usually on the table in the living room are spread out on the floor. In their place, there are three open envelopes and a fucking mound of cash. Hundred-euro bills of a poisonous green hue stacked, fanned out, and countless fifties are spread out on top. I can't even guess how much cash is lying there. The kitchen door leading to the yard squeaks, and I hear Arnim come in from outside.

"Yes. Yes. Ja. I will da sein. Okay. All klar. Ja, good-bye. Later."

I join Arnim in the kitchen. He glances at his watch, the leather strap digging into his thick arm. No wonder his hand is dark and swollen. He reaches for a greasy dishtowel covered with coffee stains and uses it to wipe his dome, as if he was polishing a bowling ball.

I swipe one of his coffin nails and take a seat next to him at the table.

"Hey, you showing your face again, my boy?" he says. His lungs produce an annoying whistle in his throat. He clears his throat. He sounds like an old moped.

"What's up? Who were you chattering with?"

"Well, I was just about to talk to you about that." He lays his knobby hands on the surface of the table, making the pack of cigarettes jump about an inch.

"Listen up. You have to help me. Those were the guuuys"—drawing out the 'i' sound—"who have the tiger for me. They drove all the way across Eurasia with the creature. Tomorrow morning, so somewhere between four and six, they're behind the border with the Polacks."

I flick the ash from my cigarette, look him in the eyes because now I'm completely serious, and say, "That pit and all wasn't just a fucking pipe dream. You're really getting a tiger, right?"

"You can bet your bony ass on that, my boy!" He makes such a satisfied face, as if he'd just received the gold medal in wrestling. "Finish that cig. Then it's time to go."

"Sure, have fun," I say, getting up, and want to retrieve a can from the fridge.

His hand wraps around my wrist. Tightens. I automatically flex my muscles, but I don't pull away.

"You're coming along, my boy. Doing a little tour. Doesn't work solo." He pulls something from beneath the table and says, "I let you live here, and I also want something in return."

He's lost it!

I say, "I already take care of the critters when you're traveling in Eastern Europe. That's compensation enough!"

He pulls his hand out more. Now I can recognize the black, ribbed transition from the grip to the barrel of a pistol. All these fucking years there was a gun under the table and I didn't catch that.

"You're coming along. No discussion. I like you, my boy, but don't ruin that for me. My dream. I won't let that slip through my fingers just because you don't want to play ball."

I can see he's actually serious. That he'd actually put that gun to my head and force me to get into his fucking car. I've always considered him fairly crazy. Even back when we met. He used to hang out in Midas, alone, and everyone kept out of his way. Then he sometimes came over to me and just started talking, probably because he needed someone to chat with. And I also thought his stories were interesting. Maybe completely wacky, but funny in a sick way. But now I recognize he's just a fucking lunatic. I could try to pull myself away now. Run up to my room, pack my stuff, and run off. If I'd even get that far. I feel dizzy. The kitchen starts to spin around me.

I say, "All right already. We'll drive there and pick up your fucking tiger."

He lets go of me. Says, "That's my boy. Good man."

I take out a beer and hand him one too. Then I take a seat.

"Don't expect I'll keep living here after that stunt," I say, with complete sobriety, opening the can and knocking back a long, deep sip.

"Only fair," he says, and raises his can.

I don't clink my can with his, just keep on drinking. He shrugs his shoulders, his old man chest briefly becoming visible under his oversized muscle shirt. He empties the can in two slugs. There's a dirty blue van in front of the house. Bremen plates. Who knows where he dug that up. The half-scratched-out vestiges of some carpentry company's logo can be seen on the side of the vehicle. Arnim bangs the hood. It sounds like he banged against a kettle.

"Off we go! Gonna get my tiger!" he shouts eagerly.

We climb inside. Slams it into reverse and turns the van around. We rumble out of the woods and over the field lane. Then we turn onto the country road toward the autobahn.

Arnim lets me take the wheel for about two hours. It's already dark. We're somewhere in the Brandenburg wasteland before Berlin and Potsdam. At the last rest stop, I stocked up with around twenty iced coffees and Red Bull cans. I knock back one after another, till I feel nauseous. Arnim is completely worked up and babbles away to himself nonstop.

"And where are we meeting with your tiger people?"

"They're Lebanese or some shit. Not tiger people." He coughs into his fist and wipes it on his seat. "In Landsberg on the River Warthe. A little town just behind the Polack border. Worked something out where we could meet. Always good to know people everywhere, I tell you. You still okay?"

"Yeah, sure," I say, "enough."

"Hey, Heiko. About what happened. Didn't mean it that way."

"Aha," I say, and focus on the illuminated surface of the road in front of us. Otherwise everything around us is pitch-black.

"I really appreciate it, you know, my boy? That you help an old warhorse like me fulfill his dream."

"That's all right," I say. "Let's just get this thing done."

I can't imagine how it'll work out, loading a fucking tiger like a load of kebab meat. But there's no going back now.

"Sure is crazy, the way life goes, right?"

"Mmmm," I mumble and roll down the window a crack. I think Arnim cut one.

"Back when I was doing my butcher apprenticeship. That I go to jail for murder. Man, oh man. Fucking vet," he mumbles, "and when ya get out. Then no one'll hire you, my boy. Be glad you've never done time. Well, did work out all right in the end. But that I'd end up doing something with live animals, I wouldn't have imagined it. Back then. And that I'd get rich, to boot."

"Rich?" I ask and look at him.

"Well, I mean for our kind, my boy. Ass-load of cash. Yep. But I'll tell you what: There's more than that. Than dough. Live your dreams. I read that somewhere, I think. It's true, for sure, yep."

"Sorry, Arnim, but could we maybe have a little bit of peace and quiet for a sec?"

He looks at me as if I'd insulted his mother. But then his face relaxes again.

"Come on, pull over. I'll take the wheel again. Way too wound up to sleep."

Crossing the border in the dark at Kustrin went off without a hitch. We didn't go through a check and didn't even see a cop car!

Three cheers for open borders! Even though I'd feel better if we'd get stopped on the way there. Better than on the way back, when we may not have a tiger in the tank but one in the back.

I ask myself what category of crime and severity of penalty there could be for smuggling exotic and dangerous animals.

Arnim doesn't know either. "Knock it off, my boy! I'm sure not going to the slammer again. There"—he points ahead vigorously—"that there is the city limits."

"Gorzów Wielkopolski," I read aloud.

Then we're past the sign.

"Hogwash, that's Landsberg on the Warthe," Arnim corrects me, giving the old German name. "Can't be much farther. So shut up."

The blurred silhouette of the city emerges from the blue morning light in front of us. Abandoned factories lie beneath a delicate shroud in front of crumbling, seemingly bombed-out facades. Like the fuzziness of a young animal. The icy blast of air whistles in through the open window like knife tips. I close it. Also to lock out the oppressive burned coal stench that seems to coat the entire region. The signs you see on the buildings and roadside give the impression they were put up decades ago and never replaced. They're usually only attached on two or three corners and flapping sluggishly in the wind. A muffled hum hangs in the air. As though the city was powered by a huge, subterranean generator. But for who? When I look at the houses, I can hardly imagine anyone living here. This is almost how I always pictured cities after bombing raids. Well, maybe that's a little worse. But I still get the feeling a nuclear power plant blew up here or something. Arnim steers us through the dead streets on a course I'm not following. The van pounds over the potholes, but the bumps are mostly absorbed by our well-cushioned seats. When I look around, I understand how the Polish hooligans can have blossomed into some of the most notorious in all of Europe. I mean Hannover isn't to be scoffed at, and I like its gray drabness. But this here. If you grow up in a city like this, then the rage starts embedding itself inside in your skull from day one. I decide suggesting a match against a Polish team back home. Surely, Tomek will still have some connections in his homeland and be able to set something up. Would just love to measure myself against the Poles. Maybe from Warsaw or Lodz. Or Poznan. So. Assuming everything gets right again. And also only once Kai is fit again. No point even mentioning it if I don't know the boys have my back. At least Kai and Jojo. Or maybe just Kai. Damn.

Arnim wakes me up. "There! There's the street. With the rental garages."

He went to the effort to lean over and poke me with an elbow.

"Yeah, sure, I see it. What kind of rental garages?"

"Belong to an old friend of mine. From the dog-fighting scene. He lives in Frankfurt on the River Oder, but he has some sticks in the fire here too. Even a stall full of top-notch bull terriers."

We idle along a street at walking speed, and it turns into sand. Halfway down, they must have run out of tar. Then we turn to the right, through a passage between two rows of garages. The grounds spread out behind that. It looks as expansive as five football fields. The lowest foundation walls of a factory complex protrude from the weeds that have overrun the place. The first tentative beams of light emerge from behind the surrounding buildings. There are two vehicles in the middle of this. A transporter, slightly smaller than ours. And a black Mercedes sedan. Both with tinted windows. I can only recognize the shape of heads inside. We stop a couple meters away from them. Arnim grabs my arm and pulls me a little closer.

"Listen up, Heiko. Those guys there are no jokers," needlessly pointing at the two vehicles. Sure, it's certainly supersmart to point a finger in their direction. Couldn't possibly be taken the wrong way. "You be sure to keep your trap shut and leave the talking to me."

"It's your thing anyway," I say.

He raises his finger in front of his face, just like my old-school principal.

"Hey! Shut up. Don't open your big mouth and no sudden moves. You might spook them. Then we'll load the tiger. And everyone can go their own way in peace. Got it?"

I nod. I can't resist rolling my eyes, but Arnim doesn't see it or just ignores it.

"And now pass me the gun from the glove compartment. But make sure to keep it down. They don't have to see it.

We stand next to each other. More out of habit, or because I think it seems appropriate in this fucked-up situation. And it's not because I'm freezing that I pull on my hoody and zip it to the top. So the collar goes over my mouth. The doors of the sedan open and three men climb out. Even from a mile away, you could sniff out that two of them are bodyguards. Both have roughly Axel's build. Or that of the Klitschkos. Well-trimmed bull necks in XXL bulky sweatshirts that barely conceal the mounds of muscle beneath. Professionally inscrutable facial expressions. Two things are immediately noticeable. The first is the guns they're holding very casually, as if they're everyday objects, beneath folded hands. The second is their round-framed glasses, which make them look like genetically modified nerds. Those glasses seem so false and completely wrong on these faces. Like a pigsty in a mosque. Or typical neo-Nazi Thor Steinar jackets on left-wing politicians. I don't know why, but the glasses make me even more nervous than the pistols. The other guy doesn't look any less strange. Bushy eyebrows like fat caterpillars mark the hard contours of a Slavic face. His slurry-black beard and hair tied in a ponytail don't fit him at all. As for his nationality, I wouldn't even know where to begin. He wears an Adidas warm-up jacket and a pair of puffy, gray jogging pants. Matched with highly polished patent-leather shoes. The two mutant nerds position themselves on either side of him. Arnim yanks the envelope stuffed with cash out of his pocket and goes over to him. I can recognize the silhouette of his gun at his waistband beneath the muscle shirt. It'd almost be smarter if I had it. But, on the other hand . . . I know how to shoot. Done it a couple times. But just for fun and at stationary objects. So maybe it's better after all that Arnim didn't entrust me with the gun. I watch as his counterpart comes slightly toward him. They shake hands. They're talking so quietly I don't catch the least suggestion of what the conversation's about. I can distinctly feel the glasses' gazes on my skin and try not to seem all too interested or even nervous. But my legs are starting to itch, from the feet up, so I'd like to shake them. Arnim holds out the envelope. The guy looks at it for a moment. Why doesn't he just take it? Arnim's hand is frozen in the air. Any moment I expect the guy to pull out a pistol and suddenly shoot Arnim in his paunch. Then he finally reaches for the money. I want to cough from the intense coal stench, but I pull myself together. The ponytail guy opens the envelope. It takes a while. My feet are falling asleep. Then he nods and pats Arnim on his relatively toddler-sized arms. He yells something in a language I can't identify, and suddenly the van's motor revs. Apparently, someone else is sitting in there. The vehicle turns till it's pointing its back end toward us. The animal dealer and Arnim shake hands one more time. Then he runs over. Even though it's walking speed, Arnim throws up his bent arms and takes awkward strides. By his standards, it's running.

"Heiko, back the wagon up," he says.

I climb behind the wheel, start the van, and turn it around. While backing up, I watch through the lowered windows, paying attention that no one gets run over. Not that they'd ever think of mowing us down just because I ran over the boss. I hear the cargo doors open, get out, and walk around the car. The fence ignores me completely. For them I'm probably just a henchman. Just like the two steam hammers wearing glasses. The doors of the other vehicles are opened. The heavy, sweet zoo smell of the animal lying there in the back immediately washes over me. The dealer says something to his bodyguards, and they slip out of their Golem posture, put away their guns, and climb into the back. The driver joins us, and installs a ramp. The bodyguards remove the cargo. A reverent gasp escapes from Arnim's mouth. I'm also at a loss for words. Zoo or no. This here is something very. Very! Different. In a huge crate, where you can see inside only through the bars, there's a monstrous big cat, unconscious. I'd put it at around a good three meters. It's lying there with its face on its front paws. Each one of them is as large as my face. It purrs slightly. Even if the purring is understated, and it sounds more like a highly tuned muscle car standing there with its motor running. Its ears flutter like an oversized species of butterfly, and the apparently painted stomach rises and falls calmly. Even the bodyguards seem not to be left cold by the critter, and touch the box only with extreme care. Their boss doesn't seem to give a rat's ass, 'cause twice he proudly pats the tiger box with his open hand after his henchmen have lugged it down the ramp. That makes my gonads retreat into the torso. But the tiger continues to doze undisturbed.

The dealer guy laughs and says in a heavy accent, "Sedated."

"What?" Arnim asks.

"Tranquilized," I say.

"Here." The dealer reaches into the trunk and hands Arnim a gun and a small box of cartridges.

"In two hours," he says and holds up two fingers, "is present."

"Huh, he'll be present?" Arnim asks skeptically as he accepts the gift.

"No. 'Present' means gift," I say.

The guy looks me up and down sinisterly. Probably doesn't please him when an employee opens his mouth. The four of us—Arnim, the stiffs with the glasses, and I—heave the tiger box up the ramp and into our van, having first opened the van doors. Puffy pants doesn't join in. He just looks at his sparkling Rolex and says, "Time. Now go."

I lock the doors, and Arnim and he shake hands once again.

"Have fun," he says, and the hair stands up on the back of my neck at the sight of his smile.

The others don't wait for us to fuck off, just get in their vehicles and peel out. Clods of dirt are thrown into the air as they speed off. We get in and, first of all, an anvil-sized weight falls from my heart. I'm familiar with this from matches. You can set the clock by it. But only now, in that minute, do I notice how amped I am from adrenaline.

"Good job, my boy," Arnim says, handing me the gun from his waistband, and turns the key. Careful not to touch the trigger, I return the pistol to the glove compartment.

We've been back over the border for less than an hour when we hear the scream of sirens from somewhere. I almost rip my arm out rolling down the window.

"Fuck, fuck, fuck, fuck, fuck!"

"Well, where are they? Where are the cops?" Arnim asks.

"No idea, man. I don't know!" I bark at him and lean out the window.

I look around. The hoodie flies up against the back of my head. I can't make out anything behind us. In front of us either, of course.

I fall back inside, saying, "Shit! Can't see nothing. Or are we just paranoid?"

"Nah, my boy. Now listen for once."

The van's motor is so loud it's hard to make out, much less locate another sound. It doesn't absolutely sound close, but the sirens are definitely not imaginary. The motor roars because Arnim's given it even more gas.

He prattles, "I'm not going back," repeating it again and again, till he can't say anything else.

"What are we gonna do now?" I ask, but don't get an answer because Arnim is almost biting the steering wheel. "Ah, fuck it!"

I unbuckle and check briefly to see if there are any obstacles or low-hanging signs ahead. Then I hold tight to the window and climb outside, twisting so I'm holding only onto the window going at full speed, with my crotch at roof level so I can better scope around. To our right, the landscape descends into a broad valley full of fields and a couple of villages. There are wooded areas scattered all around. The misty morning light and patches of fog that keep on drifting over obscure the view. But then I see a police car with flashing lights below us on the plain, and even with the rush of air, which whistles coldly in my ears, I can hear the howling sirens. I jump back inside the cab and tell Arnim the cops are heading parallel to us in the valley, but I can't tell whether they're chasing us or just happen to be nearby.

"Holy shit, my boy. They're gunning for us. I'm not going back in—"

"A deep rumble cuts off Arnim's tirade, and we simultaneously look back. Then we look at each other, eyes wide.

"Fuck, what now?!" I blurt. "The fucking tiger's awake! Arnim!"

"Shit, shit, shit. All right. Heiko. Now you take the gun and shoot a tranquilizer dart into his pelt. Don't dilly-dally!"

"What?! Have you totally lost your mind?" I scream, and I can't control my hands anymore, which are waving around my face in panic.

"Well, come on!" he bellows.

Somehow I manage to reach behind me with a wildly groping hand and retrieve the tranquilizer pistol. I tear open the box of the ammo, crack the barrel of the gun, and, shaking, slide a cartridge inside.

"And now?" I ask.

"Well, fire away, damn it!"

I turn and slide open the little window to the cargo bay. The animal stench fills my nostrils. I hastily begin to breathe through my mouth. Then I shove the gun barrel into the darkness where the menacing growl is coming from, amplified by the boxy cavern of the cargo bay. I try not to aim too high. Don't want to shoot the critter in the face, after all.

"Shoot!" Arnim screams into my ear.

"Yeah, sure," I stammer and pull the trigger. The tiger hisses and the rotten stench from its mouth wafts toward me.

"Well? And?" Arnim prods, and revs the motor again.

"What do I know? Can't see anything. Listen for a sec."

I stretch, pressing my ear up against the little window, and listen. It's still growling, but the sound is definitely getting weaker. There's silence again a short while later. I take a deep breath and ease back down. Arnim has the presence of mind to turn off the headlights. A narrow turn-off into the woods appears on the left ahead of us.

"In there!" I yell and point to the forest track.

Arnim yanks the wheel hard and for a millisecond I'm almost floating as the van's right wheels lift off the ground and we crash into the woods. Twigs and branches slap at the hood and windshield. I hold tight to the dashboard and door handle, but then the tires smash back onto the ground and we come to a stop. Surrounded by trees.

"Fuck!" I spit out. "God damn ass-fucked son of a bitch! I think I've pissed myself."

I touch my crotch. Everything dry. Wouldn't have taken much more, though.

"My, oh my," Arnim pants.

Then he drives us deeper into the woods. At this point, it doesn't fucking matter if we get lost. We park the van a little off the track where the trees get thicker, and climb out. I feel the simultaneous need to barf and pee. I calm myself by lighting up and letting myself fall back onto the wet, brown leaves beneath me.

———

What a screwed-up, shitty day! Erich Ribbeck's worthless national team had just lost 1–0 against the Brits, and I was tossing the sofa cushions across our living room while the television reporters together with the players were scrounging around for some sort of reason for the national team's failure. With the three beers I already had in my system, I didn't really care if I hit the tube . when I kicked the sneakers off my feet.

Manuela came running into the living room and screamed at me, "Heiko, are you retarded? You're making such a racket in here! I'm trying to study. Final exams. Hello-o-o-o!" she said, drawing out the last word. I hated her guts.

She pointed to the empty bottles of beer on the table: "And what's that about?"

I'd stolen the beer from Hans's stash.

"Dad'll kill you when he gets back!"

"Now calm down a little, Manuela! People drink a couple when they're watching football," I said and stuck out my tongue.

"You're fourteen, you little dick."

She slammed the door.

I yelled after her, "Hey! You don't say 'little' and 'dick' to a man. Hurts my feelings!"

I think I whipped out my pecker, grabbed it by my hand and used it to knock the beer bottle off the table, which fell onto the carpet with a thud.

"What's all this yelling?" All at once I heard my father's voice.

I put my little worm away. It wasn't any more than that, after all. Then I quickly gathered up the bottles and pushed them under the sofa. I forgot about them later. May still be under there today. He was standing there when I came into the hallway. Tanned the color of leather. Welf, his best friend, was there too. Two weeks earlier, the two of them had flown to Phuket last-minute. And by last-minute, I mean at least he told Manuela and me while he was packing his suitcase.

Welf bit the dust a couple of years later. Cirrhosis of the liver or something horrible like that. The thing just went out of service at some point, and he fell off his bar stool. Was years ahead of my father. Welf was already well lubricated when Hans had to retire and boozing slowly took the upper hand.

"Hey, Heiko," Hans said and grinned at me stupidly, "did you leave the house in one piece? Did you take good care of the pigeons?"

I nodded. Didn't say anything. Just stared at the two Asian women he and Welf were holding in their arms and who each had a big suitcase with an ugly flower pattern beside them. The whole hallway smelled of perfume.

"Come on," Welf said and snickered, "introduce the kids to their new mother."

"What? Oh, yeah."

Hans pushed the woman forward. She was half a head shorter than me. She looked at me, embarrassed, and held out the back of her hand. I looked at my father and then back at her.

"Now don't be impolite, boy. Shake the lady's hand. For heaven's sake."

I lifted my arm as if remote-controlled. My hand bumped against her and somehow we accomplished a bad imitation of a handshake. My open mouth went completely dry and sticky. Manuela jumped in front of me and bowed in front of the woman with the pitch-black hair that almost reached to her bottom.

"I'm Manuela."

The woman bowed as well and laughed stupidly.

"This is Mie," Hans said proudly, as if she was a vacation souvenir.

"My pleasure," Manuela said, and I would have liked to yank her braid.

"Well, come on into the sitting room," Hans said and winked with exaggeration. And continued with an exaggerated accent: "Coam in, pleez. Welf, you old dog, you knows where ze beer is at."

"Aye, aye," Welf joked, and saluted.

Then he pushed his wife into the sitting room and went to get some cans for himself and my father.

"I'll show you our bedroom, Mie. Our little bed cave."

She looked at him with a questioning gaze while he pushed her up the stairs before him. Every now and then he stopped and turned around to me. All at once, he made a completely different face.

"Bring the suitcases here. Pronto!"

I watched them climb the stairs and saw the disgusting sparkle in Hans's eyes and decided I'd never speak a single fucking word to that woman.

———

Over two weeks, and Kai's still stuck in the med school clinic. Indefinitely. For further examinations and treatment. If his eyes weren't taped shut, he'd almost look like a normal person. The swelling has largely gone down, and the wounds have healed. But the way he was, he looked like a dead stick figure with *X*s instead of eyes. I've made a tacit agreement with his parents. Which means I only go visit him when they're not there. They come every afternoon after work for one, two hours. I'm there almost every noon and in the evenings. Mondays and Thursdays I bring along the new *Kicker* magazine and read him articles aloud. I'm pretty good at it my now. I also read to him out of the latest issue of *11 Friends*, and he offers some commentary on each piece. Then we make our own sports talk show out of it, and I've never felt as well informed as now. I mean better than before, and not so focused on Hannover. A couple days ago, we discovered a reading plug-in for the internet browser. That way I don't have to talk until I'm blue in the face, and we can go to all kinds of internet sites and get the text read to us in a robot voice. That usually works fairly good, but sometimes it makes really funny mistakes. Mostly, when it comes to the names of foreign football players. We make a game of it by looking for profiles of the most exotic or weirdest player names. Then we have it read aloud by the laptop and laugh our asses off. Though unfortunately, that doesn't work all the time. Sometimes Kai's just Kai, like always. Makes jokes. Even about his injury. For instance, he thought about going to New York to hunt criminals while dressed in a red devil's superhero costume. And when the first movie interest came in, I should make sure that under no circumstances would he be played by Ben Affleck. But sometimes Kai isn't the Kai I know. Then he seems pressed down into his hospital bed by an invisible weight, and I can see how it churns inside him and the rows of his teeth grind behind his cheeks. The Dutch doctor is often there and every now and then even takes the time to sit down with us. He told us he comes from the same villages as the former Ajax and

Arsenal player Marc Overmars. I've already forgotten the name of the place. By now I even like the cheesy Dutch accent he speaks with. He's fairly reserved when it comes to prognoses. But he's also honest about not wanting to get our hopes up too soon. He also tried to explain all these surgeries and treatments they're trying on Kai, but at some point Kai said he couldn't remember all that crap anyway and it'd be better if they'd just do it and leave it at that.

"Do you know what I miss the most?"

"What?" I ask, but can already imagine the answer.

"Being on coke."

Crap! I'd guessed watching porn.

I pull off my shoes and sit on the other bed in the room, which has remained unoccupied the whole time. At least we've had our peace and quiet. We're watching the draw for the round of sixteen in the German Football Association Cup. I mean, I'm watching the draw. The sound on the television can't be turned on so the other resident patients aren't disturbed. Even if no one else is in the room. And sharing the earbuds was a little too stupid for us. So I'm watching the draw and commenting on it for Kai. Steffi Jones, the star goalie for the women's national team, has been hired as lady luck to pick the pairs of teams up from a jar in the tiny TV studio.

"FC Lucky Bayern," I say, "against Team 'Peg-Leg' Kiel."

The moderator takes the little ball with the club crest from Jones and makes it disappear into a tube. I picture a gigantic cellar under the studio building where all these little balls for the draw are sent with pneumatic dispatch and land on the pile of balls from years and decades past.

The draw continues and I comment, "The football division of Tennis Club Hamburg."

Even if we have good relations with the boys from Hamburg, I still can't stand their club.

"Matched against Naked Baghdad!"

"Oh, come on, Heiko, knock it off. Against who?" Kai asks while he tugs at his rustling bedding and holds his head toward the ceiling.

He looks a little like Stevie Wonder, and I ask myself if people automatically get that head posture when they're blind. Or temporarily blind, I mean.

"Against Cottbus," I correct myself.

"Dude, hopefully Hamburg will knock the East Bloc bitches out of it," he says. It sounds deadly serious somehow, too serious.

"Yeah," I say, "and hopefully they'll fling feces at them. Next match . . ."

Steffi Jones runs her hand around in the bowl as if she were making cake dough or something with it. Then she removes the next ball and gives it to the moderator. He opens it, leaving two halves. He tosses the lid into another bowl and holds up the half with the club crest.

I swallow and say, "Hannover 96." We simultaneously sit up a little in the beds. There are still some attractive teams in the bowl. Jones picks the next ball. Passes it on. It's opened. Lid gone. The moderator looks at the logo and pulls up his lower lip in appreciation, which makes his chin protrude slightly. Now, hold the thing up to the camera already! "Against," I start, and then I briefly catch my breath. I stare at the television, mesmerized. It can't be true! They made a mistake, or I didn't see it right, or it's another club. The computer graphics for the selected pair appear onscreen. In fact!

"Against? Against who, Heiko?" Kai presses me.

I let the two words melt on my tongue slowly and with pleasure: "Eintracht. Braunschweig."

"If this is just shitting me again, Heiko, then—"

"No, really!" I yell, and choke on my own spit. Two messages, one right after the other on my phone. The first from Ulf: "Oh my God! Epic!"

The second from Jojo: "You watching this???"

I can't believe it. I really have to control myself so I don't suddenly scream and tear up the bedding for joy. Then I look over at Kai and the euphoria sticks in my throat like a fat, slimy toad. He's slipped from his upright position back onto the bed. Lying on his side. His back to me. My palms radiate sweat. My neck goes cold, as if there was a draft right behind me. I bite my tongue, till the stabbing pain becomes a feeling of numbness. That lizard is gonna suffer so bad!

———

I didn't catch a wink of sleep all night. Then I drove my car to Wunstorf and sat in front of Yvonne's building till morning, watching her shadow move across the sheet covering her window. At some point the light went out. I was completely awake and went over a thousand things in my head. Made plans for how I'd make the guys from Braunschweig pay. Considered whether I should talk it over with my uncle this time or just fuck it and continue doing my own thing. I smoke till I feel sick. I go to the all-night market at the gas station and drink till morning light.

Then I helped Arnim feed the tiger. It seems to have slowly gotten used to its pit. Or maybe just resigned to its fate. At any rate, it doesn't even try to jump out to tear Arnim to pieces. You couldn't blame it. But it slips down the aluminum walls anyway. Animals can get tired of that pretty quickly. At least Arnim's having fun. He's in the basement almost all day preparing food for his favorite. He's reactivated his rusty butcher skills and hacks away happily, whistling to himself. The stench of blood from the basement has already spread over the entire ground floor. Since the tiger's been there, Poborsky and Bigfoot have grown unusually quiet. They probably sense something bad for both of them. I hope Arnim doesn't get the idea of having a test run with the tiger before the next fights. I haven't told anyone about all of this. Not even Kai. I'm saving it for a day when he's slipped back into himself and his thoughts and we're sitting across from each other in the clinic cafeteria and I can't think of anything else. I climb into the car and slam it into reverse, turning in front of the house. I hope this isn't the day.

Kai holds onto my bicep with one hand. We're strolling a few rounds through the clinic park. Jojo and Ulf are there too. Jojo's running laps around me and Kai the whole time. His arms dart out repeatedly because he's afraid Kai could stumble and fall somehow. Then he'd be there to catch him like a building-block tower that's falling over.

"Jojo, can you knock it off now? You're getting on my nerves! I've got him."

Kai's hair has never been this long. It falls in long strands over the sides of his head. The undercut is gone and has slowly grown out. Although I've brought along my clippers, Kai says it doesn't matter what he looks like here in the hospital. He goes step by step. Completely shaky. I ask myself how quickly muscles weaken when you mostly lie around for weeks, even if it's only one or two.

Maybe it's not even the muscles. It can't go that fast, anyway. Most of all, he's probably afraid the lights will go out any second or something. He also told me once he still hasn't gotten used to the fact that he'll have next to no spatial perception with just the one halfway good eye. Might sound harsh, but still. I can hardly stand watching. I'd like to let him slip from my arm, give him a little shove, and say you'll manage, you're no goddamn handicapped person. But I'm afraid he might misunderstand me.

"That sure is a fucking awesome early Christmas present," Ulf says, referring to the Cup match on December 18.

"Should I order tickets?" Jojo asks and passes out a round of cigarettes. He lights the one for Kai himself and carefully places it in Kai's mouth, as if he were feeding a baby. I want to tell him that Kai does in fact have his own mouth and hands he could use to light his own fucking cigarette, but then I let him do it.

Instead, I answer, "We'll probably have something else to do that day than sitting on our asses and watching the game."

"What do you mean?" Jojo asks, so slow on the uptake, as if we'd just met.

"You pulling my leg, Jojo? The time is ripe for those bastards."

"So you don't even want to watch the game?" Ulf asks.

"If it can be organized, sure. At Timpen or something, but it'd really be stupid to go to the stadium and wait to be escorted out by the cops at some point. The entire opportunity to start something would be lost."

Ulf groans in annoyance and says curtly: "Just knock it off, Heiko."

I suddenly stop, causing Kai to stumble over his own feet. Of course, I catch him. But Jojo's right there and stretches out his arms.

I look at Ulf and say, "I'll knock *them* on their asses. The fuckers should finally get what they deserve! And even if I have to do it alone. Don't give a fuck."

"You're just making it worse," he says, but I wave him off. Try to simply wipe away his objections.

"No fucking way, Ulf. And no one can talk me out of it," I say and feel my throat swelling closed.

Jojo asks if I've already discussed it with Axel.

"Nope. Don't know yet," I say, "like I already said. Worst-case scenario, I'll go it alone. If you guys aren't behind me . . ."

Now Ulf's standing in front of me at full stature and casting a shadow over me.

"You actually know what you're saying? You want to end up like Kai?"

He points to Kai. I look over. His head is dangling from his neck. He doesn't say anything.

"Have you given a little, even the slightest thought to how all this might end?"

I take a step toward him, leaving only a finger's breadth between our faces.

"I. Don't. Give. A. Shit," I spit out and step back a little. "You have your family, your house, your white fucking picket fence. You all have something you can look forward to at the end of the day." I can't stop, even if it'd be better if I did. Instead, I keep on barking: "Jojo's seeing this coaching thing through, and when Kai's healthy again, he'll finish his studies and get a well-paid job." I don't want to talk about them as if they weren't there, but I'm just not able to hold back. "I've got nothing"—I form a circle with my fingers—"nothing. This here," drawing a circle around all of us in the air, "is what I have. Nothing more. I don't complain about it. And you know why? Because I live for this. Because I stand for it, and I admit it. If you don't get that, then you're a lost cause for me, Ulf. Then all of this, all those years were just a fucking game for you."

I take Kai's hand off my arm and guide it to Jojo, who stares at me, stunned, and takes Kai's hand. I slam Ulf with my shoulder as I pass by. Of course he doesn't move.

"You actually know how pathetic you are?" he calls after me.

I turn my upper body, flip him off, and scream, "Fuck you, Ulf, for real. Go fuck yourself!"

———

I still remember how I sat on Mom's suitcase. Legs extended, I kicked the tips of my new football shoes against each other, and was already looking forward to showing them off to the others while kicking the ball around. The door separating the front door and the hallway was open. Mom maneuvered herself into her high heels. She even smiled. I'd come out of my room when she pulled the heavy suitcase behind her down the stairs and it bumped down every step. She didn't answer my question about what she was doing. Where she was going. She just grinned at me. Held my head and gave me a kiss to my forehead that I wiped off, whining, "Mamaaaa," in disgust. Then she walked past me. She smelled strongly of perfume and left a trail of flowery scent behind her like a bridal train. I followed her forward. Manuela stood in the open sitting room doorway and pressed against the frame. She had that ugly black neckband that was so tight around her neck and that all the girls were wearing back then. It made them look like their head was sewn onto their neck. Just like Frankenstein's monster. She had her arm wrapped around her skinny upper body and was sulking. Pouting her lips. Today you'd probably call it a duckface. At the time, I didn't understand why she was pouting. Was just a stupid little twerp.

I heard a car's motor. Groaning, Mom carried the suitcase to the front door and opened it. Then she retrieved a second bag and set it next to the first. They were still open. Clothing stuck out of the top. She waved someone into the driveway. Probably the driver of the car. Then she came over to me, bent over with squeezed together, bare knees poking out from under her skirt. She hugged me. I absolutely didn't know what to do about it, and so I let it wash over me.

With her voice—unusually deep and scratchy for a woman— she said, "Take it easy, little Heiko. Love you."

She gave me another kiss to the forehead. I didn't wipe it away. When she stood up, she glanced briefly at the glass cabinet next to the wall with her ugly figurines. She briefly considered it and said, "Oh, whatever." Then she turned to Manuela, who looked at her grumpily. Before Mom had reached her, Manuela retreated to the sitting room and slammed the door, making me jump. Mom sighed. Then she smiled again and waved at me, although she walked past very close. A man was taking the bags from the stoop by the front door and carrying them to the car. She grabbed the door, waving once more. Threw me a kiss. Then she closed the door. I heard the car doors slam and the car drove off. I stood in the hallway and froze. I went into the sitting room. Manuela had kneeled down on the old armchair in front of the window and was looking out. It'd been her favorite chair when it was still Grandpa's house. That's always where he'd sat with his beer. Or with his cup of coffee, if it was early in the morning. I grabbed the remote control, threw myself on the sofa, and turned on my cartoon about a Japanese school football team. I liked the cool, long-haired adversary of the main character much more because he wasn't so nice and kind. Never took any shit. From the grown-ups either. And because he could kick so hard. He always had the sleeves of his dark-blue jersey rolled up. I lounged around. Manuela briefly glanced over at me.

"You're so stupid," she said.

But I hadn't done a thing. Hadn't bugged her. Then she turned back toward the window. I didn't understand a thing.

———

I rush down the stairs. Almost fall on my face. Then I knock open the screen door, which bangs against the outside of the house and hangs crooked because a hinge has come loose. The bell over the door rings hollow. I quickly reach up to muffle the sound.

"What are you doing here?" I call out as Manuela and Andreas are just climbing out of their car. They look at each other in astonishment, as if they've never seen such a run-down house in all their lives. Especially Andreas can hardy conceal his opinion and lifts his upper lip with such disgust, it's as if Arnim's house were a dead, rotting whale. You ain't seen nothing, you bastard. I walk toward them. The gravel in front of the house keeps jabbing the soles of my bare feet. I ask them again what they're here for, and my sister has difficulty prying her gaze from the weathered, mold-green wooden siding of the house.

"I thought I'd been completely clear when I said that no one can just show up here!"

Without looking at me, Andreas says, "We didn't really choose to come here."

He's smartly tucked his ironed shirt with the fine, light-blue–checkered pattern into his beige pants. He plucks at the obviously extra-starched collar. Then his hair, formed with gel into an understated spiky peak, probably thinking it's hip or something. Though he looks more like a child that's been spiffed up for his church confirmation. Not to mention his condescending attitude. All of this disgusts me incredibly. I briefly consider asking them in and at least introducing Poborsky and Bigfoot. Give that fancy ape a taste of real life. Not the sheltered, well-heeled home he considers to be real life. But I can't do that. Manuela would probably lose the last shimmer of understanding for me, and her husband would call the cops, guaranteed.

"I've been trying to reach you for days, Heiko," says Manuela.

She closes the space between us and takes my hands into hers. There are bags like overripe fruit under the glasses she keeps on wearing even though she doesn't need them. Her hairline is reddened. She tends to have eczema when she's under stress. She had it frequently when we stilled lived at home.

"I turned off my phone," I say, frankly.

"Can we come inside? I'd like to sit down."

"That's not possible," I say because I can't come up with a plausible excuse so fast, "you can't come inside."

"Why not?" Andreas asks and makes a face.

Because it stinks inside of animal blood and bird droppings. Because of chemical potions and tranquilizing darts. Because there are two fighting dogs and a fucking tiger living in the backyard. Because Arnim flips out if he comes home and sees strangers in his house.

"Because it's not possible! Enough said," I say.

I have no clue where Arnim's off to again and when he'll come back. I have to get rid of them! As quickly as possible.

"We have to talk, Heiko," Manuela says.

Her voice sounds brittle. Like just before losing consciousness. There's thunder in the distance. I can see a storm brewing, past her hair, through the tips of the trees.

I hold up two fingers as a peace sign and say, "Two minutes. On the porch."

I try to give my face an incredible resolve. We walk over to the steps of the porch.

I retrieve a cushion from a chair and place it on the stairs for Manuela. Doesn't make any difference, because the cushion is dirty too and covered in dark stains. But the gesture counts. We sit down next to each other. Andreas remains standing in front of us with his arms crossed, scanning the porch derisively. I try to repress the urge to smack him. It smells like rain.

"Well, what's up?" I ask.

Manuela looks at Andreas. Then me. She gulps.

"Dad. He fell down the stairs a couple of days ago. He's in the hospital with a hip fracture."

"Aha," I say.

I can't think of anything else to say, and for some reason I'm too exhausted to simulate a different reaction. Manuela looks at me with incomprehension.

"Did you understand what I said, Heiko?"

"Yeah. Broken hip. Isn't that something senior citizens get usually?"

"Unfortunately, anyone can suffer a hip fracture," Andreas says in a pedagogical tone.

I pull my cigarettes from the pocket of my jogging suit and light one up. I feel Manuela's gaze resting on me as I smoke. She still appears to be waiting for more of a reaction from me.

"Heiko . . ."

"Drop it, dear. He doesn't give a darn," Andreas groans. I really have to try hard to ignore him. Otherwise he'll catch one from me.

"Was he shitfaced again?"

"Is that all you can think of?" Manuela asks, and moves a bit away from me.

"What do you want from me?" I ask, my voice rising. "Am I supposed to cry a little? Yell at the sky: how in the world could that happen?"

"Heiko!" Her voice cracks in accusation, as if I'd farted at a funeral.

I scrape the ashes from the tip of my cigarette by rotating it on the stair step beneath me, and say they have to go now.

Manuela starts to sob quietly. I turn my head away in annoyance and lift myself up.

"How can you be this way?"

"How can *I* be this way?" I repeat, screaming at her. "Do you suffer from loss of memory? Did you forget what happened a month ago? How you sat in his kitchen, crying?!"

I was too loud. The dogs are barking from out back. Shit! Andreas takes a step forward. His facial features are furrowed by fear.

"What is that?" he asks harshly.

"What could it be?! Those are dogs."

A growling can be heard between the barks. Oh God, please let that be thunder. But I picture the tiger is jumping from its darkened pit and touching the wooden lid with its paws.

"I think we'd better go now," Andreas says and pulls out his car keys, jangling.

"No, wait," Manuela says. She's clearly struggling to keep her composure, and manages to mask the quavering of her voice beneath firmness. "Heiko, I know that everything is going terribly wrong, but we're a family. Your father is in the hospital. And I would like . . . No, I demand that you visit him at least once. He's so stubborn. We have to make the first step. And you in particular. If not for his sake, then do it for me."

So she's making a big scene of this now. I'm just about to say no and send her away. Then I would finally have my peace and quiet. Wouldn't have to see them. But the image in my mind's eye, of how she's sitting in the kitchen and crying while Hans is raging in the bedroom, is suddenly covered over by other images. From before. When we were younger. And how she told Hans he should leave me alone. How she made me an extra evening meal after school—whether I was home yet or not—because I had silently refused to even touch Mie's food. How she came into my room and asked if I had dirty clothes that needed to be washed. These are actually completely irrelevant things, but somehow they mean more to me. My head becomes clear and bright for a second. This means that there's someone I mean something to. Not because she wanted it that way or because she considers me so sympathetic. We're fundamentally different people. Instead, for the simple reason that I'm her brother. And because it's easy for her. Maybe even as easy as always forgiving our father for his constant fuckups. Overlooking them.

"Sure," I say, "I'll visit him when I'm ready. But you really have to go now."

She hugs me good-bye. Andreas is sitting behind the wheel, motor running. He honks. Then she starts to get in.

"Tell Damian hi from me," I say and pat her on the back.

"He's already asked about you. Kicks your ball around the garden every spare minute."

"That's fabulous," I say and gently push her away.

———

A single topic has dominated all the conversations at Wotan Boxing Gym since the German Cup draw: the game against Braunschweig. Whether hooligan, martial artist, biker, bouncer, or right-wing extremist. Everyone is only talking about the match of the year. Suddenly, everyone's an expert and offering analysis. Not just about the football match as such. Of course, much of the focus is on the trappings. The historic significance. That the last time they met, in 2003, it'd also been a Cup match and 96 had been sent home without a whimper with a 0–2 result is something everyone seems to have repressed.

The last couple of weeks haven't been easy for the gym. After the raid, which everyone heard about, naturally, most of the customers stayed away to be on the safe side. Something resembling normal returned only slowly. Unfortunately, the right-wing guys were the first to come back on a regular basis. But since then, the Angels have come back, and Gaul has resumed his anabolic business in the locker-room. Axel now has a visit almost every day from the bikers, who come into his office without bidding and without knocking. He doesn't make them go back out and knock, "as you're supposed to do." I can hear sharp words now and then when I go by. Axel snorts more than ever. Talks to himself the whole time while he's stomping through the rooms. His normally reddish, seemingly enflamed skin color is duller than usual.

I'm standing at the back door when he pokes his blocky head out the office door and bellows my name without realizing I'm a couple meters down the hall.

"Come over here. Need to help me with something."

I carefully step on the tip of a cigarette I'd just lit and put it back in the pack so I can go on smoking it later. When I enter his office, he's standing on top of his massive desk, in his socks. His head disappears into the ceiling. He's removed one of the drop-down ceiling tiles from its frame.

"Need you to hand a couple of things to me here." His voice is muffled from up there, as if coming from another room.

He points a finger at the new stack of paper with lists that's lying on the desktop next to his feet.

"Don't mess them up!" he says threateningly as I'm passing him stack after stack.

He accepts them and pushes them around in the dead space. You can hear the dry sliding of the paper over the ceiling panels. A fine cloud of dust floats down. I'm supposed to hand him a bag from a desk drawer. The translucent baggie is three-quarters full of pills. Beneath it in the drawer is a bush knife at least eight inches long with a black rubber handle. The blade side sparkles sharply. The other is equipped with nasty teeth. After stowing the bag in the ceiling, he retrieves the missing tile from somewhere and maneuvers it into the appropriate spot.

I hold out my hand to help him climb down from the table, but he ignores it and climbs down on his own, groaning. We inspect the ceiling. Looks like before. I need to take a seat.

"December 18th," he says, and crosses his hands like a boss, cracking his neck, left and right.

"Braunschweig," I say, taking his pass. He nods and says, "Exactly. The preparations are already underway. As soon as the police measures are available. My friend at the station will let me know."

"Preparations?" I ask, sitting up on the edge of the chair. I can hardly conceal my curiosity.

"This is the big show, Heiko. The chance for revenge. And the chance to finally put Hannover on the map. Even more important after our defeat in Frankfurt. And after your . . . unfortunate stunt."

He doesn't blink. Watches my reaction very carefully. I don't let anything show.

"Who knows when a chance like this will present itself again. We have to take advantage." He clenches a fist and again looks like a greasy neo-Nazi politician raging against the foreigners stealing our jobs and wanting to fuck our women. "We have to do something really big. Completely in keeping with tradition."

He takes on a dreamy look, which on Axel seems more like mental illness.

"What are you thinking of?" I ask, making an effort to sound neutral, as if I didn't care about all that and my interest was only slightly aroused.

"Match on the day of the game. Not far from the stadium, preferably. Like it used to be. Before cameras, directional microphones, and surveillance systems were installed. It can't be in the stadium itself, we shouldn't kid ourselves. But beyond the immediate police radar. Somewhere in the city center."

"How about the Ihme complex?" I blurt out.

He points his sausage-sized index finger at me, smiles, and says, "That's my nephew. That's why I haven't chucked him on his ear. When you have ideas, Heiko. You're a visionary. Just like your uncle. I'll suggest that right away."

"What do you mean, suggest? To who?"

He leans back. His gaze has drifted off away from me and through the room. He rocks back and forth on his chair.

"I'm expecting visitors soon. They should show up here any minute. Sent Tomek to pick them up and lead them here."

On command, someone knocks on the door. Axel grins. He straightens his T-shirt and clears his throat.

"Come in," he says.

Tomek comes into the office. He's followed by four thick-necked, wide-shouldered guys. They smile as if they'd just shared a joke in the hallway and it was still being digested. Two of them are wearing Stone Island canvas jackets. Another a washed-out Lonsdale jacket. The last one, with a severe blond part, has a hoodie with old German script on it. Axel rises and shakes hands with each of them, saying: "Gentlemen. Nice that you were able to arrange it."

"It's an important occasion," says the guy with the part. From the roots, I can see the hair is just dyed. A fucking fake Aryan. The only thing missing is he's not wearing blue contact lenses.

"Heiko, make some space," Axel says.

I get up and give one of them my chair. He grins at me as if I'd had a big fat booger hanging from my nose that he doesn't want to draw to my attention out of consideration. He slips past me, almost touching. He stinks from his mouth like a polecat's ass.

"Is that him?" he asks one of the others and nods in my direction.

Confusion. I look at my uncle, who once again clears his throat.

"That's him."

All eyes are fixed on me and scan me from head to toe.

"And the other one?" the stinking mouth says and lights a cigarette without asking.

Axel looks at him, grinding his teeth. I can see it churning inside him and he'd like to bash his face in for it. And I hope he does. But Axel quickly opens a desk drawer and pulls out a glass ashtray he deposits in from of him. The others immediately start to puff, filling the small office with smoke in no time.

"The other one is in the hospital," Axel says and I think I noticed him darting a glance at me.

They grunt. It's what it would sound like if pigs could laugh.

"Then let's not waste any time wrapping up this deal so we can finally return to Braunschweig," says the guy who's sitting in my spot and adjusting his Stone Island jacket like a business suit.

"Heiko. Please," Axel says and makes a slow hand motion, as if we were here in the Sports Center broadcast studio and he's moderating the transition to the next guest.

"What?" I ask.

"Apologize."

My stomach contracts, as if anticipating a punch to the pit of my gut.

I ask what I should apologize for.

My uncle groans, says, "You know what for. Come on."

I don't say anything. I just look at him. My arms stiffen into ice picks at the sides of my body and prevent any further blood flow to my fists. The guys from Braunschweig are waiting. They have patience now, the stupid puddles of piss. Axel pushes off his chair, grabs me by the arm, and turns to his shitty guests, saying, "Excuse us for a sec."

He closes the door behind us. I hear them grunting with laughter. Axel pushes me against the office door. He's almost touching the tip of his nose to mine in an Eskimo kiss.

"You're gonna apologize right now for your attack on one of their people."

"I'm not doing shit."

"Heiko, listen up for a sec." His breath smells limy. Probably rubbed some leftover coke onto his gums. "I don't give a shit if you mean it, but you're going in there right now and saying you're sorry. So that we can proceed."

"What they did to Kai—"

"What they did, what they did," he mimics, hissing at me, "doesn't interest me one damn bit! If I tell you to, you do it!"

He shoves me against the door and scoots me aside. Then he pushes me into the room, walks past, and sits down in his manager's chair. Everyone has turned around. Tomek is standing between them like something foreign. He looks at me. In commiseration. But with rage in his eyes. I can see clearly that he dislikes the taste of this as much as I do. I'd like to yell at him that he should grab the knife from the drawer and throw it to me so I can put an end to these dirty fuckers. Maybe they were in Leipzig. Beating and kicking Kai. Made him half-blind. The image of ripping open their throats with the rough side of the knife sends a pleasant, warm feeling down my spine. Axel stares at me. His neck muscles are tense, making him look like wires have been run beneath his skin.

I say it. I actually say it. Say, "Sorry." And I've never hated myself more than in that brief moment. Like a dirty traitor. One like my uncle. A dirty, hypocritical, fucking traitor. I haven't even completely finished saying the word when I push open the door and escape to the hallway. I run to the toilets. Have the feeling I need to barf. Simply vomit everything out. Only sour bile comes up, and I pant and scream into the bowl so my own gagging is thrown back into my ears by the porcelain.

———

Relegation to the second league. One of the most infamous games in our history. Uncle Axel had gotten our mothers' permission to bring Kai and me along, saying he'd take good care of us and nothing would happen.

We two twerps, wearing our 96 scarves, were standing among the men in the away side's section. The songs roared around us, and the fans threw their fists in the air, and we jumped around on the perimeter fence like we were on fire. Things were going on like in a wave pool, and the sluggish masses of Hannover fans repeatedly washed against the lateral fences separating us from the other spectators. Monkey sounds rang out across the field of play. Every time our players Addo and Asamoah had the ball. I asked my uncle why they did that, and he said because they were Negros, and I didn't have the slightest notion what that meant. And I jumped on the fence, Kai along with me, and we hoped our curses reached the Cottbus fan section. No one was allowed to insult Otto and Gerald. Regardless of how! They were our best. Playmakers and goal getters. Assured Hannover's offensive attack. But we weren't loud enough. Our flat boyish voices drowned out in our own crowd's yells. A wall of faceless policemen behind heavy riot helmets set up in front of us, but we didn't care. Even back then, I'd learned there's no backing down. Even when the first beer cups filled with gravel flew into our section and a couple people next to us hit the ground, bleeding. Here in the Cottbus Stadium of Friendship, you get stones and shit thrown at you. Axel, Tomek, and Hinkel formed a circle around us. Protected us from the projectiles next to the fence. I tried to look through their bodies. Those hit were helped up. Got something to drink. They wiped the blood away or held tissues to the gaping wounds till the fabric itself stuck to them and their hands were freed to beat their fists in the air.

The game would be over soon. The score was 1–1, and 96 was gaining the upper hand. When the floodlights went out and the corner flags were cloaked in darkness. Game put on hold. The evening air vibrated with thousands of voices that were screaming their heads off and driving me crazy. But in a good way. So I would have liked nothing more than to take the monkey sounds as a reason to race up the fence, perch on top of it, and scream like mad. Scream Hannover. 96.

From then on, everything went wrong on the field. And when the lights went back on but only on one side, and Sievers, our keeper, was blinded, the fan section crowed in unison, "Fixed!" And the team's rhythm was thrown off. Cottbus got back into the game and the visitors' section boiled over. We watched as our own people destroyed a sausage stand, and a charcoal grill was knocked over. And the whole thing burned like an oversized torch in the partially darkened Stadium of Friendship. And Kai and I stood there shoulder to shoulder and cheered them on, and the light of the flames flickered against our bared teeth, and Tomek and Hinkel and Töller and my uncle brawled with the police. They beat down on us with batons, but we didn't budge. Only had our own fists. And hit back. And Kai and I looked at each other and he thought the same thing as me and we swore to ourselves we'd never budge and we'd stand there some day. In the front row. And we sealed our oath with a handshake.

———

I can barely look Kai in the eye. Can't anyway, because they're still glued shut. So it's not even possible. But even looking at him is hard for me after my denial. That'll change after the match on the 18th. Once the score has been settled. Kai's eyes will heal completely and we'll be able to get back to normal. Everything like it was before.

Kai gets up from his bed and says something. I'm scrolling through the pictures I shot with my smartphone of the winding passages and alleys in the Ihme complex. It's the perfect place for a match in the city. Enough space and room for movement for a clash between forty, maybe even sixty people. And the labyrinth-like structure and visual cover of the residential towers and empty shops offer enough hiding places to carry out the whole thing before the police force us to break it off prematurely. If it even got that far. And even if the cops do catch wind of it in time, the complex offers more than enough escape routes. But because of the low level of occupancy, it's more likely we'll be sitting in Timpen long before that and raising our glasses to our victory before a single rank-and-file cop shows up.

Kai works his way to the foot-end of his bed, expertly reaching for the other bed and pushing his way past it. Extends his hand and touches the corner of the wall behind which the room's small toilet is located. He's mastered the route by now and you don't have to lead him by the arm like a resident at an old folks' home.

He leaves the door open while he takes a piss. From where I'm sitting, I can only see his feet, over which his lowered boxers are draped. Then the flush. He washes his hands and comes out.

"Did you hear?" he asks.

I look up from my phone and say, "What? Yeah. No."

"I said that I'm thinking of doing an internship abroad," he says, "for a semester. Or maybe two."

Without looking, I turn off the phone and put it away.

"And where?" I ask, although the "where" sounds furious.

"London. One of the advisors for my masters' program has a friend at Deutsche Bank. Already said that he'd recommend me."

"London in England?"

Kai feels the dry rustling of the sheets and sits down with a groan. That's one of the annoying characteristics of hospitals. All of a sudden, everybody mutates into the worst kind of handicapped people, moaning and groaning with every move. I mean, sure, his body's probably still fucked up, but it'll heal again. The eyes are what we have to be most worried about.

His face twists in scorn and says, "Nah, London in Rhineland-Palatinate. Of course England, you idiot." A young Turkish nurse comes in, greets us, and rolls in Kai's lunch, protected by a plastic lid and positioned on a mobile table next to his bed. A while ago I'd mentioned to him that she's really cute. But he lets her go without a word. Didn't used to be this way. I ask what the hell he's thinking, going to England. He flips the lid on his food and steam billows into his face. He waves it away, wrinkling his nose. Then he touches the eye bandage and presses it tight on all sides. He feels for the cutlery.

"It's crazy. I couldn't tell you what I'm eating right now, based on the smell. You could present a fried rat's ass and I wouldn't be able to smell it. Snorted all the smell nerves." He groped the spoon to make sure it's a spoon and not a fork. Then he dunks it onto the plate and leads it to his mouth.

"Hey!" I say.

"What?" he asks, blowing a couple of times and carefully pushing the spoon into his mouth. "Whoa, disgusting. Lentil soup. Awesome!"

"When do you plan to go to England."

"Well," he says and points to his face, "this here has to be back first. Otherwise, I'll get on the wrong plane and land in Kazakhstan or something. Could be pretty embarrassing if I ask directions to Trafalgar Square."

"Hah, hah, funny," I say.

"Man, Heiko. No idea, but sometime next year. Before I start my master's thesis."

"Cool. Great. And I'm sitting on my ass all year . . ."

"Or just a semester," he says, annoyed, and lets the spoon slip back onto the plate in disgust.

"Yeah, right, completely stupid of me to assume we'd really kick some ass. The two of us in the front row. You probably don't remember, but that doesn't matter."

I can't stand my own attitude at this moment. Like a sulky kid. Manuela was always good at just letting me be when I was in this mood.

Manuela, always reasonable. But he didn't leave me any option.

"Course I remember. But maybe you missed this: I'm fucking blind!" he screams and waves his finger back and forth in front of his eyes.

"But you're not gonna stay that way, man! Once you're back on your feet, we'll get going again. At some point Axel will step down and then we can do things our way. Then Ulf will get back in gear. Just has to find a better balance with his private life."

He groans exaggeratedly, slides farther back on his bed, and puts his feet up.

"You don't seriously believe that, right?"

"What?" I ask.

"Everything, Heiko. Everything! Ulf is out and nothing's going to change that. Can't blame him either. And Axel. He won't quit in a hundred years. He'll keep at it till he falls over on some field someday."

I pull my pack of cigarettes and my lighter out of my pocket, get up, and say, "You just wait. After the match with Braunschweig—"

"Heiko, wake up! I've had enough. That's it for me. And you should finally get down to real life too."

"After the Braunschweig match . . ." I say, but don't know how to end the sentence. I open the door and say I'm going out for a smoke. I slam the door behind me. Kai calls something like wait, I want to, too, but don't stop. Need fresh air.

———

At first, I didn't get what was going on. Half-asleep, I groped through the darkness. Felt my mattress. The covers, which had slipped down to my knees. My pillow is drenched with sweat. My T-shirt, too. Images echo in my head. How I'm standing on a long street at sunrise or sunset. Although the street is straight, it rises and falls over impossibly steep hills. Everyone's there. Kai, completely healthy, and without those patches over his eyes, is grinning like a shark. Ulf, Jojo, and even Joel. Yvonne is there. She's thin as ever but looks surprisingly healthy in the orange light of the half sun. And Manuela's there and my parents. And I think we're all wearing inline skates. But I've never used them. Each of them is laughing, and we set off. The street, down the hill. Then up the next hill. I'm left behind. I just don't manage to get up the next hill, though all the others do it with ease. They're standing there and smiling at me. I panic and try to use the street like a halfpipe, get some momentum. But I don't make it, much as I try. Then they wave at me and keep on going. Disappear beyond the hills of streets. I make an effort, but can't move forward. All at once, something bangs. I'm awake immediately. The sounds come from the living room. It bangs so loud, as if Arnim's throwing furniture around in a drunken rage. I lay my forearm over my eyes and mumble, "Hey, Arnim, you old fart. Go to sleep." I try not to listen. Ignore the ruckus. Just get back to sleep, quick. He's yelling something. I can't understand it. He should just shut up. There are other voices. At first I think I'm not hearing right, and slowly take my arm off so the pillow's not covering my head and I can hear better. There are several voices mixed together incomprehensibly. But it keeps on banging and thundering. Sounds like someone's demolishing wood. Then a shot rings out and makes everything else fall silent and I jump up, ramrod straight. The dogs in their cages are the first to get loud after the shot. They're barking like they have rabies. I grab my baseball bat that's in the corner leaning against my mattress, and sneak back to the door, barefoot. The voices slowly crescendo again. I open the lock as quietly as possible and yank the door open, because it would only creak if I opened it slowly. I peer into the hallway. The ghostly light of the moon shines onto the wooden floors through the window at the other end. The stairs down start right next to it. I can't tell how many guys are down there. They talk among themselves in whispers, which is completely unnecessary after the gunshot, but what you probably automatically do when you break into strangers' homes. Can't decide if they're too quiet for me to understand them or if they're speaking a different language. I slip out the door and leave it slightly open. I'm holding the baseball bat by the middle, and I make sure not to step on the spots on the floor that creak the most. I know them by heart after years of walking back and forth. I slide along the wall. My T-shirt scrapes barely audibly against the old wallpaper. At the end of the hallway, I risk a glance around the corner. Definitely not German, what they're speaking down there. I don't want to think about why I haven't heard Arnim's voice for several seconds now. The light in the living room is off. The weak, burnt smell of propellant rises. The light of a flashlight dashes over the wall by the staircase.

"Davai," I hear someone say, then some kind of quick mumble I don't understand.

The cone of light on the wall downstairs remains still now and becomes smaller and smaller.

"Shit," I whisper and turn back. I twist the handle of the door to Siegfried's room, slip inside, and close it behind me. I hear the sound of the steps on the stairs. Since my eyes had already adjusted to the darkness, I'm immediately able to make out Siegfried's large shape. Like always, he's sitting on the edge of the chair, and his head is stuck between his wings.

"It's just me, old boy," I whisper. "I just have to hang out with you. Everything's fine," I say to myself more than to him.

I slip between the rows of paper, continuing to whisper comforting words to him and myself. The footfalls outside become louder. He must be standing on the other side now. Siegfried peeks at me from below his wings and rustles his feathers.

"Just want to get comfortable behind you for a second. No problem. Just keep on sleeping. I won't bother you."

Crouched down, I waddle around the chair, keeping an eye on Siegfried. I really don't need him to start hacking away at me. But he keeps cool and lets me pass. I press very close against the armchair, under the pitch of the roof in the corner of the room and try to keep my breathing flat. The doorknob turns and the door opens. The caustic stench of fresh vulture shit makes my eyes water. I make myself as small as possible and look between the legs of the chair, straight through the room. The black outline of a man stands in the doorway and looks inside. A quiet click. He tries to turn on the light, but the switch hasn't worked for years. Then a louder clicking follows. The man's shaking his flashlight. I can hear the batteries sliding around inside. He clicks away on the flashlight. Then he finally gets it and turns the light into the room. The cone of light falls in the corner, to the left of us, where I always dump Siegfried's food. The guy is quietly carrying out a conversation with himself. He's probably asking himself why there's a pile of bones on the floor. Then the light continues inspecting the room. The floor, the newspapers, and the bright piles of shit. Then it wanders over in our direction. From bottom to top. Shit! He saw me, but then the yellow circle of light stops on the chair and Siegfried. The guy is saying something to himself again. Fuck, fuck, fuck, fuck! Now he has me. The coarse feathers rustle in front of me. Siegfried pulls his head out, beats his wings, taking over the room. The man in the doorway emits a surprised sound. Siegfried answers him. I've never heard him make a sound. In all the years I've been living here. Much less a noise like that. It almost sounds like a hacked-off rooster's crow. If the rooster were the size of a dog, a chain-smoker, and had swallowed a live rattlesnake. Something between a rattle and a hiss. Siegfried pushes off from the chair. Jumps forward as effort-lessly as a gazelle. The huge wings extended threateningly as if he wants to shoo off a bear. The guy, who by now must have halfway grasped what was rushing toward him, yells and slams the door shut in panic before Siegfried can reach him. Too bad. The vulture stops and stands behind the door, waiting. I hear the man yelling something through the house. There's no answer from below. Then the man yells something back, sounding pretty pissed off. His colleagues probably didn't believe that a real fuck-ing vulture wanted to rip him to pieces. I can hear him walking down the hallway, cursing, and can only hope he won't find any-thing in my room that might indicate someone's still at home and hiding somewhere in the house right now. I remain seated in the corner, motionless. I feel pins and needles in my legs, which are slowly falling asleep, but I ignore it. Siegfried hops through the room, rewarding himself with something from the pile of bones, and returns to the chair. He jumps onto the seat, then onto the arm. Either he'd already forgotten I'm there or he simply doesn't care. Maybe he's just cool with me hanging with him. He shakes himself into his usual position and tries to sleep. The steps come back to our room a short while later, pausing for a moment. Let it go, boy. Siegfried will hack your eyes out. Then steps that go down the stairs. My body immediately relaxes and I exhale all at once. A splotch of feces splashes onto the arm of the chair in front of me. I wouldn't even be upset if he'd shit on me.

I wait for several minutes and listen. At some point the voices and the moving of furniture leaking through the wooden floor dies down. I slip out of my stiff crouch once I'm relatively sure no one will find their way up here. I thank Siegfried many times. He doesn't even look up from his bed of wings. While I creep through the hallway and back to my room, I think I can hear the dogs are briefly riled up. As soon as I'm in my room, I slowly lift my head from below the window and peer into the yard. I can hardly make out anything through the holes in the camouflage netting. Even with a full moon, it's actually supposed to allow very little light. I guestimate there are about five men in the yard, but I'm not sure. They seem to be discussing something. Then sudden movement under the netting and I hear the metallic clack of the makeshift cage and how the men yell at each other. Two more shots are fired, and a little later it's oddly quiet again. A couple of them come back into the house. I immediately lie down flat and press my ear to the floor. It doesn't help much, but at least I can hear them walking around down there. Then the front door rings and the door closes. I stay there, lying motionless. Several uncomfortable minutes pass. The sound of motors. Then absolute silence.

After at least a half hour, I dare to move again. I pull on some socks. I carry the shoes in my hands. In the hallway I listen again, but there's nothing to be heard. I go downstairs. The living room is completely destroyed. Cabinets and bureaus are emptied and demolished. The floor is covered with odds and ends. The sofas are slit open from end to end and the filling spills out like innards. No trace of Arnim. I risk a glance in the kitchen. The same sight as in the living room. I carefully open the front door, immediately reaching up for the doorbell so it isn't jostled. Arnim's pickup is still parked next to my VW hatchback. In my socks, I walk to my car and climb inside. I don't waste a second thinking about who might be stopped at the end of the road, waiting for someone to come from the house. I just want to make sure I get away from here. I could care less that I've turned on the brights, just so I don't run into anything. Once I come out of the woods and see the abandoned fields before me, I breathe a sigh of relief. I'm hardly back on the country road when I hit the gas in my socks and don't take my foot off till I'm back in Wunstorf.

I drive to Yvonne's after I've made a stop at the gas station, where the only person there's the night clerk, and loaded up on cheap liquor instead of beer. I spend the night in the car, in front of her house. Starting tomorrow, I'll have to figure out what to do, but right now I don't want to think. Although I'd like nothing more than to be with her and feel her presence, always beyond reach, the light in her bedroom is out and I don't want to wake her.

———

The first weeks and months after our move out to Wunstorf were terrible. And by terrible, I mean nauseatingly boring. I hadn't become friends with Jojo and Joel yet. Jojo was just a quiet boy with a head of curly hair among all the boys in my new class. I automatically couldn't stand any of them at first. And so I spent most of the time in the garden, as far from the coop as possible, pounding the ball against an imaginary goal on the garden fence. Till the neighbor shoved his face over the fence and bellowed at me, saying I'd better knock off the racket. If my parents hadn't taken away television privileges, I'd lounge a lot on the sofa in the sitting room and watch all my favorite cartoons. I was so bored to death, I even stayed when Manuela came in and wanted to watch her girly cartoons, like *Mila Superstar* and *Sailor Moon*. I didn't have anything better to do, and I was too small to jack off. The girls in my class all had little, pointy mice fists under their tops at most, and I used my dong exclusively for peeing or stretching it out in boredom and making doing-doing-doing.

One day I was tired of it all. My father had been on a construction site for a couple days, and Mom was bending over from morning till night in the old folk's home after retraining as nurse's aide. Even on weekends. I'd gone through all the cartoon series on all the channels, and everywhere there were talk shows on in which idiots were yelling at each other. I turned off the television, pulled my bike out of the shed, and rode across town to the train station. I'd completely forgotten I was still wearing my pajamas. My plan was the only thing in my head. At least I'd thought to put on my boots. It must have looked pretty retarded the way I rode through town in my pajamas and rubber boots. With a massive grin on my tiny face.

I didn't know how you got a ticket from the machine, but I hadn't brought along enough money anyway. And I've never gotten an allowance my whole life. So I just got on the next regional train with my bike. People sure must have looked funny at the little twerp riding the train in his pajamas. But no one said anything. I listened to the stops being announced and rubbed my arms. It wouldn't have been a bad idea to put on a jacket at least, but what boy voluntarily puts on a jacket? When Hannover Central Station was announced, I jumped up and was the first at the door, waiting impatiently for the train to stop and the doors to finally open. I used the elevator to reach the corridor through the station from the platform. I'd never done it before and absolutely wanted to try it. Besides, I told myself, I had my bike along and couldn't get down the stairs very well. Confused over which side of the station I should exit on, I ran back and forth. City Center or Raschplatz? I wiped my snotty nose with my sleeve and decided on City Center. Simply for the reason that the statue with the tail seemed a bit more familiar than the gray concrete of Raschplatz. I rode slalom through the crowds of shoppers. It must have taken forever, and I always seemed to come out at the Kröpcke clock on that square. But I didn't let it get me down, and tried out a different route again and again. At some point, I actually did end up on a corner I was familiar with. From there, it wasn't very far to our old home. I didn't care when other kids or teenagers laughed at me from time to time as I rode past. I was way too excited to see Kai's face when I rang his parents' bell and I'd be suddenly standing there in front of their door, completely relaxed and with my arm resting casually on my handlebars. The thought never occurred to me that there might be no one there. When I finally saw our old building, I kicked it up a notch and skidded to a stop right in front of the main entrance. I rang everyone's doorbell, and someone buzzed me in without anyone asking who's there through the intercom. I squeezed into the tight elevator with an old grandma who came in the front door after me. She stank of cat piss and musty fur coats and looked down at my trusty bike in disapproval. She had a bulldog's face, and I was glad when she got out on the second floor. The elevator stopped on our old floor. The apartment belonging to Kai's family was closed and I risked a glance at the nameplate next to our old place. It was taped over and the surname Lorkowski was written on the tape in permanent marker. I was pleased the coach from 96's Cup winners was living at our place, and I imagined he'd made my old room into a trophy room. But surely it wasn't *Michael* Lorkowski who was living in our run-down widow bunker. Whatever. That's the way I pictured it. And then the next door opened. I jumped forward and almost scared Kai's mother to death when I screamed, "Haha!" and smirked, in my pajama pants covered with mud.

"Heiko," she said and placed a hand on her chest in surprise.

I casually asked if Kai had time to play. He came out of his room, and when he saw me, joy rose in his face, and he laughed at me at first because of how I looked, and then we laughed together, and over orange juice and Nutella toast in the kitchen, I told him how I'd gotten there, while Kai's mother was trying vainly to reach someone at my home.

———

I hardly sleep anymore. After spending the first few nights in my car, I've set myself up in the gym and lie down on the middle bench in the locker-room. At least I can take showers there. Still have had no sign of life from Arnim. I thought about going to the police, but years ago he drummed into me that I should never go to the police under any circumstances if anything happened to him, and I respect his wish. After all, Arnim knows exactly what kind of life he leads, and who am I to put myself before his wishes. I'm concerned about the animals. If Arnim doesn't let me know soon he's okay, then I won't have any choice but to go home and take care of the critters. Can't just let them starve. But at the moment, I have other things to do. The match is coming up, and I want to make a final attempt to at least get Jojo at my side. When I called him, he said we should meet at Midas, but I said he didn't have to go to the trouble. I'd come over and visit him at home again.

It's ass-cold. The wind whips around the corner of the Seidel house, but my clothes are still dryer warm. I was in the laundromat earlier and sat in front of the drums in my underwear and wifebeater, waiting for my freshly washed things, which I immediately put on.

I hadn't been to the Seidels' for ages but immediately feel transported back in time when Jojo opens the door, we greet each other, and he lets me in. The familiar scent of antique farm-themed wallpaper and decades-old carpeting rises to my nose.

"You missed coffee by a couple minutes," Jojo says and leads me through the narrow hallway to the kitchen, "but I can still make you one. You want a coffee, Heiko?"

I thank him and decline. His mother is standing at the sink and washing two sets of coffee cup and saucers. She's wearing an apron in frumpy colors and has her hair pulled up in a matching headscarf. You don't see that much anymore. Maybe with elderly Turkish women. But the familiar sight of German grandmas with headscarves must have disappeared at some point in the aughts. Or the people who wore the headscarves gradually died off.

"Hello, Mrs. Seidel," I say and shake her hand.

She gives me a warm, motherly smile. I always used to like that, even if I'd have never admitted it to myself. I didn't know it from home. But Jojo and Joel's mother has a presence that makes you want to wrap yourself up in a blanket and sip on a hot choco-late. As stupid as it sounds. She's aged visibly. The Seidels were by far the oldest of the parents among us boys and even back then seemed more like Jojo and Joel's grandma and grandpa than their parents really. I take a seat at the table. Look at her infectious smile. Maybe it's the first time in her life that her appearance fits her character. As hard as I try, I can't picture Jojo's mother as a young woman or girl either. Without being asked, she places a plate in front of me with two slices of white bread and a jar of homemade blackberry jam.

"I don't have anything else to offer you, Heiko. If Jojo had told me in time, I'd have baked something." She gives him a strict look that isn't completely serious.

"Mama," he says, "we're not twelve anymore."

"Oh, all righty," she says in an artificially high-pitched voice, "the grown-up sirs don't like cake anymore, yeah?"

"That's fine, Mrs. Seidel. Thank you," I say and spread the jam on my bread even though I've hardly been hungry for days.

To be more precise, since the night I spent crouched in Siegfried's room while some random guys did God knows what to Arnim.

"What's the news?" Jojo asks, retrieving a glass from the kitchen cupboard and giving it to his mother, who fills it with Coke and places it in front of me. A well-oiled machine.

Of course, in front of her I can't really talk about how I need him to beat the living daylights out of those Braunschweig sons of bitches, and I say I just want to hear it again. When he doesn't get it, I nod my head to the side, as much to say: Let's talk about it upstairs.

We make some small talk while I'm pushing the pieces of bread in with some effort but still trying to make it look some-what enjoyable. I usually have trouble chatting, but Mrs. Seidel moderates the whole thing with great ease and asks how Kai and his eyes are doing. I'm surprised how well-informed she is, but at the same time I ask myself what Jojo told her about why Kai's in the hospital in the first place. She even knows I work at my uncle's gym in Hannover and also asks about that. I produce some random phrases I've picked up here and there. Stuff like: "Yeah, it's really protracted," and "it has to, just has to."

Then she looks at the clock and says her program is about to start. Jojo and I slip upstairs. We take a seat in Joel's old room. The same posters on the wall. One of his old jerseys has been framed in the meantime. Handbooks about football coaching are spread across the desk and every free surface. Colorful Post-its poke out from between the pages.

"Wait a sec," Jojo says and retrieves something from his own room next door, "here."

He hands me an old Diercke world atlas.

"Yeah?" I ask. "What am I supposed to see here?"

"Just open the Oceania page."

I look in the table of contents. In an open space: *Joel Seidel. Sixth grade, class B.* Then I leaf to the page way at the end of the atlas. A tiny group of islands in the middle of the blue nirvana of the Pacific Ocean has been circled with red marker. The islands, printed in yellow, are so small that at first glance you could mistake them for crumbs or boogers smeared in the book. The name *Nation of Tonga* is next to them. Also next to it, in Joel's red handwriting: *FIFA World Ranking 199.* I look up at Jojo. His face is as serious as if he'd just handed me his autobiography to have it read, and he asks, "You still remember?"

"Of course, I still remember," I whisper and watch my fingers travel from island to island.

Jojo sits down on the chair in front of the desk and, lost in thought, leafs through his football instructional manuals. Without having to look up, I can sense how he continues to watch me. For a moment that stretches like hours, I'm ripped out of the here and now and see myself back then with Joel, sitting on the tower roof of the shuttered step ladder factory, legs dangling twenty meters up. I'd scraped my chest on the handle of the heavy metal door leading up to the roof, and a thin line of blood seeps through my T-shirt. It was the night after Joel had told us about his transfer to the 96 youth squad, and we'd messed ourselves up in my new apartment in the residential tower. We'd simply left the others behind because they were lying there passed out, and our nocturnal stroll led us to the place where we'd already held more than one private party. The beer cans of countless teenage nights lay untouched at the foot of the tower. We used to roll them down the corrugated roof when they were empty, betting on whose'd be first. That's how I got fifty euros off Jojo one night. I still remember exactly the way Joel blew his parted bangs from his forehead and laughed because he couldn't believe he'd actually be wearing the Reds' jersey from then on. We couldn't even imagine back then he'd develop into one of the young players with the most potential in his age group. Even less, how badly he'd been thrown by the training injury so severe it nipped his chance in the bud. Well. And then. That he'd jump to his death from precisely this spot, where we were sitting.

"You'll hook us up with some box seats, right," I'd joked, but of course I wasn't planning to ever spend a game sitting next to all those money bags and sponsoring fuckers, who don't give a damn whether they put their petty cash into a football club or a race horse. After all, everything's just a joke for them.

"Just let me have a game on the scrimmage team first," he said and laughed, "I still think this whole thing's a huge misunderstanding and they'll give me back to the Havel team."

"Oh, cut it out!"

I thought he was going over the top with his humble routine.

"Well, let's wait and see. And even if I'm just subbed after a couple times. It's already completely nuts as it is," he said and grinned. "On the other hand, there's always Tonga."

"Why Tonga, actually?" I asked and couldn't understand why he wouldn't—with his talent—at least pick a halfway legit country where he'd want to get citizenship if he didn't have the stuff for German pro football. Which I wasn't assuming, and was completely of the opinion he could easily make the leap. And maybe he would have.

"Why not Tonga? First of all, it sounds good. Say it once: Tonga."

I repeated after him and nodded and said, "Yeah, rolls off your tongue."

"And then," he counted down his arguments on his fingers, "Tonga is so low in the international rankings they'd immediately give citizenship to any European player who can just barely hit the ball. It's sure to be enough, money-wise. I mean, you're living on a crazy tropical island. Can lie around all day on white beaches, and the bright blue ocean is only a couple steps away. You're celebrated by everyone in the country as the new Maradona of Tonga and can pick and choose between women in hula skirts and coconut bras. How great is that?! Who'd need the cash to buy a stupid sports car or something?"

"You're right," I said.

Then we lay back, ignoring the hard ridges of the roof, looking into the night sky and imagining we were on the beach in Tonga, where I'd visit him several times a year, and there'd probably be a coconut bra girl or two left over for me.

"What'd you actually want?" Jojo asks.

I have to think about it for a moment, because in my mind I'm still lying on the beach and sipping a chilled Tongan beer.

"About the 18th," I say. "The match against Braunschweig," I say, but Jojo already knows what I'm talking about.

He grimaces. Now he's thinking about how he can let me down gently, but I don't have any desire to have some excuse thrown at me.

"Let me guess: you're gonna be there. Right?"

He exhales and rubs his neck. Dandruff falls like fake snow from a Christmas-themed snow globe.

"Heiko . . ." he starts.

"No, not *Heiko* now. Say it." I was a little surprised at myself and how vanishingly short my patience is.

"I've thought it over. What Ulf said and—"

"Fuck Ulf. I get the impression he never felt it!" I give my statement added emphasis with my hands.

"I don't believe that, Heiko. No, that's just not true. But it's not just that. The thing with Kai." I try to rub the headache from my forehead. "Heiko, I never want to see a friend like Kai was that night. Never again."

"I can't believe it," I say into my cupped hands, "I can't believe all of you are abandoning me at the same time."

Jojo pushes the chair closer to me and I automatically move back.

"That's just not true. How do you get the idea that we're all abandoning you? That's not true, Heiko."

If he says my name one more time, I'll either have to scream or smack him one.

I say, "Yes, that's exactly the way it is. You're abandoning me. Leaving me to take care of it alone. If Kai isn't even ready to take revenge on the motherfuckers, then it's even more our job to stand up for him."

"Have you ever considered that Kai might not want that?"

"He's just saying that because he's so fucked up right now!"

Jojo closes his eyes and slowly shakes his head of curly hair.

"I don't believe that. No. I'm sorry, but . . . No. Besides, I've finally found something that I really want to do and do it right. And the brawling just doesn't fit in anymore."

"Yeah, great. Fantastic. The ungrateful little shits will either move up to the next age group or quit. Maybe a couple will even make something of themselves, but most of them will stay weekend warriors and move on and you can coach the next load of brats."

"Exactly. I don't want it any other way."

I get up, adjust my jacket, and pull my pants up to indicate that I've had enough and I'm leaving.

"All right," I say, "then I know where you stand."

"Heiko—" but Jojo's mother calls from below: "Jojo, our crime show is about to start. Does Heiko want to watch?"

I respond myself: "No, thanks, Mrs. Seidel. I have to get going."

One after the other, we walk down the stairs in silence.

"You don't need to see me out," I whisper to Jojo, and he looks at me with his face like a sad fucking dog, and I could just about spew. Then he sits down on the sofa next to his mother.

"Take it easy, Mrs. Seidel," I say.

She waves and smiles and says, "Nice that you came by again. You boys all have to come around for coffee when Kai's feeling better again."

"We sure will," I say and nod, but don't mean it.

I'm already on my way out, but something makes me pause again between the hallway and the living room. I turn around.

The show's intro is playing on the television. For the two remaining Seidels, I'm already out the door. Now that they assume they're alone again, the two of them seem to deflate. Their cheeks sag, as if they're filled with gravel. Both appear powerless. Mrs. Seidel's hand moves over and for a moment strokes her son's hand lying between them on the sofa. All around them, shelves and cabinets are filled with Dieter's carved figurines. Joel's trophies. The whole thing reminds me somehow of a documentary I watched once with Yvonne when nothing else was on TV. It was about ancient Egypt. Specifically, the pharaohs and how they had themselves buried with all their nearest and dearest possessions. Sometimes, even with their most loyal servants, who were simply tossed into the graves alive, together with the mummified rulers. That's about how that living room seemed. Or Joel's old room, which is more like Jojo's private altar. All at once, the air in here feels too heavy. I have trouble breathing and the sight of the leftover Seidels marinating amid their memories drives me right out the door and into the cold night. I look up. The first snowflakes of winter are falling from the dark-blue sky but hardly touch the ground before they melt to water.

———

I'm already pretty wasted when I get up from the bench in the locker-room, stumble over the beer cans on the floor, leave the gym without locking up, and climb into the VW hatchback. In the night, the thick clouds look like steel wool dunked in ink. I drive to the hospital parking lot, piss next to my car in the shine of the lights, and climb back inside. The digital clock under the speedometer says it's ten till two. An ambulance drives by with flashing lights and sirens and stops in front of the hospital's main entrance. I could try to slip inside. Wake up Kai. Hear him ask what the hell I'm doing here in the middle of the night and if I've completely lost my mind. I slam into reverse and drive from the parking lot. I myself don't really know why I got up in the first place and drive through the night like a madman. Maybe because I wanted to arrive someplace where I had the feeling I belonged. I don't know. Maybe I was just too drunk. Definitely to drive. But I was lucky. And have enough experience at inconspicuous drunk driving. Which is why I arrived safely in Wunstorf. I let the car roll slowly while I drive past the country road that leads to Arnim's farm and try to spot lights through the trees in the woods and the darkness. But there's nothing. Just a dark splotch in the middle of barren fields. I drive past and into town and end up in front of Yvonne's apartment. The light is on in her bedroom. I turn off the car, and before I can think twice, I open the glove compartment and remove the set of spare keys.

It still fits in the front door. I climb the stairs without turning on the light. Two steps at a time. I press my ear to Yvonne's apartment door. Not a sound behind the door. I bend down to the lock and place two fingers around it so the key doesn't slip in my state and betray me. This key also fits. I carefully push it all the way in and turn till it clicks and I can push open the door. The lamp from the bedroom, on the other end of the hall, casts a beam of light down the hall. Something scurries across the floor, and I remove the key and shut the door. The cat prances around my leg and nudges with its head and purrs like a model-sized moped. It smells of litter box from the kitchen. I crouch down for a second and pet the cat. Once she's had enough and I want to get up again, I feel dizzy. The beam of light splits before my eyes, and I have to steady myself against the wall. I walk into the bedroom. Taking care to place every step very consciously and quietly roll off the balls of my feet. Not so easy when you're that drunk. I push the door open and whisper so quietly I'm definitely the only one who can hear it, "Sweetheart, I'm home."

The ceiling spotlight next to the bed is on and produces a gentle humming sound. She's lying there. In nondescript, pale underwear, the color of which disappears next to her skin. Her not-at-all knobby knees she'd always been ashamed of and that I'd always kissed, precisely for that reason, to wake her up when I was allowed to sleep at her place. Between her narrow thighs, her vagina is visible under her underwear. The childish belly button. She has one of those belly buttons that don't go in, pushing out in a little ball of skin instead. I only saw something like that with her. I can count her ribs from the door, and the bones of her collarbone can be clearly seen, shimmering under the skin. My breathing is shallow. The cat purrs behind me in the hallway. She cut her hair. A strand of her bangs is dyed red. Her eyelids are closed. She sleeps like a corpse. Her eyes don't move beneath her eyelids. Her cheeks, flat as saucers, don't budge a fraction of an inch. Her mouth is open a crack and I can see the white of her front teeth. And above it her closed eyes. On the brows I love so much there are two thin, black dashes, and they disfigure the beautiful face. Why'd she do that? Why'd she scrawl those lines? I'd like to pounce on her. Press her arms down with my knees so she can't fight it, lick my thumbs, and rub those ugly black dashes off. Till she looks like she used to. Till she's my Yvonne again. And then I'd lay my finger on her lips and say, "Hush," and then we would fall asleep next to and inside each other. And early in the morning I'd wake up before her and throw away all the empty vacuum packs and morphine syringes and I'd make her a strong coffee she'd have to finish completely, and then we'd look through furniture catalogs and mark things, but never buy them, and at some point, before we're old and gray, we'd die together.

I turn on the light in the living room next door and sit down at the coffee table. I smoke slowly but can't enjoy the taste of the tobacco and quietly cough into my fist. Before I go, I take a look in the fridge. Behind the plastic door of the fridge compartment where the eggs go lies a handful more disposable syringes. How lucky it is for you, Yvonne, that you work at a hospital. And how lucky you are they haven't caught you yet. I close the refrigerator door again. The door sucks tight. I place the spare keys in the bowl in the hall and pet the cat, which was just coming out of the kitchen looking satisfied, one last time. There's cat litter still hanging on its fur. I block its path out of the apartment with my foot and then step back into the dark staircase.

We spent a lot of time at Grandpa and Grandma's place during vacation. That was only great when Grandpa was feeling good and he wasn't lying up in bed all day, his thin strings of hair sticking to his head, and tossing and turning like a walrus because of the pain. Because that's when Grandma was in charge of the place any you couldn't touch anything, couldn't be loud, and only drank that disgusting sweet fruit tea. I think that's why Gramps was usually back in the garden, when he was fit. When he didn't want to hear Grandma's nagging, preferring to have his ears cooed full by his pigeons, and didn't have to answer, Yeah, I'll do it in a second. No, I haven't yet. Just putt, putt, putt, come my bird, putt, putt, putt. There was nothing happening with Manuela. She'd quickly found friends her age down the street. I didn't have anyone and was far from knowing Jojo, Joel, and Ulf. We were only allowed to bring Kai along sometimes, but then it was also too boring in the small town. It was surrounded by fields that blandly flowed into the horizon. I liked it. Mainly because of my Grandpa. When we played football in the garden and he was in goal and I was easily able to dink the ball past him. Then I ran my rounds in front of him, across the lawn, and he provided the play-by-play and yelled, "Bandura in possession. Ladies 'n' gentlemen, feast your eyes on that technique. Takes it round the centerback. Passes to Heynckes, who's kept up with play. Takes a look, sees Rodekamp, he's calling for the ball. Great position. Heynckes back to Bandura. What are they planning? Cross. Rodekamp has it, shoots, and goal, goooooooooal!"

After our little game and before the meal, I helped him feed the pigeons and give them water, and he held out particularly beautiful specimens in his large hands. Then they kept very still because they knew that nothing would happen to them in the boss's hands. And then he stroked his finger along the feathers and I think that pleased the birds, and he showed me the beautiful play of the colors. And I listened attentively and nodded, but I didn't really understand because they were gray. Maybe a couple turquoise feathers in between. Mostly on the neck. But otherwise it was just gray leading to a darker or lighter gray, but whatever. And I listened to my gramps, how he told stories and gushed over his pigeons, which he never called critters. Just his little, dear birds. And his voice sounded as warm as a simmering stew and calmed me when I was worked up from playing football.

And then there was this one day in summer, where Gramps might not have been in bed, but you could see he was in pain. But he never said where it hurt. Much less told me. And on this particular day, because he hardly spoke and even Grandma held back with her throaty clucking and didn't fill his ears with it, and I also didn't ask when we could finally play some football because I saw his eyes were very heavy and he walked with the stiffness of a furnace. I was inside, and Grandma forced me to drink the fucking disgusting tea and said I couldn't get up till it was drained clean. So I held my nose when she wasn't looking and drank it in big gulps. I'd seen Mom do that when her friends were visiting and they knocked back clear drinks in small glasses that stank like gas. And holding my nose actually helped.

My grandma said, "Go outside and see if you can help your grandpa a little with the critters," and pulled her hair net a little tighter around the curls that were the color of snow that'd been under a car for days.

I went out into the garden. The door to the coop was ajar. The upturned trough was already lying on the grass. I called for Gramps. Then something knocked on the kitchen window, and when I turned around I saw Grandma strictly holding her finger to her lips, meaning I should be quiet. I opened the door to the loft. The pigeons had flown away, and it smelled of freshly spread straw. I blinked a couple times because it was so bright and so hazy. And when I was done blinking, I had to blink a couple more times because I saw that something wasn't right. Not completely right. But as much as I blinked with my eyes, till they hurt terribly, they didn't change the picture in front of me. On the contrary. It burned itself into my fucking brain and I knew there wouldn't be any fun kick-around anymore and no petting the birds and no mischievous jokes behind Grandma's back.

My grandpa was lying there, motionless, against the back wall of the coop. The straw had been scraped together in a pile at his feet. On his fat belly, which had always frustrated the buttons of his shirt, were the contents of the upended trough. A pigeon was picking away at him. I shooed it off, eyes moist, till it finally found the exit and flew out of the coop and I yelled after it, "You stupid critter!" There was a dark, moist splotch in the crotch of his checkered pants and it smelled strongly of piss. I didn't touch him. I didn't have the nerve. Just saw his face. Just waited for him to wink at me any second and get up and shout, "Got you!"

But that didn't happen. I didn't fetch Grandma. I must have stood there so long it got on her nerves, and because the kale for dinner had already gone cold, she came storming into the coop, but her nagging stuck in her craw when she saw us there. Surrounded by the stacks of roosts. She silently pushed me out and closed the door behind her. Then she came out, and I looked at her and she didn't look at me, and closed the door again and pushed me aside.

The ambulance came and Grandma led the EMTs to the garden. I sat in the kitchen between my parents and secretly tried to cast glances into the garden. One of the EMTs went into the coop and almost immediately returned, and shook his head. The hearse came. Because they couldn't squeeze through the path between the garden fence and the shed with my gramps on the gurney, they had to go through the kitchen and the hallway. And when they carried him through the hallway, my father pushed me into the sitting room. And closed the door. I could still watch everything from the window. How they slid him into the bulgy, black can. Like an oven. How they spoke to my grandma and my father, and everyone looked grim and nodded and shook each other's hands. Then they drove off with my grandpa. I stayed sitting in the chair under the window and thought I could still feel his body's warmth on it. Then the door opened and my father bent over me and said, "You stay here, then, right? Don't come out till someone gets you." I sat there till supper time. There were liverwurst sandwiches. The kale and meat were on top of the compost.

———

Torrents of water pour over the windshield as if from buckets. The wipers do their best to keep up but don't make headway against the flood of rainfall. The streets are covered in puddles, and the spray flies left and right every time I steer my hatchback through one. I drive past the German Air Force base halfway to Neustadt. To the hospital from my voluntary service days. The bulky, greenish Transall cargo planes are blurry on the runways. They used to circle over Wunstorf daily and descend on the Klein Heidorn Air Base. Maybe I should have done my military service in the army, just like Hans expected. Really enlisted. I might have gotten out of here then. Might have been able to see something different. The Middle East, Somalia, or the former Yugoslavia. The only thing is, it wouldn't have stopped at that. At getting out and seeing the world. Nope, that's bullshit. Going into other people's countries, forcing our democracy, our values, and our system on them with assault weapons? And also be able to enjoy McDonalds and Starbucks? Because everything works so wonderfully here? Thanks, but no thanks. I only think of it now when I see a plane like this. And because now, if someone offered it to me, I'd climb in at the drop of a hat, regardless of where it's heading, instead of going to the hospital to visit Hans. However, I couldn't run off now. Not before I get the Braunschweig gang in my fists. If there ever was something I really had to do, it's that. My phone lights up. I guess it's Manuela making sure I'll really come. I let it ring. I'm almost there anyway.

After waiting for ages at a railroad crossing for a single engine to roll by at walking speed, I finally arrive at the hospital in Neustadt. There are no parking spots left, so I have to park next door at the nursing school. The hospital hadn't changed a bit, only I'm not having to see it in early morning twilight for once. Can remember it exactly. How I always smoked in front of the door, and the block-like hospital building seemed like a huge monster in the bluish light. If Yvonne hadn't have been there, I'd have wanted to blow my brains out every morning. But she hasn't worked here for years either. Transferred to the regional hospital in Stadthagen. Can only hope none of the other coworkers from then is still here and recognizes me. I go to reception and ask where Hans Kolbe is at. Without looking up once, the reception lady says I have to go to the second floor. Room 202. Sure, I know how to get there, I say as she starts to explain the way.

I come out of the elevator, and the first thing I see when I turn to the left is Andreas. He's sitting in the hallway with his legs crossed and is swiping away at his smartphone.

"Hey, Heiko, you decided to show up?"

I ignore him and open the door to room 202. It smells like a mixture of iodine and freshly served hospital grub. I see Manuela straight ahead, wearing a light purple polo shirt. She has a sweater tied around her hips.

"Well, that sure is good news," she says and places her hand on the chrome bar at the foot of the bed. "Then you can get out of here next week." I walk around the corner of the bathroom that cuts into the room and briefly greet the group. "Hey," Hans says and blinks at me over his fork, which is planted in a large piece of gray meat.

Mie sits on a chair between Hans's bed and that of an elderly man of Turkish or Arabic origin who's wearing headphones and staring at the television, hypnotized. Mie smiles at me. I walk past Manuela and lean against the windowsill.

"Everything okay here?" I ask.

"The doctor says the operation went well and, with the screws in the bone, Papa will already be able to put weight on the affected side."

"Great," I say and tug at my sleeves.

"He's a quack," Hans mumbles under his mustache, which covers his upper lip in all its bushy glory. "Have you taken a look at him? That's a fag, guaranteed."

"Papa!" Manuela hisses, embarrassed, "that's not true. And even if, then it's none of your business."

"I'm not gonna let him touch me," he answers and opens his mouth wide to push in a chunk of meat.

"Where's Damian?" I ask, changing the topic.

"He's down in the playroom with Andreas."

"Um . . . Andreas is sitting outside the door."

She looks at me with such disgust, as if I'd wiped my finger in my butt crack and was poking it in Hans's food. Then she goes to the door. Immediately, they can be heard starting to yell at each other.

"Sheesh," my father says, "trouble in paradise."

"You would know." It slipped out of me.

"What do you mean?"

"Never mind," I say. "Then you'll be out next week?"

"That's what it looks like."

Then no one says anything more. Hans eats his ham or whatever the hospital chef calls that shoe sole. Mie tries to push the cart with the food closer to my father because the fifth pea has rolled under his covers without him noticing. And I push up my sleeves and out of boredom slap my forearm and leave a red handprint on my arm, but it always disappears immediately.

Manuela returns. She slips her phone in her bag. Unexpectedly, she puts on a smile and says, "I have a little surprise for you."

"Some real food?" Hans asks, and the next pea rolls toward his crotch and leaves a trail of brown sauce on the sheet.

Manuela taps her fingertips in front of her stomach and says, "Mother's on her way here."

"What?" I explode. Mie stops fiddling with the table, and Hans lets his fork clatter on the plate.

"That's right," Manuela says, "we've been back in touch since a couple of weeks ago. I thought it'd be a nice opportunity to bring the family back together again. She's bringing her boyfriend along."

My chin drops.

"You're in touch? You?" I can hardly hold back my surprise.

All these years, my sister has never said a single word about our mother, and now she pulls this out of the fucking blue.

"Are you crazy?" Hans yells, and his fellow patient looks over and timidly pushes his headphones from one ear. "Why are you bringing her here?"

Manuela gives Hans an ice-cold look and says with a bossy teacher voice, "Because. I think it's the right thing to do. Just look at us! Just look at us! This is no family. All I want is for it to get better." The authority seeps from her voice and is transformed into an insistent whimpering. "Maybe not like with Andreas's parents. But a little normalcy, is that too much to ask?"

Hans pushes the table aside, hitting Mie's upper arm. She squeaks in shock or pain. The fork thuds to the side of the bed and from there to the floor.

"If I can overcome my fears and call Mom, then you could come my way a little! Especially you, Heiko. I thought you of all people would be happy."

"I don't want to see the dumb bitch!" Hans bellows. "She's not coming in here. And no way in hell with her squeeze. I think I'm losing my damn mind!"

Looking for help, Manuela glances my way, but she can't expect anything from me. Hans continues screaming that he wants to get out immediately, but with every new motion he grimaces in pain and remains prone, completely exhausted, and is still grumbling insults to himself, several for each of us, while Mie pats his arm.

"Out! Everyone out!" he screams. "Get lost!"

"Heiko," Manuela says and leaves her mouth open.

But I just shake my head. I feel my nostrils flare and suck in a deep breath. Then I push away from the windowsill and very quietly, so it almost disappears under Hans's curses, say, "You're all completely crazy," pushing myself sideways past Manuela so we don't touch. She turns along with me. "Just leave me alone."

My sister calls after me, but I slam the door shut behind me. Andreas is coming up the stairs. He's pulling Damian behind him by the hand. Andreas opens his dirty, untrusting mouth, but before he can say anything, I slam my fist into his face. Not with full force, but hard enough so it's more than sufficient for him. He falls half backwards. He pulls on Damian's arm, who yells, "Ouch!" I'm already stomping down the stairs when I hear Andreas yelling after me that he'll press charges and what all else. He should go ahead. I don't have anything anyway. That stupid son of a bitch.

———

Tomorrow's the day. Tomorrow's when the boys from Braunschweig will pay for what they did to Kai. Axel filled me in on the crucial details by SMS. The whole thing is going to take place in the passageways of the Ihme complex, as I suggested. At 5 p.m., so we can, in the best-case scenario, follow the broadcast of the game at Timpen. Or the others can. I'll be getting in my car and driving to Kai in the hospital. And even if we can only follow the game on the radio or internet, I'll smuggle in some beer and we'll make a toast, regardless of how the game ends up. And then everything will have come to an end. Kai will be healthy again, we'll be able to start again. Axel will transfer the leadership to me because I've proven myself. Jojo and Ulf will come back, and together we'll shake up the whole damn scene.

They all stare at me when I come into Kai's room. Jojo and Ulf are sitting next to his bed. Look at me with googly eyes, as if I were a passerby who'd stumbled into a secret meeting in some random dark alley.

"Kai, can we have a word? The two of us," I stammer.

Ulf sits up. Wants to open his mouth, but Kai holds up his hand and says, "No problem."

Then he heaves himself up from the bed with their help and staggers over to me. We walk down the corridor, through the cafeteria and its glass facade, out into the park. He's now wearing patches over both eyes. The right eye's is white with ventilation holes. There's a transparent patch over the left one.

"Can you see stuff again?" I ask and point to my own left eye while we walk side by side and the headwind makes us go even more slowly.

"Not bad. Everything's still blurry, but the doctors say my left eye is healing so well that I'll soon be able to see again. Almost like before."

"And the right side?" I ask and the feeling that everything will turn out all right spreads across my chest.

"They can't say yet. The tear is much worse than with the other eye and the doctors are holding back with a prognosis."

We take laps over the prescribed path for a couple minutes and I pass out cigarettes.

"I have to go back in. The draft isn't good for the eyes," Kai says in a hushed voice.

"I'll be there tomorrow," I blurt out, and I give Kai a pat on his bicep, "then we'll celebrate. I'll come here and we'll celebrate."

"No, Heiko," he sounds weak. Maybe we've already gone too far, done too much; "not me. You're going to have to celebrate without me."

"I'm telling you, they're going to suffer something terrible, the sons of bitches." I clap my hands together symbolically. "Score settled."

Kai stops abruptly and literally pierces me with his one eye. He hits my chest with the back of his hand. The translucent cup makes his left eye seemed cruelly distorted.

"I don't want anything to do with it anymore! Get that through your head. I'm out. That's it for me. How many other ways do you want to hear it?!"

I just stand there. In his eye cup there's a flat, brown reflection of me blurred beyond recognition. A tiny figure without a face, copying every turn of my head. A human residual image in front of a gray backdrop.

"Come along," he says and swallows hard.

"Where?"

"To London. You have enough saved up. And here? What's keeping you here? Not a fucking thing, man. Let's get away. Just for a while."

I can't look him in the eye. Instead, I watch how his gown flutters around his ankles. The path around us begins to shine with moisture. Rain drops fall on my head and run down my forehead and over my face, along my nose.

"Besides, I could use a good guide dog," he says uncertainly when I manage to lift my head again. He laughs in the hope I'd join in and we could laugh together. I grab his forearm with my left hand and shake his hand with my right and say, "Take it easy, brother."

As I walk past him, I think I hear my name whispered but must have been mistaken. I pull my hood over my head, drawing the elastic drawstrings tight so I can take the jacket collar in my mouth, and press my fist so deep in the pockets that two bulging balls press out from under the fabric of the windbreaker. I walk through the rain to my car with a numb humming in my chest, making all of my movements automated. I still have a couple of things to do, a couple scores to settle, before the day can start tomorrow.

———

The lane to Arnim's farm is soggy and soft. The car gets stuck halfway between the county road and the woods. I put it in neutral, open the door and push. It's pouring like crazy, and a little puddle forms on the driver's seat. At first the vehicle seems just to sink even deeper into the mire. I gather all my strength one last time and push almost horizontal against the frame between the door and the interior. The hatchback goes over a stone or something. Then it starts to roll and I'm able to push it out of the hollow. I make to jump back onto the seat, but my left shoe remains stuck in the mud. I pull and tug and my foot slips out. Fuck it. I climb in, close the door, and step on the clutch with my foot covered with muck and the sock only halfway on, while the seat of my pants soaks up the water.

Arnim's pickup truck is parked in front of the house. As if he'd come through the screen door any second and call out, My boy. With his gun in one hand and an Elephant beer in the other. I go inside. The house, still destroyed, is quiet all the way to the roof the rain is drumming against. I can hear the refrigerator humming out in the living room. The acrid stench of old blood rises in my nostrils. Even the sound of the doorbell didn't rile the dogs. I curse myself for not having had the balls to come here sooner. Something rustles through the newspaper and the other stuff scattered everywhere. Probably a rat or a field mouse that's found its way into the house. In the kitchen it stinks like a stale cellar and mold. Maggots wriggle in the leftovers in the sink. I walk out into the yard. One side of the camouflage netting has fallen over and a section as big as the clock in a clock tower snakes across the tiger cover. Nothing moves in the cages. The bowls inside are spread around and overturned. I put my middle and index fingers between my lips and let loose a shrill whistle. No reaction. I'm such a damn, cowardly asshole.

"Bigfoot!" I call and make an effort to imitate the Russian accent of the previous owner. "Poborsky!" But neither dog comes storming out of its house as if snake-bit in the fruitless attempt to seize me by the throat. Even worse, when I walk around the cages, I see they're both wide open. I hold tightly to the fencing, feeling my body go heavy and sluggish. It hangs numb, supported only by my fingers and my shaky legs, and all of it is so overwhelming. And by all of it, I mostly mean the guilt. The guilt that I didn't do anything but hide upstairs behind Siegfried and waited for the coast to clear. The guilt that I also didn't initiate anything later and postponed returning again and again. And even more than about Arnim's possible fate, I feel bad about Bigfoot and Poborsky, who couldn't do anything about being thrown into this miserable life, never had a choice except to play along or lie down and wait to starve to death. I'd like to cry right now. Really. Till my face dissolves and my body collapses in dehydration. I let go of the fence, but my wish doesn't come true. I wipe the raindrops stuck to my fingers over my face and roll up my sleeves, trying to prepare myself for the worst, and pull the cover of the tiger's pit to the side so I can look through the crack. There's water in there, reaching halfway up the tiger's legs. Its fur hangs down wet and limp. It immediately looks up at me and growls deeply, but it's visibly weak. Too weak to try to jump up the walls. There's something floating on the surface of the water that looks like bits of clothing. The shreds float on the water like water lilies and rock with every wave. A shiver runs down my spine, but I force myself to look a little longer and search for additional evidence. I don't find anything. And right now, in this moment, a tiny glimmer of hope should be flowering within me, but there's nothing. Nothing moves. Because for some reason I know I'll never see Arnim again, even if I turn the damned Earth upside down. The tiger quickly loses interest in me. We didn't even have time to give him a name. He turns away from me and wades through the knee-deep, slaggy water. Knowing full well it can't expect anything from me. Except for one thing. A last service I can render the creature and that I have to do, as little as it pleases me. Because no one else is there. Should I call the zoo? Wouldn't change a thing. I wouldn't be doing the animal a favor because the result would be the same. I pull the cover closed again and go into the house. I dig through the chaos, push the sofas to the side, and lift the broken cabinets. But Arnim's gun remains missing. The fucking losers must have taken it. I sit down in the trash, smoke a cigarette, putting my ashes wherever. And contemplate. I consider calling Gaul. He could surely provide me with something. But it'll all take too long. I'd have to drive to Hannover first. Maybe it'd take a couple of days for the goods to arrive. No, all that is out of the question. I can't leave till it's done. Then I remember the gun Arnim pulled out from under the kitchen table. I jump up and slide over the greasy kitchen floor to under the table. There it is. Hangs flat in a holster made of layers of black duct tape. That wily bastard! I sit down at the table and pull it out. It's so easy. I weigh it in my hand. It lies heavy there. I remember how everything works. The magazine is fully loaded. I push it back into the handle till it clicks, get up, release the safety, and pull back the slide. A round slips into the chamber and I release the slide. I go back outside. The heavy black thing dangles from my hand. Careful not to accidentally touch the trigger with a finger, I place it on the lid, pull the lid over again, and take up the pistol. Then I place my index finger on the trigger. The tiger has only a fleeting glance and a brief hiss for me. I check one more time if the safety is really off and aim into the pit.

"Hold still," I whisper, "please hold still."

I'm shaking. This isn't working. Then I remember how detectives on the crime show always hold their pistols, and I support the gun under the grip with my free hand. I squint my left eye and aim again. I try to breathe calmly and bring the notch and bead into line under the tiger's head. Then I finally pull the trigger. You always have the image or know from the movies that something crazy happens then. But no way. It just bangs. The bullet enters the head of the tiger. The gun's kick makes my arm flip back. And the tiger sags into the water. At first I think that I didn't hit it properly, and I'm already cursing myself, but when the slight waves subside, the body of the dead tiger is also still. I collapse to the ground in relief and my knee sinks in the moist earth. My breathing is loud and hoarse. I wait till all the raindrops have slid from my face. I need a second. Just a second. Then I pull the cover over and go back in the house. The rain has taken a break, and you can only hear the dripping of the gutter. I put the warm pistol on the kitchen table as I go past, maneuver around the trash in the living room, and climb the stairs. My legs work as if on automatic. Don't need my brain any more to make them move. I turn the handle to Siegfried's room and open the door. Pale light falls through the window missing curtains. As usual, old Siegfried is sitting on the back of the chair. He's made himself small. Well, as small as possible for an oversized vulture. The wings are folded flat against his body. Handfuls of his feathers are standing up on end. His breast is plucked bare. There's a tattered pile of feathers lying on the chair in front of him. I walk to the window. Don't make the effort to encourage him or me. I turn the handle on the window. Old, rotten wood creaks in the window frame. I rip it wide open. Fresh, cool air streams inside. Siegfried shakes his feathers and they fly around as though from a torn down pillow and slowly float to the ground. I hope he's not too overwhelmed. He's had to breathe the stale, dusty air in this room for years.

I step back from the window to give him some space, and say, "That's it, old boy. You're free. We want to see if you can still fly, right?"

Nothing happens. He moves his talons in one place, as if his feet are cold.

"Hey!" I call out and bang against the wall with my closed hand, "Wake up! You can finally get out of here."

The stupid fucking bird remains motionless. Just hides his head deeper behind his wing.

"Now fly away already, you old shit! Get lost before I get other ideas!" My voice gives way, with only the crumbs of words in my mouth.

He doesn't make a move. Doesn't even look outside.

"As you wish," I say. "Then make sure you take care of yourself!"

And I kick the door open, banging it against the wall. I pause one last time in the doorway. Then his eyes flash over the feathers and draw me in. His one good eye. Like with Kai. My lips quiver, and I have to clamp my mouth so it stops.

"Take it easy, old boy," I say, and close the door.

———

It was so hot I ran around in underwear a couple sizes too large that my skinny legs poked out of like toothpicks from a piece of cheese. I ate my coiled sausage, even though it was still real hot. I rested my feet on the arms of Manuela's chair and sometimes I slipped a little farther down on the chair and held my feet against her nose and yelled, "Finger or toe? Finger or toe?" and then Mom or Grandma scolded me, saying I should leave my sister alone, because she got all whiny and waved her hands wildly and squeaked, "Gross!" And my grandpa laughed and his belly shook, and he turned the sausage and the meat on the grill. Sometimes my father would join him and douse the BBQ with his beer, and Grandpa would chase him off and say, "That's enough, man! You're drowning it."

And my uncle had his knee on Sabine's knee. The girls were far from being born, and Manuela and I were the only kids in the family. When we were still something like a real family. Mam, Dad, Grandma, Grandpa, Uncle, and Aunt. Just like it's supposed to be. As far as I can remember, this was the last time it'd been that way. And Uncle Axel coughed into his big ham of a fist and said, "Father, think about it, we have to talk about it again," and Grandpa brushed him off and said, "Yeah, yeah. That's the way it is for now. Everything in good time. We're not six feet under yet." Manuela unloaded the fat she'd surgically removed from her meat onto my paper plate, and I literally gulped it down and gnawed on the gristle. I like that it tasted like meat but could be chewed like gum, and Grandpa laughed and said, "Well, take a good look at that boy. He eats everything. That tickles me," and I was happy and asked for more.

Then the BBQ was over, and the coals faded, and my grandpa wanted Dad to hand him his beer so he could put it out, but Dad didn't want to give up his beer and Uncle Axel groaned and soaked the coals with his own. Grandma came out of the kitchen with a tray. There were six little glasses on the tray and just as many long-necked bottles, and all of the adults could choose what kind of shot they wanted to drink. Most took Grandma's home-distilled schnapps, which she saved for days like these. They made toasts, and Grandpa smiled and said he'd come right over, and I kicked the ball into the garden and said I'd start warming up.

I kicked the ball back and forth and tried to juggle it with my knees, but I never got more than three before it dropped to the ground, out of range for my short legs. I yelled for my grandpa, saying I was getting bored and asking when could we finally play again, and then he would comment, but there's no answer. So I stuck my ball between my arm and body and snuck up to the patio from behind the coop. I think I wanted to kick the ball over the grown-ups. But I'd certainly get into trouble with Grandma. Especially if something got broken. I crouched behind the coop and scanned the situation. Uncle Axel and my father were standing at the edge of the patio. My father with a bottle in hand. Both of them wearing wifebeaters, and Uncle Axel's skin glowed in the sun like the charcoal on the grill earlier. They were snarling at each other. Uncle Axel's voice rolled over the lawn like thunder: "I'm the eldest. Just get in line behind me, Hans!"

And my father answered, but much more quietly than my uncle. This fit the size difference, because Dad was a whole head smaller than his big brother. Behind them, the women were silently carrying the dishes back into the kitchen. Manuela popped out of the patio door, but Mom grabbed her by the arm and pulled her back inside. Uncle Axel and Dad started getting up in each other's faces and yelling, and Dad said stuff like, "Oh yeah, you think so?" and "That's sure what I think!" Grandma and Grandpa sat on the bench like spectators and watched their sons give each other hell. I slowly crept out from behind the coop, and Grandma must have seen me and she made a waving motion for me to go away, but I just stood there. Let her try to come and shoo me off. I was much more agile than her. And then Uncle Axel and Dad got even louder and tossed words at each other that I wasn't allowed to say or didn't even know, or knew and used though I didn't exactly know what they meant, and got in trouble for. But they didn't get in trouble. And then they started to push each other. I think Dad was the one who started it, and then Uncle Axel's face got as long as a fiddle and he pushed back. I thought my father would fly backward onto the grill, but he managed to catch himself. He threw his beer in the grass and ran at Uncle Axel and shoved his chest with both hands. He didn't even budge. But his face got even redder, as if it was about to explode, and then he pulled back. My father didn't see it coming. And bam! Uncle Axel smacked him one. The punch had such force that my father fell down and held his face.

That was probably plenty for my grandparents, and they yelled, "That'll be enough now!"

And then my grandpa pointed toward the street and said, "Axel, you leave right now," and his fleshy toad's throat wobbled under his chin, and Axel spat on the ground and went past them and called for Sabine. They drove off, and we didn't see them for a long time, and there was no more playing football with Grandpa that day, but he turned on the television for Manuela and me in the sitting room, and he and Grandma and Mom and my father sat in the kitchen for a long time that day and we kids weren't allowed to get anything to drink and had to keep on watching television even when there wasn't anything on that would interest kids.

———

The only thing I took along from home was the pair of shoes that I have on now. Everything else seemed like unnecessary ballast or things I could buy new. Either way. I'll never set another foot on Arnim's farm.

The rain started up again as I drove through Wunstorf's industrial area. By now it's turned into hail that pounds on the hood of the hatchback and rolls down or collects in long piles along the wipers. It's already dark. There's no light on at my parents' place. There's no car in the driveway. Everyone's gone. I hope that's also true for the pigeons. I leave the car there without locking it. It'll only take a couple minutes. I open the trunk and remove the canister I bought on the way to the gas station and filled with super at the pump. In long strides, I push through the overgrown path along the shed. Stomp down on stinging nettles and thistles. My feet have become blocks of ice. I should have put on fresh socks too. My pants are soaked and covered with mud, and I ruined the fresh pair of shoes with the dirty socks. With swinging steps, I wade through the tall grass that bends heavily under the weight of the weather. A fine sleet pounding down stings my face like needle tips. I bet I'll be knocked out of commission with a fucking cold next week. But that's okay. When tomorrow's come and gone,

I think I'll want to sleep a month anyway. After that, in the new year, life can go on. Refreshed and cleansed.

The pigeon coop stands before the garden like a dark, musty mausoleum out of a horror flick. I grab the handle of the canister tighter and reach into my jacket pocket with my free hand. I briefly put the canister down and bang against the coop. I managed to get here in time, before the pigeons have returned. I open the door. Inside it's relatively dry and almost cozily warm, so I feel an overwhelming urge to just lie down in the middle of the coop on the hay. I grab the bright orange gas canister and unscrew the cap. It dangles down the side on a plastic string. I grab the cap, rip it off, and toss it behind me in the grass. Then I place one foot inside the coop and shake out the gas vigorously, so it goes everywhere. Till the canister is three-quarters empty. I don't know if it'll do any good, but I pour the last quarter over the steel roof and let it run down the side walls. I toss the canister back behind me. It produces a whistling noise as it flies through the air, then lands with a thump, softened by the grass. I bend over again. The gas fumes smell fucking great. I take a deep breath. They make my head very light and give my stomach a pleasant nausea that I need right now for some reason. As long as something changes. To notice again that a body exists around myself that reacts to the outside environment. I pull my Zippo out of my jacket pocket and light it. I hold it in front of my eyes for a moment and expect a flame to shoot up, followed by an explosion coming toward me out of the gas-drenched coop and catapulting me into the air. I'm forced to note with disappointment that nothing like that happens. I fling the Zippo into the middle of the coop and watch as the floor immediately catches fire. It looks like the almost transparent flames are floating over the gas. As if it wasn't the gas itself that burns. Within a couple seconds, the circle of fire spreads in all directions and reaches the walls, the shit-covered perches. The straw spread everywhere does its part. At some point, it's so hot my body reacts by itself. My head jerks back. I close the door to the coop and sit down on the patio. It crackles. Reminds me of fires the five of us always used to light in the field behind the Seidels' property. While Jojo, Kai, Ulf, and I fell asleep between our empty cans, Joel preferred to go inside and sleep in his bed. Then he woke us the next morning and brought us a thermos of coffee that Mrs. Seidel had brewed for us. I want to light a cig and pat down my pockets till I realize my lighter is in the middle of the flames. This makes me laugh and I can't stop. I sit there a couple minutes, watch the gigantic torch that used to be the pigeon coop as its blaze successfully fends off the sleet, and laugh my head off like a fucking psycho. Till I tell myself, That's enough! Then I flip the cig into the fire. The steel roof is already drooping and falling away. I leave the garden the way I came. Before I climb into my hatchback, I listen out into the night. Still no sirens to be heard. And I slip away before that changes. I drive to Wotan Gym. Maybe I can find some sleeping pills somewhere there. Not too many. Just enough to knock me out till tomorrow morning and I'm fit. 'Cause tomorrow's a big day.

———

My eyes literally pop open. I frantically search for my phone and look at the time and date, firmly believing I've dozed for days and slept through everything. It's December 18th. Ten after nine. I've got such a dry mouth, as if I'd dissolved a fizzy tablet in my oral cavity. I undress and take a shower, motionless. Use one hand against the tiled wall to support myself and let the stream of water wash down from my head over my body. The previous day seems unreal and more like a dream the tranquilizer made me imagine. But the sight of my wrecked clothes is enough confirmation that yesterday really happened. I wad them together, throw them into the trash can, and pull my athletic clothes out of my locker: T-shirt, jogging pants, and tracksuit top. The knees on the pants are grass green. Old, brownish blood stains on the T-shirt. The stuff I was wearing a couple of months ago against Cologne. I take a stroll down the street to the nearest bakery and choke down a Coke and two rolls with meat spread on them. No idea when the last time was I really felt hungry.

An hour and a half later, Axel comes into the gym. He's clean-shaven and smells freshly showered, making his boxy jaw and asshole chin stick out even more.

"Ready?" he asks. "Want to see a straight-A performance from you today." Then he places his hand on my shoulder and turns me like a water faucet, so I have to look at him. "Once everything's gone down to my satisfaction, we'll sit down together, okay?"

"Hmm," I mumble and stare straight through him.

Deep inside, I feel the urge to swat away his hand and slam the heel of mine under his nose. He presses his lips together and makes a fatherly sound. Then he pats me on the cheek and goes into his office.

The others slowly dribble in during the next few hours. All of them are talkative. Like kids before a field trip. Can't keep their traps shut anymore. Töller comes through the door and immediately starts to loudly proclaim that the central train station is full as fuck with police in riot gear. Fences and barriers everywhere, and you could see cops with binoculars and walkie-talkies on the towers across from the station. After he's finished his monologue and joined the other rowdies who were chattering away like the worst gossip girls, I slip back into the locker-room, stick the earbuds of my MP3 player into my ears, and crank up Grime to the max till the battery quits and it stops. The inner circle of fifteen men divides up into the cars. My uncle says the rest of them will join us at the Ihme complex. People from the fringes of our "operation," friends and acquaintances, former members who wanted to prove their mettle again on this occasion, a couple from the security scene at Steintor, and a handful of guys from Hannover's Angels chapter. As we climb in, Axel says there won't be a dress code today, that "everyone has to make sure he doesn't go off on one of our own." Then we drive off, staggered a couple minutes apart.

I'm standing on the fire escape of one of the residential towers in the Ihme complex. I can hear a helicopter circling in the distance. I guess they're flying over the city center but can't make out anything because of the foggy conditions. The view is just enough to see a hundred yards down the River Ihme. I have a hand in my pants pocket and I'm kneading my mouth guard. I left my phone in the car. I had to switch it to vibrate during the ride because Kai had called me four times in a row. Under me, in the middle of the meandering concrete paths and corridors, I can see the gang around Axel, standing around him like toy soldiers. It reminds me of the first Grand Theft Auto video game we used to play till we passed out at Ulf's. As a change of pace between the hard-fought FIFA matches, where we more or less insulted each other to the max. With GTA you always saw the people and cars from above. As if you were looking down on them from a helicopter. I hold my hands in my field of vision in front of the play figures down there and act as if I could steer them from up here with a twitch of my fingers. Then all at once, something catches my attention on the fringes of my field of vision. I'm just barely able to see a group of some twenty to thirty men turning into the Ihme complex from the street. Then they disappear under the various levels and paths of the complex. I shove my fingers in my mouth and send a piercing whistle down the concrete walls. The figure I recognize as my uncle looks up at me and waves. I start to climb down the fire escape. It groans and squeaks under each of my steps. I swallow the mouth guard. Only in that moment do I notice something's missing. What's wrong about this situation? There's nothing floating inside me. No helium feeling in the stomach area. No adrenaline shooting through my veins and nerves, or wherever it flows. Head, arms, legs, fists. All of these are objects attached to me as if repaired and screwed on, and they function automatically. I should actually be feeling something like joyful anticipation right now, but there's simply nothing. The only thing in my head is what my eyes give my brain. My feet, which move down the grated rungs of the fire ladder, and the gray and sand-colored concrete that comes ever closer below.

Axel claps his hands and rubs them together. He smiles and calls out to the pack of mean, joint-cracking piles of flesh with eyes popping, "Get it done, men! History will be written today. They'll be talking about this in twenty years. So we'd better win this thing."

I remain standing where I came down from the ladder. Don't make the effort to reposition myself. I know my target. A single shout rises and resonates through the loose rows of men. Braunschweig must be coming around the corner in a second. All the muscles in my body go tense, relax, and tighten again.

The first shoulder shows from around the corner. Then another. Skinheads. Clenched fists. A slow-motion of legs in billowing jogging suits. They call out: "BTSV! BTSV!" We respond. A deep thundering that carries the name of our city over the asphalt becomes a yell. The echo reflects off hundreds of concrete walls, making the names of the cities mix in the air. Braunschweig turns onto a straightaway, directly toward us. I roll on the soles of my feet, back and forth. I look at my uncle's neck, shaved clean. Give the sign! Come on! He waves us forward. The group stomps forward as one. I search through the opponents. The faces on the bodies that seem to merge into one in front of my eyes. A thirty-headed monster. One kisser uglier than the next. Where's the wart? The blond side part? Where's the fucking son of a bitch? The air between us becomes thin. Becomes completely used up and drawn into the countless nostrils and comes back out of us, in huffs. I move to the side within the ground. Don't step on anyone's heel or bump into anyone. We've become an organic unit. Then I see the blond hair. The dirty smile and the red, blinking wart next to it. The tunnel vision sets in. I see only that one face in front of me. Everything around me disappears into a black cloud. Then there's Axel's voice again. He's calling out something to us. But I only hear a dull rumble. I push off the ground. The sprinting heads in front of me rock back and forth, but I keep my eyes on the wart. Run around the others like trees. I think I'm yelling because air is streaming into my mouth. I don't know. Nothing else matters. I run at the Braunschweig gang. My fingernails dig into my palms. I lock down fists with my thumbs. Before I get to him, I see Ulf's and Jojo's faces flash in the corner of my eye. I see them yelling and running forward at my side. Feel Kai's hands on my back and how he screams in my ear, euphoric, "Go, go, go!" I close my eyes for a second and tell him it's not necessary and we'll get him. I open my eyes again and the wart is in front of me, dancing excitedly back and forth. I pull back. Way back and put everything into that first punch. From that moment on, when my fist reaches his dirty face and I feel bones and teeth give way beneath my bones, everything blurs into a jumble of sounds and images. The taste of blood under my tongue and how it sprays when I scream. The shiny, wounded, open skin of my finger bones that don't stop slamming into that face. Axel's voice from far away, in my head. Or is it penetrating my head from outside? He's yelling something I can't understand. A muffled explosion under my chest that steals my breath. The rough feeling of hair between my fingers and how I slam a head on the concrete. The useless flailing of the blocked arms under me. Blood-encrusted, throaty choking and the red-rooted teeth that are coughed out. Countless warm hands that reach for me and pull me away. The movements of my eyeballs that I feel underneath my palms. And underneath flickers all this rage. But also the satisfaction that shouldn't be there, and despite the voices that rain down on me, but don't reach me, and the feeling lets me know that everything else doesn't matter.

———

I still remember how my father called me into his bedroom. How he took his treasured vest from the coat hook and slipped it on, looking perfectly happy and content. Then he bent down and held me tight and tapped a finger against one of the many patches sewn onto it. The big black 96. And he said, "That sure is something, you know. 96. Yep, Heiko. Sure is something."

I nodded and looked at the patch under his yellow finger. We bid good-bye to Mama and Manuela, and I still remember how I hoped they'd be so jealous of me because I was a man now and going to the stadium, but they kept on watching television and weren't even interested, and I was sure they were just pretending. Because what I was doing was something only grown-ups did, and only the men.

Uncle Axel picked us up. I'd hoped we would drive in his big car with the great seats the color of vanilla ice cream, but he picked us up on foot.

"What ya got there?" he asked me, and I held up the apple Mom had pressed in my hand. He took it and threw it away and said I wouldn't need that, and that there'd be real food in the stadium, and he and my dad grabbed me by the hands and swung me back and forth. The streets were full of other men. Men like us. And all of them were walking in the same directions and clapping their hands and singing something about an old love. Many of them were wearing red and green scarves or had 96 jerseys on. Just a handful of men were wearing denim vests with frayed armholes instead of sleeves like my dad was, and these other men's vests were also covered with patches like medals on a veteran's parade uniform.

After we'd walked through the big gates at the bottom of Niedersachsen Stadium, my uncle bought me a hotdog and a Coke. Just for me. The bottle was ice-cold and wet, and I had to be careful it didn't slip through my fingers. I was hardly ever allowed to drink Coke at home. And never when we were at Grandma and Grandpa's. Grandma always said it'd give you black feet like a Negro and I wouldn't want that, but I didn't understand what was so bad about that. What I would have liked most of all was if we'd go to Grandma's after the game, when I'd drunk the big Coke all alone. Then I would have proudly marched into her sitting room and taken off my socks and shown her my black feet, and I would have run off, laughing.

I was so busy drinking that I'd just taken one bite of the hot-dog poking out of the roll like a fat, brown worm. But my dad was pulling me farther because the game was about to begin. I wanted to start whining because he'd grabbed me so roughly by the upper arm, but Uncle Axel rubbed my head with his hand. It seemed as big as an umbrella. He winked at me and took the Coke off my hands so I could eat in peace, and all together we went into the stadium. We were down at the bottom of the stands. Close to the fence separating us from the field, and my uncle had to put me on his shoulders for me to see anything. Dad was busy yelling at the official that it'd clearly been a foul, but I thought the whistle was blown ages ago and a free kick given. The Reds, that was our team. Hannover. And the Blues, from Meppen, our opponents. The free kick went in the direction of their goal, and all of the players had gathered in the box and were pushing each other and then the ball came and bounced through the rows and was headed here and there. Till it fell at the feet of the Reds' number 5. He swiveled with the ball on his foot and shot. I jumped in shock because the completely filled stands behind us let out an ear-splitting yell, and I hopped up and down on my uncle's shoulders, and my Dad bellowed his head off and screamed, "Yeah, Wojcicki! He plays till all their backs are against the wall!"

That stuck in my memory. That strange, magical name that sounded like something from another planet. I tried to silently form the name with my lips: Woit-chiky. Woy-chikki. I was so stuck on that name that I kept on getting on my uncle's and dad's nerves, asking when number 5 would get the ball again, and if he'd score another goal, and sometimes they found time for a curt answer between the yelling and thrusting their fists in the air and the beer drinking. But I just wanted to have them pronounce his name again. And again. Till I'd have the courage to say it right, because at some point I had the feeling that it'd lose its magic if I mispronounced it.

It took a while till the flaring celebration died down in our section. I'd joined in at some point and also called out "96!" but then the game and all the spectators above had calmed down, when a deep voice like a bass drum said, "Axel, you old salamander." Axel turned around fast, and I whipped around too because I was sitting on his spacious but hard shoulders. A giant stood in front of us. He was even bigger than my uncle, and though Uncle Axel and I were standing on a step, the two of us just barely came up to the level of the giant. He had very dark, bushy eyebrows. Like thick building blocks. And a bald head that was a little pointy. This was accompanied by a puffy bomber jacket whose orange was so bright it almost pierced my eyes. Axel took me off his shoulders and told me I should go to my father. He was sitting in the row below us and trying to keep up with the rhythmic clapping of the other fans.

"Damn toothbrush," my dad said and held me tight, pointing up at the floodlight pole that had just gone out.

But it was still bright enough that the game went on without it. And I anyway, I was much more interested in the scary, bright giant, and I kept secretly turning around to see him while my dad talked about the terrible electrical system and the like. Uncle Axel and the giant stood next to each other like two towers of a knight's castle and looked into the distance and whispered something to each other, and even though I was a real man now because I was allowed into the stadium, I noticed that there was something beyond that, and the two of them were sharing a very special grown-up-man experience. They pointed their fingers straight over the field to the other end of the stadium, where tiny fans in blue could be seen. And when one of them pointed, the other nodded, and vice versa, and I really would've liked to know what it was about and wanted for them to let me in on their manly secrets. But the orange giant also sent a shiver up my spine, so I turned back around to Dad, and because I didn't want to seem like I hadn't been listening, I wanted to ask something. I don't remember what. Something about why toothbrushes, because I couldn't make the connection yet that a pole mounted with flood-lights sometimes looks like a toothbrush. But my dad had turned around too and was looking at his big brother and his giant buddy, and his mouth moved slightly, as if he wanted to say something. Then he reached for his beer and spilled some on my shoes, but I didn't say anything, that kind of thing happened among men. Sometimes beer gets spilled. And Dad took a sip and the suds stuck to his mustache and popped in tiny bubbles, and he wiped his sleeve over his mouth and called out, "Hey there, Dirk!"

But he didn't get a reaction, so he called out again, this time just a little louder, and my uncle and the orange giant interrupted their secret exchange and looked down at us, and the giant nod-ded briefly but didn't smile friendly, and then they continued whispering. Mom had tried to teach me that you should always have a friendly greeting, but when you're that big, I thought, then you didn't have to follow the rule. My dad turned back around and drained his beer in a long gulp. And then he looked at me and said, "Well, Heiko," draping his arm around my shoulder and pulling me tighter, making me smell a little of armpit. "Wait a sec," he said and pulled off his vest. He briefly held it in his arms like a baby, and then he swung it over my head and all I had to do was slip my arms through the holes. He looked at me and grinned, and then he said, "Yeah, Heiko. 96." He pointed to the logo on my chest, "Sure is something."

———

The fields behind Wunstorf go blurry under opaque patches of fog, becoming a watery gray soup. The surrounding villages no longer seemed to exist. I roll down the driver's side window, and my whole arm thanks me with a stabbing pain that vibrates down to the tips of my nerves. Only now, as the cold places a stranglehold over my neck and cheeks, do I realize I'm about to bounce over the frozen path to Arnim's house, and every little bump pushes into my spine.

The pickup in the driveway hasn't moved an inch. Its windows, and those of the house, are covered with frost. Through the holes in the trees, only gray can be seen. The world has become still and smells of practically nothing. The bell rings when I open the front door. I jump, scare myself so bad a pinching pain shoots through the top of my skull. Nothing has changed, aside from the spiderwebs that have spread across the ravaged living room landscape and on which single little drops of condensation hang. It's musty and damp in here. I climb the stairs. The creak of the steps echoes through the whole house. I feel dizzy. For days now. Maybe because I've been eating too little, hardly drinking. That's why I support myself against the doorframe in front of Siegfried's room and listen. Nothing. Something goes through my arm, wants to press the handle, but I don't give in. Don't want to know what or if I'll find anything inside. I stagger into my old room instead. I put down my backpack, though I'd forgotten till now I was even carrying it, and let it slip down in front of me on the wooden floors. Was it on my back the whole ride? No clue. Doesn't matter. My stuff is spread across the room in the usual chaos. I crawl through it on my knees. Layers of dust stick to my pants legs. I reach around randomly, grabbing clothes semi-intentionally that I want to take along and stuff them into the backpack. Then I push my mattress to the side and pry up a loose piece of wood flooring in the corner. Underneath is a bundle of bills I've set aside for emergencies. It's not much, but it's enough for a while. I could have taken it along last time, but I was in a trance and just wanted to get away after what I'd discovered and what I did. In the end, I take my decrepit laptop and cable and cram them between the stuff in the backpack. That's everything I wanted to take care of here.

When I turn around one last time in the front doorway, I see Arnim's gun lying on the kitchen table. That's enough for me. I don't go back into the kitchen, don't cast a final gaze into the yard. There's nothing left for me here. I have an unpleasant feeling of pressure on my ears. It'll get better when I'm finally gone, far away. I'm sure of that. I'm about to pull open the front door when I hear a muffled clatter. Just once. It came from upstairs. I don't move. The door handle is ice cold under my bruised, still-injured fingers. There's nothing for a moment. I already think I misheard, but then there's another sound. I can hear it clearly through the thin wooden ceiling. The unmistakable beating of wings. Rustling feathers.

The pack I'd tossed onto the backseat of my car falls down into the footwell behind the passenger seat. When I drive out of the woods, the fog has lifted slightly and is now at the level of the treetops. For the last time, I drive the track to the road at walking speed. My head is a little lighter. I let my gaze scan through the windshield. From left to right. The gray boxes of the industrial area behind the fields seem almost brilliantly white. All at once, I whip my head back around to the left because something was in the corner of my eye. I stomp on the brakes and come to a stop halfway there, in the middle of the fields. Without looking, I turn off the ignition and the VW's motor dies under my gaze in the middle distance. I awkwardly unwrap myself out of the seat belt, finding the release button with my hand. Don't want to lose the white point that's moving quickly over the fields. I get out. Don't blink. My eyeballs start to burn. I blink briefly. Testing. But the white point is still there and shoots straight over the fields toward me. It's not a white point anymore, either. But rather a body carried on four muscular legs and a massive head with a nearly square muzzle and pointy cropped ears.

Poborsky abruptly comes to a stop a couple yards from the car. His wide tongue hangs out the side of his jowls. Slobber drips from it. We look at each other. He barks a couple times, rearing up. I walk along the car, not letting him slip from my gaze. His jowls twitch in front, so I can see his teeth. He growls. I freeze next to the trunk. Then he's quiet again. Just looks at me. Turns his head. His fur is dirty. Dried mud clings to the white. He takes a couple steps toward me and the hatchback, then pauses. I don't move. Just watch. He continues. With swinging steps. Then he makes a leap and jumps into the car. I bend over and look through the angled rear window inside the car. He carefully moves over the middle console to the passenger side. I continue staring. He's just sitting there and looks out the window. His warm breath makes the window fog over. I approach the driver-side door a pace away from the car so I can keep an eye on him. No reaction. I get in. No reaction. I close the door. Nothing. Hand on the ignition. I start the car. Poborsky looks out the window. There's a warmth exuded by his body, which has become skinnier. I put it into first gear. We drive off. We're almost on the county road, almost have asphalt under our wheels, when he turns his head to me. His nose is sandy from digging. He follows my hand as it goes to the stick shift, into second gear, and back to the steering wheel. Then he looks into my eyes. He pants. I think when dogs pant it looks like they're smiling. We look at each other for a moment. Then he turns away and looks out the window. We turn onto the road.

I would like to offer thanks. To Kathi for so much in so few years. To my grandparents. My entire family. My friends (now we're even, Laura). To Valentin and Elisabeth and the ERA team. To Tom and the people at Aufbau. To Mr. Gleitze and Mr. Watermann. To all those who supported me, whether while I was working on the book or before.